FRIENDS AND FOES

Kelsey's Burden Series – Book Three

KAYLIE HUNTER

This book is a work of fiction. All names, characters, places, businesses, incidents, etc., etc. are the imagination of the author, and any resemblance to actual persons or otherwise is coincidental.

Copyright 2016 by Kaylie Hunter
All rights reserved. No part of this book may be used or reproduced in any manner without the written permission of the author except when utilized in the case of brief quotations embodied in articles or reviews.

KELSEY'S BURDEN SERIES:
LAYERED LIES
PAST HAUNTS
FRIENDS AND FOES
BLOOD AND TEARS
LOVE AND RAGE

Chapter One

Forcing myself out of bed before the sun had even peeked over the horizon, I dressed in sweats and a sports bra and snuck barefoot through the house to the basement gym. Hopefully, working out would help me focus my rapidly spinning mind filled with troubled thoughts.

Sitting on the small bench in the gym, I pulled on clean socks and laced up my favorite tennis shoes before stepping on the treadmill. Turning it on, I built my pace until I was pounding against the conveyor belt.

The day prior had been a grueling day of research. But, hour by hour, I could feel us getting closer to finding my son, Nicholas. For almost three years, I waited, watched, secretly searched, while I created a new life for myself and hopefully someday, a life for my son. Between my store, my books, and a multitude of investments, I generate more than enough money to buy whatever I need to rescue him and provide a safe haven for him. I trained in weapons and hand-to-hand combat, and though I still wasn't able to best Donovan, Wild Card, or Bones in a sparring match as of yet, I was getting closer.

Feeling the tension rise up my neck, I pressed the button a few times to increase the speed. My already rapid heartbeat, raced to a new level, as I struggled to keep up with the machine. My thoughts cleared. My body heated. And, my muscles stretched. *Keep going, just keep going.*

Wild Card descended the stairs, but I kept my attention on my run. One misstep and the treadmill would likely throw me into the wall. I didn't look at him again until sometime later he was reaching over the machine's panel and selected a slower speed. I quickly adjusted my pace, and he lowered the speed again to a walk. I sighed and rolled my eyes.

After tossing me a towel, he returned the dumbbells he was using to the rack and sat on a nearby mat to stretch. While still tender on one side from a recent bullet wound, he was able to complete a variety of stretches, without gasping aloud. The bullet had gone through him and grazed me. I looked down at my ribs and confirmed that the stitches tacking the skin together were still holding, and the wound appeared to be healing on schedule.

"Did you sleep?" he asked.

I walked over and turned on the scrambler I had left sitting on the bench. "A few hours. I caught up on the audio recordings last night of Sam and Penny."

Despite needing to keep a tight lid on the investigation, I needed help to find Nicholas. The inner circle now consisted of Katie, my sassy slightly bitchy army vet friend who also served as store manager of my resale store, Tech, our store security, club member, and computer wizard, and Cooper, aka Wild Card, military expert and ex-fake-husband. The ex-husband part is a long story, but the story ends with him becoming someone that I'll always be able to count on in my life.

"How's the Bones and Penny thing going?" he asked.

"Not well. She's suspicious, and he's being flakey."

Wild Card stepped onto the treadmill and set a slow jog.

"You can't blame him. He has no idea what's at stake."

Bones is the Sergeant of the Devil's Players, a local motorcycle club. I am completely addicted to the man and his luscious muscular caramelized body but recently had to ask him to get back together with his ex-wife. I couldn't even tell him why. He was pissed, but somehow Wild Card convinced him to do it anyway. So, he's off playing the happily married husband while I try not to think about it.

In the meantime, we are tracking and listening to the devices that we planted on his beautiful wife, Penny, who happens to have a questionable history with human traffickers. We didn't tell Bones about the devices we planted, but I think he suspects.

"If I explain it to him, he could slip up and expose us all. That could get Nicholas killed. I can't take that chance. Until Penny takes off, Bones has to remain in the dark."

"And if he doesn't convince her that he's in love with her, she could also figure it out," Wild Card scolded with a raised eyebrow and a pointed look.

Over the last few days we had had this same argument at least a dozen times, and I was unwilling to have it again. I glanced out the slider door and saw the sun was starting to rise.

"I need some coffee and a shower. Any idea where the coffee pot is?"

"It was in a stack of other kitchen crap in the family room the last time I saw it."

The kitchen remodeling began yesterday and everything was removed from the kitchen and dining room and jammed into multiple locations throughout the house. Even my atrium, my private sanctuary, was storing a good number of supplies.

"Have no fear, Katie's here," Katie laughed coming down the steps. In her hands, she carried a cardboard tray with four large coffees.

I quickly scanned the cups for the one marked 'Dark Roast –Black' and snatched my cup.

"Oooh. I could kiss you," I grinned.

"I didn't run to the café for you. I did it for the rest of the family that doesn't deserve to be trapped with you in a house while you go through caffeine withdrawal."

"I'm not that bad," I snapped.

Tech came down the stairs grinning and winked at Katie, carrying another two carriers of large coffees. Wild Card shut down the treadmill and retrieved his cup, as I gave Tech a fake evil glare and took my coffee upstairs with me.

Ok. So maybe I was a little addicted to caffeine.

At the top of the stairs, I looked about at the chaos that used to be our kitchen. Yesterday the contractors tore out the wall between the dining room and the kitchen and removed the upper cabinets along the outside wall. They were making good progress, but we weren't used to the house being so unorganized.

Hattie walked up next to me and looked around.

"Good Morning, Hattie," I grinned.

"Please tell me you know where the coffee pot is, Sunshine," Hattie sighed.

"I heard it's somewhere in the family room, but Tech and Katie bought some this morning. You'll find them in the basement. I would go steal one before everyone else wakes up."

Hattie grinned and padded in her fuzzy slippers down the stairs. I smiled as I watched her leave. Hattie, our rock, works at the store when she wants, but mostly takes care of our personal lives and ensures we have enough food and alcohol to keep up our stamina. She also lives with me in the main house along with gentle soul Anne, and her genius of a daughter, Sara, aka Little-Bug. They're all a permanent and vital part of my family now.

Whiskey, the Devil's Players VP, is currently staying with us in Anne's room while he recovers from a recent bullet wound of his own. I wouldn't be surprised if his residency becomes more permanent, as Anne has barely left his side since the shooting.

Katie lives in the apartment above the garage, supposedly by herself, but I see Tech making a lot more trips up and down the back entrance stairs these days.

Lisa and Donovan live next door. They're getting married in the store in just a few weeks, on New Year's Eve. Lisa's New Jersey mafia based family is expected to attend, so it should be interesting. We are hopeful that Lisa's father doesn't find out that there is a bun in the oven before the wedding.

Alex lives in the third and final house on our road. He also works at the store overseeing laundry, restock and purchases. He's been recovering from a head injury, so he's been a bit out of the loop lately. Haley, formerly one of the club girls, now a pre-med student, has been taking care of him. When she's not with Alex, she's either studying or working the registers at the store, and she now lives with her friend Bridget in my old house a couple miles away.

The biker club, the Devil's Players, have come to terms with Haley and Bridget stepping away from the club. Since the Players are at my store and home more than they are at their own clubhouse, I don't think they have even noticed much of a difference.

I guess there is a silver lining to all the violence and danger that has happened over the last year. It has brought my family and the club closer, some closer than others, and that friendship has saved my ass on more than one occasion.

After showering, I went back to the basement. Hattie, Anne, and Alex were enjoying coffee at the bar while James, Tyler, Bones, and Whiskey were working out. Lisa was setting the coffee pot up, and Sara was scouting out the bakery boxes.

"How are you feeling this morning, Alex?" I asked.

"Back to normal, Luv," he grinned, kissing me on the cheek. "Haley and Bridget left on their vacation this morning. They had six suitcases for five days of laying on the beach," he said, shaking his head. "Now, I like to accessorize as much as anyone, but I couldn't possibly fill that many suitcases with bathing suits and beach towels."

I didn't share the fact that at least four of those suitcases were supplies that I sent with them, thus the reason that I booked them on a private jet so their bags wouldn't be searched. One of the bags contained tracking and audio surveillance equipment that Bridget would use to tag a few cars for us, as well as, some get-out-of-Dodge cash, in case things get dicey for either one of them. The story we told everyone was that the girls were flying to Florida for a much-needed vacation. Neither one of them hesitated when I asked them to partake in some illegal activity. When I told them the bad guys they were targeting were dirty cops, they both grinned. Bridget was excited to put to use her pickpocket skills that have lain dormant for too long, and Haley was up for anything if it included eighty-degree weather and a beach.

"It's a girl thing," I shrugged, confiscating another large coffee.

"Donovan!" Lisa squealed and ran over to the bottom of the staircase where Donovan swooped her up. Donovan was back to work for his security firm in Chicago and had been out of town a few days. Pregnant Lisa without her man was whiny and bored, so we all grinned at seeing that he had returned so soon.

"About damn time," Alex said. "Your soon-to-be-wife has been driving us nuts."

"I can only stay a few days, and then I need to fly back," Donovan said. "But boy, did I miss you," he said to Lisa, leaning over to kiss her.

"Well, all, I need to get some work done. Call for me when Carl gets here," I said walking off down the hallway.

I felt Bones' eyes watching me the entire way, but I never turned to look at him. It was better this way. He needed to focus on Penny.

Chapter Two

After entering the passcode, I opened the door to the War Room where Katie, Tech, and Wild Card were already busy reading files and listening to audio devices. I started working through the records that Maggie emailed me yesterday on Ernesto Chaves, Penny's former lover and keeper. So far, none of the contact references or phone numbers held any meaning to me, though I was still researching a few Miami addresses.

I was an hour into my research when Hattie announced over the intercom that a car pulled into the driveway.

I grabbed my coat before walking out the front door to greet Carl and Maggie. Carl jumped out of the passenger seat, cupping his privates with both hands.

"I gotta pee, I gotta pee," he said before dropping his pants and underwear to his ankles and peeing in the snow. Carl's long hippy gray hair wasn't long enough to cover the wrinkly hairy ass that now clouded my vision.

Sara giggled behind me, and I reached back and covered her eyes. To the left, I heard male laughter and looked over to see Bones, Donovan, Tyler, and Wild Card openly laughing at Carl's antics.

Just wait, this is nothing, I thought.

Carl completed his business, turning a huge section of snow bright yellow.

"Kelsey!" he exclaimed in excitement, heading right toward me.

"Stop!" I ordered holding my free hand up.

Carl froze in place.

"What are the rules after you go to the bathroom, Carl?"

"I have to wash my hands, with soap," he looked around frantically.

"We'll show you where the bathroom is so you can wash your hands, but first, you have to do up your pants. You can't show your boy-parts in front of Sara."

"Oh no," he pulled up his pants and secured them.

I uncovered Sara's eyes.

"Are you going to send me to jail?" he asked Sara.

"No, Mr. Carl," Hattie answered walking up beside me. "But you have to be more careful. Sara lives here too, and you need to make sure you're properly covered at all times, or you will be in big trouble with me. Understand?"

"Yes, sir," Carl nodded.

Carl's odd, to say the least. It's going to be interesting to see how everyone adapts to him living with us. Highly intelligent in science, mathematics and all modern languages, Carl reads a dozen newspapers daily – often nude, because someone needs to remind him to put on clothes. He also needs to be reminded to brush his teeth, eat, bath, and not to adjust his boy-parts in public. I wonder how he will adapt from the Miami weather to Michigan in December. Today's temperature is expected to top out at a high of 28 degrees.

Hattie seemed pleased by his response and led the troops inside. I lit up a cigarette as Maggie walked over.

• • •

"I owe you," I laughed.

"Yes, you do. And, I am going to think of something absolutely horrible to pay you back," she laughed. "I like him. He's really out there, but once you figure out his quirks he's a lot of fun."

FBI Agent Maggie O'Donnell is a newer friend but earned her place of those I consider loyal. She found the evidence against the bad guys in the Miami PD, DA's office, and ME's office. She is sitting on the information for now, giving me time to use it to find my son.

Maggie offered to transport Carl to Michigan when I discovered he was in danger. He's an old friend from back in the day when I was a cop in Miami. He left an odd witness statement that was intended to be a message for me, but I only recently received it. To ensure his safety, Maggie brought him to Michigan. It wouldn't be good if the bad guys found out that he had witnessed the murder of seven women and a child.

"You want to share custody?" I offered.

"No, I think I'm good. Maybe I'll just visit from time to time."

"I understand," I grinned. "We have a room ready for you if you want to wait to head back until tomorrow. You're more than welcome."

"Thanks, but I plan on leaving this evening. I'm excited by the prospect of driving at night, slightly over the speed limit, without a co-pilot screeching: *We're going to die*!"

"My bad. We didn't have a chance to talk much before all this happened. I could have given you a few tricks to get around that."

Donovan, Wild Card, Tyler, and Bones had walked up and were listening to our conversation.

"Do tell," Wild Card said as he leaned in and gave Maggie a hug. Bones and Donovan hugged her as well before they turned back to me.

"Well, to drive at night, you give him night vision goggles. He can't tell it's dark out that way. And, to speed, I have a CD of a police siren that a buddy burned for me back in the day. You put it on really loud and drive as fast as you want. He doesn't screech anymore, but he will yell about every five minutes: *Get out of the way – Police Business!*"

Maggie laughed. "How in the hell did you come up with those tricks?"

I shrugged. "He used to wander off a lot. When the group home director couldn't find him, my phone would ring. I would check his favorite spots and bring him back."

"He still wanders. You'll need to watch him. I almost lost him twice getting here."

"I have that covered too."

I stepped on my cigarette and gestured everyone inside.

"Hey, Carl!"

Carl flew around the corner and plowed into me. He hugged the crap out of me before I was able to finally force him back.

"I get it. I missed you too, my friend," I laughed. "I have a present for you. Do you want to see it?"

"Seventy-eight percent of the population likes presents," he answered.

"And, are you part of the 78% or the 22%?" I asked steering him into the family room. Tech was already in the room getting our new gadget ready.

"I am 78% under these circumstances."

"Good. This is my friend, Tech. He's going to put a bracelet on your ankle. What do you think about that?"

Carl leaned over closer to the device in Tech's hand.

"It's a Mini OFT-210 GPS tracker! For me?!" Carl clapped before sitting in the chair, pulling his pant leg up to his knee and thrusting his foot in Tech's face.

"I think he likes it," Sara giggled.

"I'll know where I'm at now," Carl said.

"Better than that Carl, everyone in this room will be able to find you if you go missing. Tech hooked the GPS up to their phones. You don't have to worry about getting lost anymore and getting hurt."

"I won't sleep outside anymore?" he asked tearing up.

"Never again," I answered leaning down to give him a hug.

"Look, Carl," Sara said, showing him her phone screen. "This dot blinking is you."

Carl grinned and held the phone screen under his nose.

"And, Aunt Kelsey got you a Kindle and had me subscribe to all your newspapers, so this is yours too."

"Kelsey's not your Aunt. You have German and Indian genetic tracers, and Kelsey's are Scottish and Irish. You are not biologically related."

"We pretend, Carl," I said.

"That's okay then, as long as you both know the inaccuracy of the statement."

Bones and Donovan had to step out of the room. They were laughing too hard to control themselves. Wild Card looked confused, and Hattie just shook her head. Sara smiled.

With it being Carl's first night with us, I asked Tyler and Bones if they wanted to join us for dinner. They accepted the invitation and Bones left to go back to the clubhouse to check in with Penny.

I called Goat to make sure he and Amanda were invited as well.

After the invites, Hattie reminded me we didn't have the use of the kitchen yet, so I called a catering company I had used before, and they assured me that they could prepare dinner on such short notice. Having money had its advantages.

Chapter Three

Maggie helped me unpack Carl's suitcases and after I gave them a tour of the house, they followed me back down to the basement. The contractors had cut the openings in the exterior wall to install the new windows, so it was frigid cold upstairs.

I nodded to everyone sitting around the basement bar talking, but continued toward the hallway that led to the War Room. Sara stepped in my path, hands on hips.

"Little-bug, what do you think you're doing?" I asked.

"I want to help," she insisted. "I'm good with secrets, and I'm good finding stuff on computers. You've always let me help before."

I pulled a scrambler from my pocket and turned it on.

"Sara, these people are dangerous," I said.

"Let me help find Nicholas. Please, Aunt Kelsey," Sara said.

"How do you know about Nicholas?" I stammered.

Tech stepped up beside me and rested a hand on my shoulder. I looked up at him, but he shook his head that he wasn't sure how Sara knew about Nicholas.

"Who's Nicholas?" Donovan asked, standing up with Lisa to stand beside Sara.

Hattie, Whiskey, Anne, and Alex moved to her other side, adding to the barricade between me and the War Room.

I looked at them before looking back at Katie. She shrugged before saying, "We need all the help we can get. When the other trackers go live, we need more people to help monitor everything."

I looked back at Tech, and he nodded his agreement.

I looked at Maggie.

"You're what – two or three puzzle pieces away from needing to disappear and go after the bad guys? To stay safe, they're going to need to know what's going on before you leave. So, you might as well tell them now."

"I'll keep watch of the house," Tyler said, jogging back up the stairway. Tyler was a prospect for the club, but I had recently hired him to keep an eye on my family. He was young, but had good instincts. He was the one that had let me know that Sam, another prospect, was watching me and acting suspicious.

I looked around at the worried faces that surrounded me. It was time to tell them some truths.

"Alright, let's go," I said leading everyone to the War Room.

Katie and I scanned everyone as they entered. Anne and Lisa both had bugged phones that we set back in the hallway before closing the door.

"Why did that gadget light up with our phones?" Anne asked.

"They've been bugged," Katie answered.

"No way. Penny couldn't have gotten to my phone," Anne insisted.

"But Sam could have," I answered.

"I'll kill him," Whiskey growled.

"Relax, big guy. We are taking advantage of the situation and spying on the spy. It's all good," Katie assured him.

"So this is the storage room," Hattie said looking around. "I thought it would be smaller."

I looked around from her perspective and was actually pretty impressed with myself. The 15ft by 20ft room offered long rectangular workstations in the center area filled with multiple laptops and secondary monitors. The far wall contained racks that were stacked with file boxes and equipment. Two other walls were covered with corkboards filled with maps, crime photos, and other important documents. The remaining wall had cupboards and shelves with miscellaneous supplies.

"Welcome to the War Room," I said.

Carl was immediately impressed with the computers and equipment, and wanted to change the security access panel to fingerprint identification, but I told him we had more important things to do.

"Sara, how did you know about Nicholas?" I asked again, sitting at my preferred workstation.

"Duh, the internet," Sara said rolling her eyes. "Of course, the internet says that he died. But I don't believe that. You wouldn't be all secretive if he were dead. And, it's the only reason that makes sense as to why you're making Bones stay with Penny. So, what's first on the list?" she asked climbing onto one of the stools and turning two of the laptops toward her.

"The newspapers had it wrong, Kelsey," Carl stammered. "They all got it wrong. Nicky wasn't there."

"I know, Carl. I know he wasn't there, and you were trying to find me to let me know. I'm sorry. I didn't see the statement you gave to the police until the day I sent someone out looking for you. I didn't know you were missing. They wouldn't let me read any of the files," I tried to explain.

"It's okay. You have to find Nicky, though. Do you know how to find him like you found me?" Carl asked.

"No, it's not that easy. The woman that took him is hiding him from me. But I'm looking."

"The woman that burned the others? Is that who has Nicky?" Carl asked tearing up.

"Dear Lord," Anne exclaimed, and Hattie reached out to hold her hand.

"Yes. The woman that hurt the others has him. But, I'll find him, Carl."

"I'll help. Nicky's my friend," Carl nodded to himself, as he began looking through the boxes on the shelves.

"Who's Nicholas?" Hattie whispered.

"He's my son," I admitted.

"Oh, no," Anne whimpered.

"I adopted him when he was barely a year old, when I was still a cop in Miami. When he was five, his babysitter was murdered, and he was kidnapped. His biological mother Nola then faked his and her own death to throw me off the trail and convince every cop in Miami to stop looking for him.

"Everyone except my cousin and I did. Since then, we have been running an undercover investigation to find him, but we've had no clues to follow. Until now.

"Maggie found the links to the corrupt city employees. Tyler reported Sam's suspicious behavior. And, I found the statement that Carl left. So now we are buried with leads and busy trying to put the pieces together. Tech, Katie, and I have been working all the data, and Bridget and Haley are on their way to plant some bugs in Florida."

"I knew those girls were up to something," Alex grinned. "Nobody needs that many bikinis."

"The fight training, the weapons training, the obsession with making money?" Donovan asked.

"You were preparing to go after them," Whiskey answered for me.

I nodded. "I need help. I can't wait much longer to go back to Miami. I need my son. I need to bring him home." Tears started to pool, and I looked away and blinked quickly to clear them.

"Put us to work then," Lisa said.

Katie provided me with a mental break and continued answering questions and providing more details of the investigation. I turned back to the audio equipment and passed the earbud of the audio feed of Sam off to Tech and placed Penny's in my ear.

I couldn't tell what she was doing, but could hear drawers and closets opening and closing so I assumed she was in their bedroom at the clubhouse.

I heard a door open and close, and then Bones' voice.

"Hey, beautiful. Did you miss me?" he asked.

"Of course, I did. What took you so long?" she purred.

"I had some club business to handle and Tyler's training. What did you do this morning?"

"Slept in again, by myself," she emphasized the last part, seeming annoyed.

"I'm sorry. We will spend some time together today. And, we were invited over to Kelsey's house tonight for dinner."

"Lovely. Another evening with your ex-girlfriend," Penny snapped.

"Kelsey's not my ex-girlfriend. She's just a friend."

"I think we need to go to Pittsburgh. It would be good for both of us to be with family and have a chance to reconnect."

"Let me check the schedule and see what I can come up with," Bones answered.

I could hear him kiss her, but it was brief.

"I'm hungry. Let's go out for breakfast," Bones said.

Frustrated, I passed the earpiece to Wild Card. Bones needed to make a move on Penny, and soon.

Katie had finished filling in the details of my past, some of which they already knew. The rest of the information had completely blind-sided them. They watched me, waiting for me to acknowledge the truth of what they had just heard.

"How sure are you that he's still alive?" Anne asked with tears in her eyes.

"I'm not," I admitted.

"Now, don't lie," Maggie said pausing from her perusal of the documents posted on the corkboards. "You know Nola better than anyone. What's your gut telling you?"

"That's not evidence," I said.

"Evidence – no. But you're a natural profiler. That's why the FBI keeps trying to recruit you. I've studied your cases, and as a profiler myself, I'm a little jealous. So, what's your gut telling you?"

"She won't kill him," I said, standing and walking up to the corkboard, looking at the crime photos. "Not unless her life depends on it or I push her over the edge. She'll keep him alive to fulfill some jealous fixation she has with me and to protect herself if I ever get too close. If I don't know where he is, I can't kill her. So, she keeps him healthy, but at a distance, always just far enough away to offer her protection."

"I agree," Maggie nodded. "Keep going, why the murders?"

She was referring to the burned bodies that were left with a message for me to leave Miami.

"She needed the cops to believe that he was dead so the city-wide search would stop. Her picture had become public, so she needed to be perceived as dead as well." I answered the question robotically, as I had recycled the thoughts over and over again in my head for years.

"If Nola and Nicholas were not among the bodies, who did those bodies belong to?" Maggie asked.

I knew this question was driven by curiosity. I had years to figure out the victims and profile them. She had been only on the case a few weeks.

"Six of the victims were correctly identified. They were all prostitutes. The child was Benny, age three, a son of one of the prostitutes. The victim that was identified as Nola was Nola's younger sister Tessa, who had moved to Miami a year earlier in an effort to reconnect with Nola.

"I already informed Tessa's parents and relocated them to California under fake names so Nola can't find them. They admitted that as a child, Nola terrified them and that they tried to stop Tessa from going to Miami. When they didn't hear from her for six months, they had already assumed the worst."

Everyone was listening to Maggie and I work the case back and forth. Other than a gasp from Anne, the room was silent.

"What do you need?" Donovan asked.

"I need to follow every trail until there is nowhere else to turn."

"Hattie and I will monitor the rest of the house, and keep people away," Lisa said. "Donovan, Whiskey, Alex, and Sara, will go through the files. Anne can organize all of the boxes and make sense of this room. Maggie, are you staying?"

"I can stay until tomorrow morning," she agreed. "After that, I'll need to jump on a plane and report back to work."

"Where do you want me to start?" Sara asked.

"Figure out who Pasco is," Katie answered while pulling out one of her notebooks.

I felt all the blood drop out of my body to my feet. I leaned back against the cold cement wall and slid to the floor. Maggie reached out a hand and helped guide me down.

"Shit, shit, shit," Maggie stammered from above me.

Everyone in the room watched me as I tried to move out from under the weight of that one name.

"I need a drink," I whispered to no one in particular.

Through fuzzy vision, I watched Katie dig out a bottle of premium vodka from the cabinet, open it, and pass it to me. I took a large drink.

"My turn," Maggie said, sliding to the floor next to me and stealing the bottle.

We passed the bottle two more rounds before my throat became scorched from the alcohol.

I turned my attention back to Katie. "Where did you hear that name?"

"Penny said it. She was in her room and muttered '*Shit, not Pasco. Anybody, but Pasco.*'"

"Pasco? Penny was the one that used that name?" I asked.

"Yeah. She was by herself, so she must have been talking to herself."

"Shit, it's her phone," Tech said. "She must be going online with her phone. She was reading something on the display."

"We need to clone it," Sara said.

"That's great kid, but I don't know how to do that," Tech said. "That kind of spy shit is only in the movies as far as I know."

"It's easy," Carl shrugged. "You just need to copy her sim card."

"He's right. Not many people know it's a real thing, but it is pretty simple to do," Maggie said.

"I'm sure Kelsey can come up with a scheme to get access to Penny's phone," Donovan smirked.

"If she can't come up with a scheme, I can talk to Bones and see if he can take care of it," Wild Card said setting down the earbud.

He seemed mad. Most likely Bones was still doing a lousy job pretending to be husband-of-the-year.

"So, the phone will be dealt with, but Kelsey, who's Pasco?" Hattie asked.

"He's the Antichrist," I dryly laughed, taking another swig of the vodka.

Wild Card took possession of the liquor bottle and drank some himself before looking down at me.

"Explain," he ordered.

"Darrien Pasco is rich, powerful and has no limits when it comes to his sexually violent games. Men, women, children, they're all on his radar. The bigger the challenge, the more money he's willing to shell out. The authorities have been trying to pin something on him for years, but he's careful," I said.

"His prey are delivered onto his private island which is manned by his handpicked security team," Maggie continued for me. "His victims are never seen again. Rumor has it that he turns them into chum and feeds them to the sharks."

"Sweet Jesus," Hattie said.

She took the bottle from Wild Card and took a swig. The bottle was promptly passed around the room, with only Sara and Lisa skipped. Lisa followed it with her eyes looking jealous.

I pushed off from the wall and moved over to the workstations. I was wasting time and needed to focus.

"Tech, Sara, I need you guys to dig up everything on Pasco's property you can find. I have a file on him that I might be able to access, but the property details and building designs were very basic, mostly from aerial photos. See if you can find out more. Carl, you can help guide them and offer ideas, but under no circumstances are you to touch a keyboard."

"I can help get them started with background on Pasco," Maggie said gaining her feet again and moving over to the computers. "I'll also reach out to my little computer genie and see if she can send some untraceable data from the FBI computers."

Lisa led Hattie out of the room to work the upstairs cover stories.

Chapter Four

I retrieved an unused burner phone out of one of the boxes and called a number that I had listed in my little black book. I was waiting for the other line to answer when I saw Anne pull a stuffed animal, a puppy with the lopsided grin, from one of the boxes marked with Nicholas's name. I walked over and took it from her hands.

She turned to me and hugged me.

"We'll find him. I promise," she whispered.

"Hell-ah," a woman answered the other end of the phone call.

I tucked the stuffed animal back into the box and turned my attention to the call.

"Shauna, that you?" I asked.

"Girly, I'd know dat voice anywheres. How's you doin'?" she asked.

"Alive and kicking. I need a favor, Shauna."

"Any-ting for you girly."

"Get to Charlie. Tell her to call home. Don't let anyone else hear you tell her, though."

"Got me a blow to finish, then head dat way. You can count on Shauna, girly," she said before disconnecting the call.

I snorted as I broke out laughing.

"Now what?" Alex asked.

I looked around to confirm that Sara hadn't returned yet. Anne had sent her to her room to get dressed.

"Shauna had to finish giving a John a blowjob before she could run my errand."

"And, this woman is a friend of yours?" Wild Card asked.

"Hey," I shrugged holding up my hands. "I worked undercover vice. I have all kinds of strange friends."

"Shauna's a nice girl," Carl said without glancing away from Tech's computer screen. "She said if I wanted a freebie to come see her and she'd *hook me up*."

"Mr. Carl, you are not to accept anything from Miss Shauna, or I'll be very upset with you," Hattie instructed setting down a tray of beverages. By tomorrow, I figured Hattie would have the cabinets fully stocked with snacks and liquor. I had my fingers crossed for a mini fridge too.

"Ok, Ms. Hattie," Carl agreed.

Tech looked up and winked at me.

"So who's Charlie?" Anne asked, as Sara came running back into the room and climbed up on one of the workstation stools.

"My cousin. We grew up together and moved to Miami to become cops. Everyone knew we were cousins, but we worked different units and had very little interaction at work. So when all hell broke loose, I knew I needed to leave, but Charlie wanted to stay behind and become the inside man at the department. I knew the department was dirty, but couldn't prove it."

"Dang, I bought it," Maggie grinned. "I read that she had you committed and figured for sure that she didn't believe you."

"Your cousin had you committed?" Anne squealed.

"We needed everyone to believe that we were on the outs, or she would be in danger," I said. "It was only a 24-hour psych hold and evaluation. Which I failed, of course, but they didn't have a choice but to release me."

"So, you faked a big fight, and she had you committed for 24 hours. No one would ever believe you'd forgive her after that," Donovan grinned.

"I could never think up shit that messed up," Alex said.

"It's a special skill," I grinned.

"What about the case file?" Maggie asked. "She worked in the department, so why didn't she send a copy to you?"

"She couldn't get her hands on it either. My old boss Trevor convinced the lead detective and the Chief to have restrictions placed on access since the case involved family members of the precinct. The DA backed the decision."

"Why didn't you tell us any of this? Didn't you trust us?" Anne asked.

"Kelsey knows that everyone in this room is loyal," Donovan said. "But in cases like this, any one of us could say something that is overheard, and it'll be her son and her cousin that suffer the consequences. Now that we have been looped in, we'll all need to be very careful."

Anne stared past me at the map on the wall. Several others looked away trying to understand why I kept so many secrets.

"So if I'm up to speed, you just asked a prostitute to go track down a Miami cop?" Alex asked, changing the subject.

"Yup," I grinned.

"And, how does that work?" Whiskey grinned.

"Shauna is going to do something to get arrested. When they book her, they'll see her file is flagged and call Charlie. Charlie will try to get her a pass on the charges, and if that doesn't work, Shauna will get a 3 to 6 month vacation that includes free dental, compliments of the county."

"And this Shauna person is okay with getting arrested?" Whiskey asked.

"Well, yeah," I shrugged.

"And, why would she be okay with this?" Donovan pushed.

"I worked undercover vice. I made a lot of enemies, but I also made a lot of friends. I helped some people get off the streets, others into rehab. When I left Miami, I couldn't trust anyone in the police department, so I reached out to my criminal friends. We set up different ways for them to reach out to Charlie. They agreed to help because they felt they owed me."

"What did you do for Shauna?" Anne asked.

"I beat the shit out of her pimp," I mumbled quietly.

"*You what?*" Donovan yelled.

Whiskey, Tech, and Alex grinned.

"He wasn't a nice guy!" I defended myself. "I usually didn't resort to police brutality, but I couldn't nail this guy without taking down all the girls. And, since he made the girls handle most of the illegal stuff, they would have been the ones to do hard time. So, I rearranged a few body parts and encouraged him to leave Miami." I turned away and noticed Maggie standing there. "Oh shit, Maggie, I keep forgetting you're a Fed!"

"It's all good. I completely understand," she grinned.

"How is it that I was married to you and didn't know this other side of you?" Wild Card asked.

"I don't know. Jackson pegged me as a cop in the first two minutes. Reggie saw something else. You were just my fake husband."

"So, Jackson dragging you out of the strip club in Vegas– was that a lie too?" Wild Card asked.

"No. I had already left the department and was really stripping at that bar. We just didn't tell you that I was working on my own undercover human trafficking case. As I said, Jackson pegged me as a cop right away, so when everything blew up that night, he helped me get two women and a kid out of town in a hurry. Pasco owns that club."

Everyone looked at me with huge eyes. I don't think they had a real grasp on what I was willing to do to find my son. Well, maybe Maggie understood, as she was the only one still grinning. Or maybe she had put herself in just as many stupid situations as stripping in a club that was known to traffic women.

"So you know this guy? That's why you were running?" Wild Card asked.

"I was running because the bouncer caught me snooping around when they went to move the women and the kid. He saw my face. I needed to clear out and lay low somewhere. I never met Pasco personally."

"Did you wear those sparkly tassels on your boobies?" Carl giggled.

"No, Carl. They didn't allow anything to cover your breasts in that club," I answered honestly.

Wild Card groaned and ducked his head in his hands.

Hattie giggled and chose that moment to do another tour of the upstairs and to check on Lisa.

A few hours later the red laptop on the top shelf started ringing. I retrieved the laptop and moved it to the center workstation, answering the call. Charlie's face appeared on the screen. Her eyes darted around at the unfamiliar faces standing beside me.

"Hey there, girlfriend. You seem to have company. Should I call back?" Charlie asked.

"Nope. They're with us," I said.

"About damn time," she grinned. "What's on the agenda?"

"Pasco's name came up in a surveillance job I have going. Can you get to my old files and send them to me?"

"Shit! Tell me you're not going to try to get close to that psycho again! Kel, he'll kill you and enjoy every minute of it," she argued.

"Relax, Kid. I'm just building a bigger file. I've no intention of going in blind again. But, I need the information in my old files. Can you get to them?"

She watched my face for a long moment to ensure I was telling her the truth before she nodded. "Sure, no sweat. Anything else?"

"I have the list of what I hope to be all the Miami players in the department. I meant to reach out to you with the names, but things got a bit dicey here."

"Yeah. I heard about a shoot-out in your neck of the woods last week involving a biker gang. And, I swear I heard your ex-husband's name on the injured list. What the hell?"

"All the good guys lived," I assured her while avoiding the subject of explaining the whip-lash relationship that Wild Card and I shared.

"I also heard that. A little fairy stopped by and filled me in over a beer. He didn't want me to worry," she grinned.

I rolled my eyes.

"So whose name popped up on the naughty list?"

"Trevor Zamlock and Feona Hughes were confirmed. Also on the list was a clerk in the DA's office by the name of Sue Cratler and in Internal Affairs we have Tim Simpson. Consider yourself warned."

"Both Trevor and Feona? *Shit!*" Charlie stammered, throwing her fists on her hips and looking down at the floor.

Trevor and Feona had once been considered close friends. Trevor was my old boss and mentor in the Vice unit for the Miami PD. Feona was one of the medical examiners, and we became friends over some gruesome cases that involved mutilated bodies. They had been regulars in my personal life and knew Nicholas.

"It's okay, Kid. I didn't want to believe it was them either."

"I'm going to kill them. Especially Trevor! I'm going to stare him straight in the eyes as I put my gun up to his head and pull the fucking trigger," she ranted, pacing on the other side of the screen.

"Whoa," I said holding my hand out toward the computer screen, wishing I could touch her shoulder and help her calm down. "We may need those bullets for the bigger fish. Some federal warrants are set aside with their names on them. Until then, are you going to be able to keep from blowing your cover?"

"Yeah. I'll keep my shit together," Charlie grumbled.

"You better. This is Maggie O'Donnell, as in *Agent of the FBI*, Maggie O'Donnell, and she just heard you threaten murder, so we're going to pretend you were joking," I grinned.

"Ooops," Charlie grinned.

"Maybe you'll feel better if you get to meet some of our allies." I turned back to my friends, and they eagerly took over the laptop and started overwhelming Charlie with their charms.

Alex stepped up behind me, wrapping his arm around my shoulder as we watched everyone carry on in excitement. Even Donovan was jovial trying to dig up dirt on me.

"You two are close," Alex said.

"Yes. We've been close since Charlie was a toddler."

"You don't seem close to anyone else in your family. You occasionally spend time with your brothers, but only at the store. I figured there was some bad blood."

"Not with my brothers, but they were caught in the middle. I sided with Charlie against my parents, my aunt, and my uncle. It tore some holes in the family fabric, but I never regretted it. I got the better end of the deal."

Alex nodded and we laughed at the questions everyone was asking Charlie. Her loyalty to me was unwavering, and while she never revealed any of the juicier stories, she dropped plenty of hints that she knew some. Finally, Wild Card was able to voice above the others the only question I cared about.

"So, is Shauna in jail or back on the streets?"

"*Please*. Like I would let Shauna sit in a cell. I hooked her up with a one-way ticket out of town and enough money and clothes to start over somewhere fresh."

I could see the monitor from where I stood. Her eyes gleamed, and she had her devilish grin on full sparkle.

"Kid, where did you send Shauna?" I asked.

"Texas," she grinned and winked at me. "I have to end this call. Let's plan on touching base in a week, same time. Be safe, Kel."

"You know the Fairy will be seeking revenge," I said.

Her smile expanded as she disconnected the call.

"Jackson is the fairy of this story and your cousin just sent a prostitute to Reggie and Jackson's house. Didn't she?" Wild Card asked. Wild Card's family had split the ranch up years ago into three huge parcels. Pops had the property furthest to the West. Wild Card had the middle property. And, Jackson recently moved in with Reggie in the eastern most property.

I shrugged but didn't answer.

"Holy shit," Wild Card grinned.

"Isn't calling Jackson a fairy a little offensive?" Anne asked.

"Not when Jackson was the one that introduced himself to Charlie as my fairy godmother," I grinned.

"Why do you call her Kid?" Maggie asked.

"Because when the shit hit the fan at home, I told her it wasn't her fault, she was just a kid," I answered. "It stuck and became our only fight over the next several years. I was only two years older than her, but she was my kid-cousin, and I had to watch out for her."

"Is that why you moved to Miami to become a cop?" Anne asked.

"No," I laughed. "By then I told her it was time for her to be the grown up and I was going to be a beach bum while she became a cop. But somehow she convinced me to go through the academy training with her, said it was a good angle for my writing. But when I discovered I had some untapped skills, she was pissed. She had been planning on mopping me off the floor and at graduation I reminded her again that she was just a Kid."

"I feel so sorry for her," Donovan laughed. "She never had a chance."

I grinned, leaning into Alex. "Don't feel too bad for her. She graduated second in our class right on my heels. She's good."

Chapter Five

Hours later, Maggie kept working while the rest of us quickly changed and prepared for dinner. Maggie had bowed out of attending dinner, saying she wanted to catch up on some of the files, but I think the real reason is that she had no interest in sharing dinner with Penny when she was aware of the role Penny had played in Ernesto's trafficking business.

We had barely regrouped in the dining room before the doorbell rang and our guests arrived.

Dinner started out with Carl insisting everyone had to sit in specific chairs, or the table would not be properly emotionally balanced. Everyone complied, and I was happy to see that the new placements put Penny out of my direct vision. Carl sat down across from me and smiled brightly. It was almost like he did it intentionally. I laughed out loud before I corrected myself.

Everyone glanced at me with big eyes, but then Hattie distracted them by ordering them to fill their plates.

"Penny, you must be dying to get out of the clubhouse," Lisa said. "I have to sort some evening gowns at the store tomorrow for the new addition. Would you be interested in joining me? It would give you a chance to get away for a bit?"

Go Lisa. Though I suspected Lisa's intent was to give Bones a break—Penny would have the opportunity to reach out to Nola.

"You should go," Bones said. "I promised Tyler we would train tomorrow. I can drop you off at the store and pick you up on my way back through."

"I suppose that will be fine," Penny replied giving nothing away.

"Clubhouse? Is it a strip club?" Carl asked.

"No, Carl, it's a motorcycle club," I answered.

"Do the women wear strips of leather over their girl parts and chain their boyfriends naked to the wall?" Carl asked taking a mouthful of roasted potatoes as he awaited my answer.

Katie spit her wine up, staining the front of her satin blouse. James and Tech smiled, waiting for me to answer. Hattie covered Sara's ears as Goat covered Amanda's.

"Carl, where did you see something like that? Have you been on the computer without supervision?" I asked.

"No. My TV has movies for only $5.99," he grinned.

I turned to Tech.

"On it," he laughed and went to Carl's room.

"I have to pee," Carl announced.

"Not at the table, young man. To the bathroom," Hattie pointed in that direction.

Listening to Hattie scold a man ten years her senior was cute enough. But Carl running into the bathroom and without closing the door, dropping his drawers to his ankles to do his business, was the icing on the cake. We all buried our faces and started chuckling. Well, all except Hattie.

"Carl, close the door, or I swear, you're going to get a spanking!" Hattie yelled.

"Is that a little boy spanking or a sexual spanking?" Carl asked.

Hattie turned bright red and huffed while the rest of the table, including Penny, laughed louder.

"What did I miss?" Tech asked hurrying back into the room.

Katie, Tech and I joined Maggie in the War Room after everyone else either left or went to sleep.

"Penny should be able to easily report that Carl isn't a threat after witnessing everything tonight," Tech said.

"Yeah, I would say when he tried to snort his green beans, that pretty much sealed the deal," Katie agreed.

"Sounds like I missed quite the event," Maggie grinned.

"Kelsey picking the green beans out with tweezers was the best part," Tech said.

"I preferred the whips and chains discussion, myself. Though I felt bad for not warning Goat before we exposed Amanda to that dinner conversation," I said.

"I'm sure she's heard worse from her mother," Katie shrugged.

It took Katie and me a minute to digest what she said, and we looked at each other simultaneously. The last time we saw Amanda's mother, she was drugged and moved into the back of one of our freight trucks. The club drove away with her, and we never thought about her again. I could see the same question in Katie's eyes that was running through my own head. Did they kill her?

We both looked at Tech.

"Don't ask," Tech grinned not looking up from his laptop.

"I suppose it's for the best if we don't know," Katie nodded.

I was sleeping on one of the couches in the family room when loud pounding woke me early the next morning. Throwing the pillow over my head didn't muffle the noise so I grudgingly decided to get up. Hattie was sitting next to Henry on the floor in front of the oversized coffee table on the other side of the room.

"Good morning, Sunshine," Hattie giggled.

"Good morning, Hattie. Good morning, Henry," I said as I crawled across the carpet to their makeshift breakfast bar. Henry poured me a cup of coffee from the carafe as Hattie selected a glazed donut from the bakery box and placed it on a plate for me.

"I take it that the kitchen is off limits this morning?"

"They're installing the new wood flooring after they finish tearing out that stone cold tile," Hattie said.

"I asked them to try and save some of the tiles so I could use them at my house, but Hattie threatened their lives if a single piece survived the tear-out," Henry laughed.

"I assume the contractors are following Hattie's orders?" I grinned.

"Of course, they are. I promised them burgers on the grill for lunch," Hattie grinned back.

"Cheater," Henry laughed.

Sara came stumbling in and crawled onto my lap at the same time that Wild Card dragged himself into the room and took possession of one of the recliners. Sara started nibbling on my donut as Hattie poured her a glass of orange juice. I passed a donut to Wild Card, and Henry passed him a cup of coffee.

"I thought with the store closed for a couple weeks, we would be able to sleep in around here," Anne grumbled entering the room with Whiskey trailing behind her. They both sat on the loveseat, and we passed the breakfast supplies their way.

"No rest for the wicked," I grinned.

"Ha! I'm the non-wicked one, remember?" Anne insisted.

"Hey, Mom, what about me?" Sara asked.

"You aren't fooling anyone," Anne winked.

Sara giggled and moved over to sit on Whiskey's lap so she could snitch part of his chocolate éclair. Sara preferred to eat just a bit of each kind of donut rather than sticking to just one flavor so I knew her moving to Whiskey wasn't a betrayal.

"So, you camped out on the couch again last night?" Wild Card asked.

"Yup, and before you decide to rub it in, last night was your last night in my bed. You're officially evicted," I grinned.

"Should I make up Katie's old room?" Hattie asked.

"No. James said Wild Card can stay at the clubhouse. He will still be here during the days to use the gym downstairs for his physical therapy, though. And, I'm sure he'll be mooching meals off us, but other than that, his butt sleeps there."

"I'm right here you know," Wild Card said.

"Believe me, I know!" I quipped back.

"You need a nap," Wild Card grinned.

"I need my private suite back, including my extremely comfortable mattress, and my thousand-plus count sheets," I said.

"It is one hell of a bed," he agreed.

"Well, consider it gone," Bones growled entering the room.

James followed Bones into the family room and made a beeline for the bakery box. "We were told to be here early to pack your ass up and ship you out."

"Y'all are mean in the mornings," Wild Card complained.

"Not me," Sara grinned.

"No, but you're the most devious. I got you all figured out, little-bug," Wild Card said as he leaned over to tickle Sara. She squealed and giggled before moving over to Bones' lap to partake in a bite of his lemon custard donut. Bones winked at me as he tore her off a chunk. Anne just shook her head at her child.

"Well, this has been fun, but I got places to be, and shit to buy," Henry announced, getting up from the floor.

"Where are you storing the inventory while the store is closed?" I asked.

"Alex is letting me use his garage, free of charge, as long as I build enough stock for the main store and the additions. Piece of cake," Henry grinned.

"Good to know," I grinned back. "Do you have a minute to go over a few more business items?"

"Sure," Henry asked and followed me out of the room.

I looked back and pointed to Wild Card and Anne, who stood and followed us into my bedroom.

• • •

Once I was in the atrium, I turned on a scrambler and explained to them that I needed some supplies transported to Dallas's house. Anne agreed to pack the clothes I needed, and Wild Card agreed to gather the equipment. They would move everything through the tunnels, and when Henry dropped off his afternoon delivery at Alex's house, he would pick up the supplies and relocate them for me.

Chapter Six

After Henry left, everyone scattered to start their day. I was halfway down the basement stairway when Bones caught up with me and wrapped an arm around my waist, turning me to face him on the stairs. I looked around and verified no one was in sight before pulling the bug scanner out of my pocket. The lights lit up when I held it over Bones' cut, and his eyebrow rose. He pulled his cell phone out from the inside pocket.

Pulling him by the hand down the remaining stairs, I set his phone on the bar and rescanned him before scanning myself. The lights stayed blank. I walked down the hall and unlocked the furnace room. Bones followed me inside.

Bones was already lifting me in the air, as the door slid shut. He kissed me deeply as he pressed his body into mine against the cold cement wall. A searing heat rushed through me as we started pulling at each other's clothes.

It was wild, frenzied, and instinctual. I needed him, and he needed me. With my legs wrapped around him, he lifted me away from the wall, lowered himself on top of our pile of clothes, settling me to straddle his body. He slipped my nipple into his mouth, sucking deeply, as I guided his cock home.

Damn. He stretched me to my limit as I glided down. I was already on the verge of an orgasm and didn't dare move. Bones took the decision away from me by lifting me up and thrusting me hard and fast back down on him. My body exploded, gripping him tight as he swore and rolled us to switch positions.

Still in the throes of my orgasm, I held on tight as he pounded deep inside of me. Desperation, lust, and fear gripped our bodies in a vice and fueled our movements as he sent me further over the edge, followed by his own release.

Bones rolled over to the cold cement floor, pulling me with him, tucking my head to his shoulder.

"Tell me there is no other way, Kelsey," he whispered in my hair as he kissed the top of my head.

"I wouldn't ask this of you if it wasn't important, Bones. I'm sorry, but it has to be this way for right now."

"Is Sara in danger?"

"No. Why?"

"I've been racking my brain trying to figure out what could be so important. It's the only thing I could think of."

"No, she's safe," I said kissing his jaw line. "Bones, I need to ask for another favor. You won't like it, but I need you to promise me something."

"What do you need?" he asked while stroking my hair.

"If I ever come up missing, I need you to get my family to safety. All of them."

I moved my hand over his heart when I felt him tense at my words.

"If I'm dead, they're safe, but if I'm missing, they're in danger. Don't let them have a say in the matter. They can go to New Jersey or Texas, but they need to be moved where people can protect them."

"Tell me what's going on, Kelsey. I can help," he begged, rolling to his side to face me. He raised my chin and wiped the single tear that slipped past my guard.

"I can't. Not while Penny is still around."

"I can't keep her out of my bed much longer, Kelsey."

"I know. I don't like it any more than you do, but it has to be this way. And, I know she has asked about going to Pittsburgh. It might be easier if you do."

"I can't leave you," he said, tightening his arm around me.

"And, that's the problem, Bones. You're going to destroy me if she catches on to how you feel about me. People could die. People that are important to me. And I don't think I could ever forgive you if that happens."

He was quiet for a long moment. His hand slid gently up and down my side. He stared at me, waiting for me to change my mind, to tell him everything. I shook my head no, and he rolled to his back and sighed.

"Make me a deal—Promise to pull Wild Card into this mess. Ex-husband or not, he cares about you and will help."

"I told him everything a few nights ago. But don't even think of speaking to him about it. We have at least five bugs in the house. Your phone is the fourth phone we have found wired. And, we suspect the club and store are bugged as well."

"There's no way Penny could have covered that many locations so quickly without getting caught."

"She's not the only spy in our circle."

"Shit, babe. How bad is this thing?"

"As bad as it gets," I answered curling into him one last time, kissing his chest before I pulled away. "We're out of time. We need to separate before one of the bad guys catches us."

We both reluctantly dressed. Bones snuck down the hall as I crossed over to the War Room.

Tech and Katie were already inside working.

"Did you have a nice visit?" Katie grinned.

"None of your business. Any updates?"

"Maggie left. She said she would stay in touch. Sam is expected to make his check-in call today, and thanks to Lisa, Penny will have an opportunity to make a call too," Tech said.

"I'm available most of the day. So is Wild Card."

Carl and Sara entered. Carl claimed a box of electronics he was busy taking apart. He had decided that the listening devices we had planted were inferior products and was in the process of inventing an improved model that would pick up a more detailed recording. It not only kept him busy but could prove helpful as well. Sara pulled two laptops over and started working with Tech on whatever current research they had going.

Alex, Anne, Whiskey, Wild Card, and Donovan joined the room, and I doled out assignments. Hattie was in charge of snacks, refreshments, and monitoring the rest of the house in case visitors arrived. Lisa would be at the store keeping an eye on Penny.

"Carl, you better sit between Tech and me so we can keep an eye on you," Sara said. "After last night, I can't trust you near a computer."

"What happened?" I asked.

"It's okay, Aunt Kelsey. I covered his tracks," she said.

"Sara?" I asked again.

Sara sighed, and looked up at me. "I went to the kitchen to get a glass of juice, and when I came back, Carl seemed a bit too happy. I checked the computer's history, and he hacked the cable company. We all have unlimited access to triple X movies now."

Carl was grinning, quite proud of himself.

"Please tell me that includes my house," Alex laughed.

"It was actually the whole county, which made it easier to cover his tracks," Sara explained as Carl pointed to something on her screen.

Three hours later, I was getting a headache from reading all the data that Maggie copied from the FBI files. Most of it was outdated, but I was taking notes on anything that might prove useful in the future. One of the burner phones on the counter rang, and I leaned over to retrieve it.

"Hello."

"It's Haley. I'm on a payphone in the grocery store."

"Are you safe?"

"I don't know. We are still in Key West, but Bridget says we are being followed. I don't see anyone, but she's better at the sneaky stuff than I am."

"You are being followed. You have some bad guys on your tail, but some good guys are tailing them. Stay in populated areas and if something looks off, run or scream. But the good guys have orders to jump in if it looks like either of you are in danger."

"Shit. So, exactly how many people were watching us at the nude beach yesterday?"

I was laughing too hard to answer. Katie took the phone and started talking to Haley.

"Haley and Bridget have a spa treatment set up for today, and Bridget is planning on making her move," Katie said after disconnecting the call. "She'll sneak out the back of the salon and jump over to Miami."

"Good. We need those trackers going. We also need to get Penny's phone cloned today," I said.

Penny wasn't the type to leave her phone lying around, so getting access to it wasn't going to be easy.

Carl, being in his own little world, jumped up and went out into the hallway. I followed him out and watched as he started drawing with a black marker on the long white hallway wall. I grinned after a few minute, realizing what he was doing. He was drawing a scaled map, freestyle, of Pasco's island, including reefs and land elevations. I returned back to the War Room.

"Carl's drawing out the island on the hallway wall. Katie, can you call Goat and see if we can get a door installed at the end of the hall to secure the whole area?" I asked.

Katie nodded and stepped out to call Goat.

"Sara, do we have anything on the interior of Pasco's mansion?"

"Pasco was stupid enough to allow an interior design magazine to do a feature on his island mansion. But it only had a few photos of rooms on the first floor and the master bedroom on the second floor. And, the house descriptions were too vague to be helpful."

"There would be a lot more pictures," Carl said reentering the War Room and resuming his work on the electronic gadgets at his workstation.

"Carl's right. The photographer probably took hundreds of pictures, and they narrowed it down to a handful," Tech said stopping whatever he was doing on his laptop and opening another laptop. "Sara, do you know the name of the photographer? I might be able to access the rest of the pictures."

"Coming up," Sara said moving over next to Tech and starting up another laptop for her to work off from. Between the two of them, they now had six laptops and eight monitors going. We were going to need a bigger War Room.

I saved my notes on the laptop that I had been working on. I felt restless and needed to clear my head, so I went upstairs.

Arriving in the kitchen, I was surprised to see that the new cabinets and flooring were installed, and the walls were being mudded.

"I can't wait to see it when it's done. It's already looking so much nicer," Hattie grinned coming up beside me.

I had to agree. The new space would be an open layout with room enough for everyone to hangout and plenty of sunlight to brighten the large space. I just couldn't get as excited as Hattie while my head was so cluttered with everything else.

"Hattie, did you catch the weather report?" I asked.

"No snow in the forecast for a few days. The roads are clear. It's bitter cold, but the sun is shining," Hattie said with a slight smirk.

"Good," I grinned back. "I'll be gone for a couple hours. Cover for me?"

"Go let your hair down," Hattie said as she dug into the coat closet for an insulated leather jacket and gloves. "I'll let everyone downstairs know that you're taking a break, and we will keep an eye on Carl."

I didn't need any more encouragement. I changed into some insulated clothes and my riding boots before retrieving the coat and gloves from Hattie.

Chapter Seven

I pushed the bike from the shed through Chops' backyard and into the parking lot. Chops came out and shook his head at me, but didn't try to stop me. He had refused to sell me the bike when I asked about it. Being a club member, he was probably worried about Bones' reaction. But his longtime girlfriend Candi had worked with me in secret to buy the bike and taught me how to ride.

"You go, girl!" Candi cheered walking up next to Chops as I started up the bike.

The small engine pitched and whined in excitement beneath me, vibrating through the seat, egging me on. I double checked the gauges and secured my chin strap before waving to Candi and ripping through the parking lot and down the road.

The wind pressure was intense, but the leather and insulated clothes kept me warm, as I continued to speed up, turning down secluded roads out of town. I was heading toward farm country, where the roads were straighter and less traveled by commuters and police. I opened the bike up and let her fly. Leaning forward into the bike, I zipped past fields of dead crops until I noticed the speedometer was well over the 100 mark, and reluctantly slowed down. If it weren't for Nicholas, I would have liked to have seen just how fast the bike could go.

An hour later, my hands and feet were starting to get cold. I had crisscrossed through the farming districts to the

Southwest and was somewhere between the southern outskirts of South Haven and Bangor. I pulled into a small country hole-in-the-wall bar, opting for a drink and to warm up before I drove home. There were a whopping three vehicles in the parking lot, and I assumed one of them was the bartender's.

Entering the bar, I pulled my helmet off and tucked it under my arm as I peeled my gloves from my chilled fingers. Two young women sat together at the far end of the bar. A middle aged woman that looked like she would make a good ally in a fight worked behind the bar. Three drunk men sat at a nearby table, laughing too loud and ogling the young women.

Everyone in the room turned as I entered and I nodded a silent greeting before picking a stool at the bar that allowed me to watch the entire room, as well as the door. I ordered a rum and coke as I piled my outerwear on top of the barstool beside me.

"Kind of cold out to ride," the bartender commented.

"I bought the bike just before the snow started to fly, so haven't had much of an opportunity to play. It's cold, but it's worth it," I grinned.

The bartender nodded with a knowing grin.

I felt my phone vibrate and pulled it out to read the text from Candi: *Bones just left. He knows about the bike. Not happy.*

Damn it. Bones needed to chill, or Penny was going to figure out what the hell was going on.

The three drunk patrons were getting louder, and two of them got up and moved over to the younger women at the bar. I set the phone down and moved my messenger bag behind the bar. The bartender watched me do so and nodded. We both pretended to be distracted as we listened.

"So, you ladies looking for some company?" the first man chuckled as he stroked his hand down one of the women's arms.

"We make real good company," the other man added stepping up behind the other woman and placing his hands on her hips.

"No thank you. My brothers will be here any minute, so you need to back off," the woman closest to me said, trying to push him away.

She managed to stand and turn, but he used her new position to push her back into the bar and proceeded to paw at her.

"The company I'm planning to give you isn't the brotherly kind," he said as he leaned in, trying to kiss her.

Both women now struggled to gain distance from the men, and both men continued to paw at them.

"They said NO," I stated loudly gaining their attention. I rose from the stool and slowly walked their way.

"Why lookey here, boys. One for me too," the third man said as he stepped into my path and reached for my arm.

I pivoted to the side and pulled his arm forward, propelling him past me into the bar. As his chest ricocheted off the bar, I slammed his head downward onto the bar top, knocking him out cold.

Both his buddies stood shocked for a brief moment before barreling toward me. I grabbed a nearby chair, swinging it with force into the closest man's face. Several of his teeth and some blood splattered about as the chair broke away in pieces.

Stepping back and to the side, I back-kicked the last man in the gut, before turning to face him with a heel punch to the throat. He dropped to his knees, holding his throat.

Snagging two empty beer bottles, I smashed the ends of the bottles off on the edge of a table. I held a defensive position with the broken beer bottles at the ready while two of the men slowly pulled themselves up off the floor.

"Gather your idiot friend and leave before I finish this," I warned.

The two rushed to drag their buddy out the door without looking back. As the door closed, I walked over to the trash and discarded the broken bottles.

"Sorry about the mess. I'll pay for the damage and help clean it up," I said as I reached down to pick up some of the chair parts.

No one responded.

I looked up to see the bartender grinning, a shotgun resting in front of her on the bar. The two young women stood staring at me.

"What? Never saw a girl that can fight?" I smirked. "You two – make yourselves useful and help me clean this mess."

The young women jumped in and quickly the bar was back in order, minus a chair.

"I wouldn't count on those guys going far," I said re-occupying my bar stool. "They will be pissed. You should call someone to escort you home."

"I already called Trinity's dad," the bartender said as she set a fresh round of drinks down. "From where I was standing, if they want revenge, you'll be their target."

"I'm not concerned about a couple of rednecks," I said.

And, I wasn't, but to be on the safe side, I pulled my gun from my shoulder bag and strapped on my shoulder harness. I had just secured and covered my weapon when I heard motorcycles approaching. I tensed.

"It's just Trinity's dad and brothers," the bartender said reading my body language.

In walked six Hispanic bikers wearing leather cuts. On the back of their cuts, their club name was branded across their backs: Demon Slayers. I hadn't kown that there was another club this close-by and wondered if they were allies or enemies of the Devil's Players.

The young women greeted the bikers and excitedly began talking over each other about the drunk men. The bikers listened as they removed their outerwear and claimed their beers that the bartender lined up along the bar-top. An older man with a goatee kept glancing my way, and I rolled my eyes as the story was beginning to become a bit embellished.

"Enough," the older man interrupted. "You—," he said turning to me. "What happened?"

With him now facing me, I read his patch confirming my suspicions. His cut declared him to be President of the MC.

"Three drunk rednecks didn't understand the word no. I intervened, and they decided it was best to leave. The end," I said taking another drink of my cocktail.

"She kicked their asses," the bartender grinned. "The one guy was still out cold, maybe dead, when they dragged him out."

"He wasn't dead," I rolled my eyes again. "These girls with you?" I asked the head biker, pointing to the two young women.

He nodded.

"You need to teach them to fight. Having them depend on the club to keep them safe, isn't realistic. They need to know how to defend themselves," I said getting up from the bar.

"After they get their asses spanked, we just might do that," he said scowling at the girls.

"You leaving, hon? Those guys could still be out there," the bartender asked.

"I'll be fine. My bike is fast, and as you know, I'm armed."

"I would feel better if you had an escort," she said.

I sighed but pulled my phone out and called James. He answered on the first ring.

"Hey, Bones is pissed," James chuckled answering the phone.

"Don't care. Look, I ran into some minor trouble out of town and if I don't make it home in the next thirty minutes, send the cavalry my way."

"Where are you?" James asked, his tone turning serious.

"Just leaving The Last Season bar outside of Bangor," I said.

"That's Demon territory. We don't have a beef with them, but we don't have a relationship with them either. Does your minor trouble involve their club?"

"Two of their women were being mistreated by some rednecks. I set the rednecks straight. The bartender is worried about retaliation."

"I can have some guys meet you at the county line and follow you the rest of the way in. Get on the bike and open it up till you see them," James instructed.

I disconnected the call and proceeded to glove up. "All set. My friends are meeting me at the county border. They didn't want to cross the line and have any misinterpretation of their intent unless I was in danger," I said eyeing the President.

"So, you're one of the Devil's girls?" he asked.

"No," I snorted, both at the notion that I was a club whore and the way it sounded to be called the Devil's girl. "But, we're good friends."

"It'd be bad if a friend of the Devil's Players was hurt on our side of the line. I'll send some of my guys to escort you for a mile or so to make sure you aren't followed," he said holding out his hand. "The name's Renato Gonzalez."

"Kelsey Harrison," I said as I returned his handshake. "Teach the girls how to fight."

"I will. And, we owe you one."

"I'll remember you said that."

Chapter Eight

Three of the bikers followed me out of the bar and road behind me out of the lot. Two miles down the road, they slowed to turn around, and I opened up the throttle and sped to the county line. Devil's Players met me and followed me home as promised.

My SUV was parked in the driveway, and the garage door was up. I drove into the garage and parked the bike in the extra space at the back. Shutting down the engine on the bike and removing my helmet, I watched as someone pulled my SUV inside and the garage overhead was closed. Bones climbed out from behind the wheel and stalked toward me. I pulled out the scrambler and turned it on. It was enough of a warning for Bones to walk back to the SUV and set his phone inside. As he walked back, I tossed my helmet on top of a nearby counter followed by my gloves.

"What the hell do you think you're doing? You have no business going out riding a bike by yourself!" Bones yelled.

My fury spiked, and I slammed my palms into Bones' chest, knocking him back into the SUV. The car alarm blared as I stormed up to a stunned Bones.

"You need to understand me, Bones," I glared. "This morning's interlude was a mistake. You need to stay away from me until this is all over. Don't talk to me. Don't track my movements. Don't breathe my direction. You will *destroy* me if you fuck this up. Do you hear what I'm saying? I won't just be mad. I'll HATE you for the rest of my life."

Bones stood shocked, still leaning against the blaring SUV. I grabbed the keys from his hand and shut the alarm off before throwing the keys onto the nearby counter.

"Kelsey, I can't do this. I can't sleep with Penny. I can't pretend that I'm not in love with you," Bones said reaching for me.

I pulled away from his touch and turned my back on him. "Penny is smart, Bones. She watches you, and she watches me. She can't know I'm on to her. And, right now she's suspicious of every move we make. The way you and everyone else around us keep reacting, she's going to figure it out. The only way she is going to let her guard down is if you sleep with her. There isn't any other choice."

"I can't do it."

"You have to."

"Damn it, tell me why!" Bones yelled, dragging his hand over his face. "Why is this so important?"

Wild Card stepped into the garage through the kitchen door. He walked over and cupped my face in his hand, turning me to face him. I saw the resolution in his eyes. He was going to tell Bones what was going on. And, as furious as I was at the moment, I knew he was right. Keeping it a secret wasn't working. I was making the situation worse by not trusting Bones.

I nodded, and Wild Card released me, turning his attention to Bones.

"Penny may know the people that kidnapped Kelsey's son. It's the first solid lead she's had in years, and if you can't sell this charade of a marriage to Penny, then Kelsey may never get a chance to find him. Or worse, Penny figures out what we are doing and sends word back to kill him."

"What? No. Penny wouldn't do that," Bones insisted.

"Brother," Wild Card said stepping in front of him, "Penny would do just about anything. She's never been the person you thought she was, and I think you already know that. That's why you're struggling with sleeping with her."

I walked away.

Inside the house, everyone was gathering for dinner, but they moved quickly out of my path as I stormed passed them toward my private suite.

I swept everything off the top of my dresser in a fit of rage. Picture frames, perfumes, lotions, bounced off the wall. *Fuck him!* He was going to ruin everything. I turned and smashed a fist into the full-length mirror.

"Bastard!" I screamed.

My back to the wall, I slowly slid down to the floor.

Resting my head in my hands, I tried to calm my breathing. I heard the door open and shut and knew there was only one person brave enough to venture this close when I was this angry.

Wild Card sat down beside me, careful to pick an area clear of glass. He pulled a scrambler out of his pocket and turned it on, setting it between us.

"Bones is going to fuck this up. I can see it coming and don't know how to stop it," I whispered.

"I think he has a better idea of how serious you are about this charade after you bounced his ass off the SUV," he grinned, trying to lighten the mood as he wrapped an arm around my shoulder. "He knows the stakes now. We'll just have to hope that he helps. I'll keep an eye on him."

"There's no choice for me between Bones and Nicholas. I'll always pick Nicholas," I said.

"I know. He's trying, Kelsey. But leaving him in the dark was a mistake."

"I need to change plans. I need to be ready to go on the offense."

"Don't count Bones out yet. Now that he knows about Nicholas's life being on the line, he may just pull through for us," he said as he got up and started to pick up the glass and debris from the floor.

A knock on the door was followed by Hattie entering with a broom and trash can. The three of us cleaned up the mess that I had made.

"Feeling better?" Hattie asked, grabbing my hand and inspecting the small cuts from the mirror.

"I'm okay now," I nodded. "I'll be out in a few minutes."

"Glad to hear it, Sunshine," Hattie said, before her and Wild Card left.

I cleaned and bandaged my hand and was ready to return to the dining room when Carl walked in followed by Tech.

Carl had earbuds in his ears that were connected to a cheap looking MP3 player.

"I DON'T UNDERSTAND WHY IT STOPPED WORKING," Carl shouted.

Tech shook his head and pulled out one of the earbuds from Carl's ear. "It's called a scrambler," Tech said picking up the device from the floor. "It interferes with the frequency."

"Ok," Carl said taking the scrambler from Tech and walking back out of the room.

Tech pulled out another scrambler and turned it on. "He's going to rebuild the bug so the scrambler doesn't interfere with it, isn't he?"

"That would be my guess," I grinned. "I'm going to grab some food and then work downstairs for the rest of the night."

"I'm going to go eat while I watch Carl continue to blow my mind with his mad electronic skills," Tech laughed. "It's Katie's shift in the basement. Can you take a plate of food to her?"

I nodded as we walked back down the hall.

Entering the War Room, I balanced two plates and a bottle of wine.

"You read my mind," Katie said taking the bottle from me.

I set the plates of spaghetti and meatballs on the other end of the table. I grabbed two plastic cups off a shelf but by the time I turned around, Katie was already swigging straight from the wine bottle. That will work, I thought as I tossed the cups back. We sat and ate our dinner while sharing the bottle. The wine was sweet and had a hint of green apple.

"Anything interesting happen while I was gone today?" I asked.

"No. I had to listen to three hours of Lisa and Penny talking fashion and Sam whining all day about Bridget being gone. According to Sam, Bridget's extremely flexible."

"Didn't need to know that," I laughed.

"Are you sure? Because I can rewind to the section where he describes to Goat in great detail Bridget riding him reverse cowgirl style." Katie tipped the bottle again.

"I think I'm good. No one has made any phone calls?"

"Not yet. I wondered a few times if Penny was reading something on her phone, but I have no way of knowing for sure."

"We need to get the phone cloned," I sighed.

I had been trying to think of an angle we could use on Penny to separate her from her phone, but so far I was coming up blank on ideas.

Shaking the thought off for the moment, I turned around to the printers and started looking at the pile of pictures that were printing at warp speed. There were at least sixty already printed. The photos were a jumble of both interior and exterior photographs of Pasco's estate and would take a while to sort through. Having finished my dinner, I grabbed the first stack and a roll of scotch tape and crossed the hall, entering the furnace room. I started hanging exterior shots on one wall and interior shots on another. By the time I was through the first pile, Katie and Sara joined me with more stacks and started helping me sort and hang them.

We were just hanging the last of the pictures when Tech entered with a final stack. We all groaned but started to work them up onto the walls.

I looked around the room at Katie, Sara, and Tech. "Who's watching Carl around all those computers?"

"Shit!" Tech said as he ran from the room.

"I don't even want to know. But, if you guys can try to prevent him from going to prison, I would appreciate it," I said to Katie and Sara.

Sara giggled, and Katie smirked.

I gathered the dirty dinner dishes and carried them out. Entering the gym, Bones and Tyler were working out on the mats. Bones was teaching Tyler some basic offense moves. When Bones saw me, he stopped what he was doing, and Tyler accidentally cross-armed him in the face.

I couldn't help it. I laughed as Bones stumbled back.

"Oh shit – sorry, brother," Tyler said as he distanced himself away from Bones.

"I'm fine. It's my fault for getting distracted," Bones said glaring at me.

"Yes, it is. Distractions can be deadly," I agreed as I moved past them to the stairs. "Lesson number one Tyler, never let your guard down."

I had just walked back into the War Room when the red laptop on the shelf started to ring. All eyes turned to the laptop as I jumped to retrieve it and answer the teleconference call.

"What's wrong?" I asked before the screen even blinked from black to a picture of Charlie.

Charlie was laughing so hard she had to lean her head on the table in front of her.

"What the hell is going on Charlie?" I asked.

My immediate concern was quickly evaporating, and I was more curious than anything. It wasn't usual for Charlie to randomly reach out, but she obviously wasn't panicking about anything.

She was finally able to ebb her laughter enough to wipe the tears from her face and look at the display again. "I have to know. Who the hell is the little pixie-looking chick?" she laughed.

"The pixie-chick is with us. Please tell me she didn't get caught!"

"No, No. She's good. I mean really good. I was loading the boxes you asked for into my car and was distracted by something going on in the parking lot. It was so entertaining that I turned on the video recorder on my phone. Here, watch this," she said.

The screen blinked and then a video app appeared. I hit play and watched the scene unfold.

"Holy shit. Is that Bridget?" Katie asked over my shoulder.

Bridget was wearing a skimpy bikini top, short hot pink shorts, and a cute little hot pink helmet with matching elbow and knee pads. She was also flaying about on rollerblades, slamming into multiple vehicles and people as she squealed and giggled.

My old boss Trevor Zamlock was trying to help her maintain course and guide her to his car. She skidded away and bent over abruptly, offering a pleasant view of her backside. He was so focused on her ass that he never noticed her attach the tracker. Then she abruptly swayed the other direction, breasts-first into his face. He stared openly down at her breasts as he backed her up and settled her neatly in the passenger seat of his car.

The video couldn't make out all the audio from the distance, but Bridget's squeals and giggles could be heard across the lot. I watched her lean back into the car, appearing to relax and I grinned. She had not only tagged the outside of the car with a tracker during all of her slamming around but, if my suspicions were right, she dropped a bug inside the car as well. *Hot damn.*

"Bridget, I could kiss you!" I yelled at the video in excitement.

"Did she really just drop a bug into a cop's car?" Tech asked in bewilderment.

"That she did. And, she probably already tagged Feona's car, so get the tracking and audio equipment going."

Charlie's face came back on the screen, still grinning ear to ear.

"Damn, she so reminded me of you during that drug bust on the beach in Southside. Where the hell did you find her?"

"She's a friend of the family. I like her too. She helped me out with a pickpocket job last summer. She has some mad skills that she's been teaching me."

"Well, I know you weren't expecting a call from me this soon, but I had to share the laugh and wanted to let you know to turn on the gear in case she can't reach out anytime soon."

"I appreciate it. We will jump on the computers and get things going. Did you find all the information I asked for?"

"Sure did. It wasn't a problem. I told them I wanted to sort out all your old boxes and clear it all out. They have sat gathering dust in the corner untouched. Everyone assumed I was just sick of looking at a reminder of you," Charlie grinned and winked at the screen.

"Feeling the love, feeling the love," I laughed.

"Ha. There are plenty of good cops that are still pissed as hell at me for locking your ass up in the nuthouse. It hasn't been a smooth couple of years to deal with, so don't start any shit with me, cousin."

"So there are some loyal friends on the force after all? That makes me feel better. I busted my ass for that department. Sometimes it's hard to see past all the betrayal."

"I know, Kelsey. But don't blame them all for the actions of a few. I'm sure the majority of them will be on our side when this all blows up."

"Alright, alright, this isn't getting us anywhere. Anything else to report?"

"FedEx will be delivering your boxes Saturday morning. As for me, I have a date tonight so I have to go."

"A date, huh," I teased. "Anyone I know?"

"Probably, but it doesn't really matter. Just scratching an itch, Cuz. No reason to snoop into my personal business."

"Ugh. Kid, be sure to use protection and don't tell me any of the details," I laughed and disconnected.

Chapter Nine

There was a knock on the War Room door, and I opened it to see Goat standing in the hallway. I pulled him inside, and Katie quickly scanned him.

"Sorry, Goat. I haven't meant to exclude you. You've been busy at the store and ended up out of the loop on some things." Goat was a club member but also a good friend and was overseeing all the construction projects at the store.

"It's all good. I figured whatever was going on, you would let me know if I can help. I don't need to know any of the details," Goat nodded.

"Good, then I can give you the highlights. I have a son, who was kidnapped by really bad people. Sam is spying on us, but he's not doing it because he's evil, he's being blackmailed. Penny is also spying on us, but she really is evil. That's the basics, and oh, the house, store, clubhouse, phones, cars, etc., consider it all bugged."

"Damn," Goat said, leaning back with both eyebrows raised in surprise.

"Yeah, so our operation has expanded, and we need more space. I need to know if you can install a door at the end of the hall, and open up the real storage room with our fake storage room so we can move some of the boxes back and make our workspace larger."

Goat looked around and then stepped back into the hallway. He opened the furnace room, seeing all the pictures posted to the wall, and shook his head before closing the door. The next door beside the furnace room was an empty room with several cable bolts secured to the wall and a floor drain. This gained a grin and a head nod from Goat. It was a similar setup to the storage room I had at the store, which had held unwelcome guests on a few occasions. The other room was adjacent to the War Room and was a real storage room, but it only had a few boxes of kitchen and linen supplies.

"I can build a new doorway tonight at the end of the hall and install the locks. You will need someone to move the security panel."

"I can do that," Carl volunteered.

"I can also open up the real storage room to your fake storage room so you can move some of the racks out of your way. Who from the club has access and permission to help?"

"Whiskey is the only one that knows what's going on, but I trust Tyler and James too. Bones is already juggling his sneaky time. As I said, I didn't intentionally leave you out. They kind of barged into my personal business, well except Tyler."

"Stop fretting over it," Goat grinned. "I'm not that insecure."

"Good to know," I grinned back.

"I'll go grab Whiskey, and we'll get started. Should only take a couple hours as long as you don't care about the wall opening between the two rooms looking pretty," he said before turning and leaving without asking any questions.

I always liked Goat, but he just moved up several notches on the scale.

I pulled out a fresh oversized copy of a Miami-Dade County map and started marking Trevor and Feona's travel history from the tracker logs. The old theory of 'know your enemy' was a little disconcerting being I used to consider them both friends and recognized most of their stop locations.

Tech started researching the few addresses I didn't recognize as Katie pulled the audio files so we could catch up to real time listening again. Katie listened to Sam's outdated feed, while I listened to Penny's with one ear as I worked the map with Tech, who was listening to Sam's real-time feed.

Goat returned with Whiskey, James, and Tyler and they opened the wall between the two rooms and constructed the new doorway at the end of the hall. They also removed the doors from the War Room, storage room, and furnace room for easier access.

While Carl and Goat were adding the final touches to the new entranceway and security panel, Whiskey and James dragged the shelving units into the new space. Tyler got a text and had to go back to the clubhouse. Anne and Lisa helped clean up all the drywall and stack it into trash bags.

The audio for Penny was about two hours behind real time, so at first, it was strange to listen to Lisa talking with Penny in the earbud while she was in real time talking to Anne only a few feet away from me. By the time she and

Penny left the store, it was obvious that Lisa's feathers were ruffled and that she was ready to escape all things Penny.

"Rough day today, Lisa?" I laughed pointing to the earbud I was listening to.

"That woman is the rudest human being I have ever met. You might call me Princess, but if I ever act that snobby then you have my permission to slap me," she grumbled. "I really hope she doesn't take me up on my offer to come back tomorrow, but the odds aren't in my favor."

"So glad it was you and not me," Anne giggled.

I could hear in the earbud, that Bones and Penny were back in the clubhouse and that Penny was in their room moving things around. It seemed she spent most of her time in their room when they were there, not bothering to socialize with the rest of the Players.

I heard the door open and moments later Bones' voice.

"Did you have fun with Lisa at the store today?" he asked.

"I would have rather spent the time in bed with my husband, but it was better than sitting here all day waiting for you."

"I'm sorry. I've been neglecting you," he said.

When moments later I heard Bones moan, I pulled the earbud out in a rush. Wild Card looked at me in concern, before picking it up and listening. He looked back at me sadly.

"He's going to make it believable," I said.

"Yeah. Sounds like he's willing to do what it takes," Wild Card answered. "You okay?"

"Okay? No. But if it gets me closer to finding Nicholas, I can live with it."

"And, if it doesn't," he asked.

"I don't know if Bones will ever forgive me if she's not involved," I answered truthfully.

"It's almost time," Tech said, taking his earbud out and putting Sam's audio on speaker.

"What's about to happen?" James asked.

I had Katie update James, Tyler, and Goat with an outline of everything that we had been working on and why, but it was a lot of details and moving parts to keep track of.

"Sam has to call Nola with an update on his spying," Katie said.

"I just don't get it. He seems like he genuinely cares about everyone," James said.

"I think he does. But Nola has his sister, so he doesn't have a choice. I'll try to get her out of it if I can, but with Nola, the girl could be dead already, or worse," I said.

We could hear Sam dialing an outgoing number before it started to ring. We all held our breath as we listened.

Nola: So, you are capable of calling in on time.

Sam: I don't have much to report, and I don't dare stay away from the clubhouse too long. James is watching me all the time.

Nola: Why is he watching you?

Sam: Probably because I'm only a prospect, and you have me sneaking all over the fucking place spying for you!

Nola: Did he catch you?

Sam: No. He's just been paying more attention to everything going on since the VP is staying with his girlfriend and the Sergeant is off fucking around with his wife most of the time.

Nola: So she bedded him then?

Sam: Why the fuck would you care if Bones is getting laid by his wife?

Nola: It's none of your business why I care, just answer the question.

Sam: Yes. About an hour ago, she was screaming her orgasm loud enough to hear from the clubhouse bar. I would say they're definitely fucking.

Nola: Anything else?

Sam: No. They've kept me busy on club runs lately. I haven't been to Kelsey's house the last few days.

Nola: Report in next week.

Sam: Can I talk to Bianca? Please. I just want to hear that she is okay.

Nola: Since you asked so nicely, you have 30 seconds.

One of the phones beeped, and then background noises became more pronounced. We could hear a female crying. Nola had put her phone on speaker.

Bianca: Sammy? Sammy, is that you?

Sam: Bianca, it's going to be okay. I'll get you out, I promise.

Nola: You shouldn't make promises that you aren't sure you can keep, Sam.

Bianca's screams drowned out any further conversation until the phone was disconnected.

Sam's voice: *Fuck!!*

"She's insane," Anne whispered.

Whiskey pulled her into his good shoulder to comfort her.

"Yes, she is," I said.

I turned away and stared at the box that contained Nicholas's stuffed animal and other keepsakes.

"We will find Nicky. He's waiting for you just like I was," Carl said.

I nodded and offered a small smile to Carl.

"Carl, I need you to explain to James how to clone Penny's phone. He can work with Bones to get access to it, but you have to teach him how to do it," I said.

"Easy-peasy," Carl said, taking Donovan's smartphone away from him, and within seconds he had it laying on the table in multiple pieces.

"Damn it, Carl," Donovan grumbled.

Carl was explaining to us a third time the parts of the interior of Donovan's smart phone when the buzzer on the in-house intercom signaled.

"Kelsey," Hattie called over the intercom. "Motorcycles are pulling up."

I checked my gun clip as did Wild Card, Donovan, and Whiskey.

Carl jumped up and hugged me before releasing me abruptly and returning to his chair. I gave Tech a questioning look, but he just grinned and shrugged.

Donovan and Whiskey led us out of the room, and Wild Card was trailing behind me. He seemed to be recovering quickly from his recent gunshot injury, and even the stairs weren't bothering him today. I would still have to watch him, and make sure he didn't overdue it.

"Quit mothering me inside that head of yours," he grinned. "I'm fine. I'll take a break and lay down when I need to."

I smirked, but didn't say anything.

Donovan sent Hattie to the basement to wait as the four of us stepped outside. A very distressed Sam and a watchful Tyler were just getting off their bikes.

I raised my gun to Sam's head and with the other hand signaled for him to remain silent. Wild Card emptied a flower pot and with Whiskey's help, frisked Sam and relieved him of his phone and anything else electronic. We moved into the garage and Donovan scanned all of us and turned on a scrambler.

"Sam, why are you at my house in the middle of the night?" I asked.

"I don't know what else to do. I didn't want to help her, but she has my sister. She's hurting my sister. She is fixated on you and makes me call her and tell her what you're doing," Sam cried, grabbing my arm. "She's going to kill her. I don't know what to do."

He was a wreck. Hearing his sister's screams must have sent him over the edge.

"How can I trust you, Sam? Your first priority is going to be to Bianca, not to the club or me. How do I trust you with everyone's lives?"

"*Please.* She's going to kill my sister. Just tell me how to stop her," he cried.

Whiskey stepped up and held Sam in brotherly comfort until he calmed.

"Sam, she also has my son. You have to understand that while I'll try to get your sister out, I have to consider my son's safety too. If you report back to her that I'm searching for her, she'll kill him," I said.

"Your son?" Sam looked up at me with tears streaming down his face. "Fuck. I didn't know, Kelsey. She didn't tell me."

"If you betray me, or I get even a hint going forward that you're a threat," I said, stepping forward and pressing the barrel of my gun to his forehead, "—I will kill you. I don't want to, but I'll do it to protect everyone."

"I won't betray you. I swear it. Nola's never going to let Bianca go like she said."

"No. She'll never let Bianca go. She'll either sell her or kill her. To Nola, your sister is either a witness or a commodity. And, she won't let you live either."

I holstered my gun.

"The house is bugged. Some are from you, but some are Penny's. So don't speak as we walk downstairs until we are in a secure area."

"You'll help me?" Sam asked.

"We'll help each other. You might have information that can help me find both Bianca and Nicholas. But you have to trust me, and do whatever I tell you to do, Sam."

We silently walked into the house and moved to the War Room.

Chapter Ten

Several teary faces greeted us when we opened the door to the War Room. James stood and greeted Sam in a brotherly embrace. Anne hugged tightly to Whiskey seeking comfort. Sara and Tech grinned at Carl who sat sipping a soda through a bendy straw.

"What the hell?" I demanded.

"Carl fixed his new and improved bug. It's not only impervious to scramblers, but it's undetectable by our scanners too," Tech grinned.

My brain finally caught up, and I reached into my pocket, pulling out Carl's latest creation. He must have stuffed it in my pocket when he spontaneously hugged me.

"Carl, do not bug me. You can bug anyone else in this room, but not me," I scolded.

"Sorry, Kelsey," Carl pouted.

"It's okay, Carl," Sara said. "Aunt Kelsey doesn't have her mad face on, so you're not in the real kind of trouble. Next time let's practice on Whiskey or Aunt Katie though."

By midnight, both Feona and Trevor had settled in, and we were at real-time on the audio recordings. Penny was snoring loudly over her mike, and I could hear Bones tossing and turning in frustration. He was probably regretting giving her so much wine during their late dinner.

We all took turns grilling Sam for any scrap of information he possessed. We had a lot of new leads to follow, but nothing definitive. He also gave us remote access to all the listening devices he had planted and told us their locations. We were able to remove several since he never told Nola in any detail where they were placed. He admitted hearing several conversations where James, Whiskey, and Bones had been trying to figure out whatever I was hiding. And, Anne and Lisa had spoken enough near a mike to send red flags to anyone listening that my behavior was different as well.

"Damn," Anne said. "I get it now. It's way too easy to say the wrong thing and get caught. You couldn't risk telling us."

"I'm sorry," I said hugging my friend.

"No, I understand now."

Sam had already proved his loyalty by not giving any of this information to Nola. In the end, I believed Sam had provided us with everything he knew and that he was as willing to help me find my son as I was to try to save his sister. We both knew the odds were against us.

It was late by the time I packed up for the night. Upon exiting the War Room, I was surprised to see that Carl had indeed changed the security access. A tablet was secured to the wall, and I grinned as I placed my palm onto the screen. 'Good Night, Big Mama' displayed on the screen, and the latch buzzed, unlocking the door. *Oh, Carl.* I shook my head.

Sometime in the night, a noise woke me. I turned to the atrium and recognized Bones' silhouette approaching. I held up a finger to my lips, letting him know my room was bugged. He nodded, before stripping down in front of me and joining me in bed. I pulled out a scrambler and turned it on as he slowly kissed down my body.

"You shouldn't be here," I panted as he removed my underwear.

"I won't make love to you while I'm sleeping with her. But, that doesn't mean I won't claim your body in other ways," he said while his tongue started to dance down my body.

"Oh," was all I managed to say as he worked his magical tongue and fingers.

Two orgasms later, I was panting heavily, trying to recover my breathing as I pulled back the sweaty sheets and Bones trailed kisses back up my body. He grinned at me before he claimed my lips and ravished my mouth.

"You shouldn't be here," I warned when he moved beside me.

"I have Tyler watching Penny," he said as he nuzzled my neck. "He'll let me know if she makes a move. I got her drunk on some expensive wine I stole from your cabinet, and she was snoring when I left."

"This is too risky, Bones. One screw up –," I started to say.

"I know. I just needed to see you after… I just don't know how we are ever going to be right after all this."

"After what? After you had sex with your wife? Do I want to see it, hear about it? – Hell no. But when this is all over, we'll both know we did what we had to do."

"I hated every minute of it. You have to know that," he said as he pulled me close and held me.

I closed my eyes and enjoyed the peaceful moment, but the guilt of what I was risking forced me to pull away. "As much as I want you here, it's not safe. And, it's not smart. You should go back to the clubhouse."

I heard my phone vibrate on the nightstand. Reaching over to retrieve it, I read the text message from Wild Card: *Bones was seen leaving. James covered -said club errand. Send him back.*

I slid away from Bones and passed him the phone. Wrapping in a robe, I quietly retrieved a gym bag from the closet and filled it with stacks of cash I kept in my desk drawer. I zipped the bag and handed it to an already dressed Bones.

He took the bag from my hands but didn't move away. I looked up and saw the question in his eyes. He wanted to know if it was worth it. If almost getting caught was worth being together. Shaking my head, I walked away into the bathroom and closed the door. Nothing was more important than Nicholas.

Chapter Eleven

I tossed and turned for a few more hours, before finally drifting back to sleep. The much-needed rest was short-lived, though, when I heard Anne, Whiskey, and Hattie yell: "PANTS, CARL!" from the other side of the house. I decided it was safer for Carl if I got up.

I took a long hot shower before dressing in my favorite badass bitch gear, made complete with my knives securely tucked inside my heeled leather knee high boots.

I found Carl sitting, dressed, on the edge of his bed, looking down at the floor.

"Good morning, my friend," I said, sitting next to him. "You okay?"

"I keep getting it all wrong. I wanted them to like me," he pouted, his lower lip quivering.

"You're not getting it all wrong, Carl. They just have to get used to you. And, because of Sara, we need to figure out a way to make sure you have pants on," I said nudging him with my shoulder.

"I'm sorry, Carl," Hattie said from the doorway. "This must be hard on you to be somewhere new. But we do like you. We will figure out the pants thing, and I'll try to remember not to yell at you, okay?"

Carl stood, ran over to Hattie, and gave her a hug.

"Are you going to come join us for breakfast now?" Hattie asked while patting his back.

"Can Kelsey come to? She needs to have her coffee or she gets grumpy," Carl said.

"Oh, I know all about Kelsey's caffeine addiction," Hattie said, leading him down the hall.

"Caffeine is actually a stimulant that depending on the quantity ingested, can either spike sexual energy or diminish it," Carl said. "I don't recommend you drink too much Kelsey, or you won't be able to enjoy yourself like you did last night."

Carl's voice had projected down the hall, and when we reached the dining room, six sets of eyes locked in on me. I could feel my face heat, and started to turn around to flee when Hattie grabbed me by the arm and propelled me forward.

"Uh, thanks for the advice, Carl," I said. "I'm sorry if I disturbed you last night. I was under the impression that the wall between our rooms had a bit more sound-proofing."

"I built a sound magnifier and attached it to the wall. I wanted to be sure you were safe."

"So, you can hear everything in my bedroom now?"

"Yes," Carl said as he carefully inspected the food offerings on the table.

"Splendid," I grumbled as Anne handed me a cup of coffee.

Katie laughed.

"What did you use to build your sound magnifier?" Tech asked.

"My phone and television contained all the parts that I needed," Carl said before he stuffed half a croissant in his mouth.

Tech got up and walked down the hall. Minutes later he returned with Carl's electronic masterpiece, and Sara and Tech started grilling Carl with questions about how it worked. I just hoped that they disassembled it.

"Damn. It's going to be a good day," Alex teased checking out my outfit.

"I felt like stepping it up a notch this morning. I've been in sweatpants too many days this week," I winked.

Hattie entered setting a plate of eggs in front of Alex. I scrunched up my nose at Alex's breakfast, and Hattie noticed the expression.

"Is there something special you want this morning?" Hattie asked.

"Is there any leftover spaghetti? Breakfast just doesn't sound good," I answered honestly.

"I think there is enough left," Hattie grinned going back into the kitchen.

"I can get it. You don't have to wait on me," I called.

"Shush. You've been on the run for days. Sit and relax while you can. You have a busy day today," she added glancing at the basement door.

I sighed.

"I'm going to the store with Anne and Lisa this morning," Alex said. "Do you need anything?"

"Not that I know of, but if things change, I'll give everyone a call."

A few minutes later, Hattie returned with the leftover spaghetti and meatballs, and my stomach rumbled as a dug in. She had even made some fresh garlic toast to accompany my meal.

"Dang, that looks and smells delicious," Alex said as he looked disappointed back at the rest of his breakfast.

"Believe me, it is," I said as I placed a huge forkful in my mouth grinning.

Hattie giggled as Alex tried unsuccessfully to steal some.

I finished my food in record time and then helped Hattie clear and wash the dishes before the contractors arrived to work in the kitchen.

Moving downstairs to the basement gym, Wild Card and Whiskey were working with the physical therapist that I hired to strengthen their damaged muscles. Bones and Tyler were working on defense training on the mats. Donovan was lifting weights while James spotted for him. I nodded to them all but continued down the hall.

In the War Room, Tech, Sara, and Carl were nose deep in laptops. Katie was working on the cloned phone.

"Anything on the phone?" I asked.

"We have the information and I've been going through her data and browsing history. So far I can't see where she is communicating with anyone."

"Does she have email accounts on her phone?"

"Yes, two. One is an account that her family uses, and the other one is empty. There doesn't appear to be any history of emails sent or received and it's in a dummy name. Maybe she bought the phone used, and it's the prior owner's email account."

"Anything in the drafts folder?"

"I didn't check. Hang on," Katie said as she turned back to her own laptop. "Damn. One drafted message exists and says: *'Pasco's looking for fresh blood. Have other buyers and sellers in need too. Can you get to FL?'* That's all there is."

"So, she hasn't answered yet. She read the message and should be responding back either today or tomorrow."

"How will we know she responded?" Sara asked.

"The draft message will be changed. They both have access to the email account. A lot of criminals use draft messages in email accounts to communicate without actually sending the messages."

"We might be able to pull the history," Tech said.

"Let's hold off. The past stuff is likely related to Ernesto's business and not our present day situation. If we get caught messing with the data, the FBI wouldn't be able to use the information to prosecute."

I paced back and forth letting my thoughts gather and formulate a plan. I retrieved the burner phone from the counter and called Maggie. She answered on the first ring.

"No, I'm not coming back to pick up Carl. He's all yours," Maggie laughed answering the phone.

"Wouldn't trade him for the world," I said. "I need a favor that might benefit both teams, but I need to know if it will get me in legal trouble first."

"Why doesn't that surprise me?"

"So, Penny's phone has been cloned, and she has a dummy email account that is being used for human trafficking. The older information is all yours, but the newer stuff is in my wheelhouse. How do we divide the line without me being arrested with violating privacy laws?"

"I have no idea," she laughed, "but I'll find out."

"Sounds good. I'll have Katie send you the email address. If you pile the information in a folder and wait to take action on it, I would appreciate it. I think she's close to bouncing out of Michigan."

"You got a handle on keeping track of her?"

"All over it."

"Anything else?"

"Not at the moment but things are speeding up."

"Keep me in the loop," she instructed before she ended the call.

I walked into the furnace room and sat on the floor staring up at the pictures of Pasco's estate. Within minutes, my cell phone rang.

"Kelsey," I answered without looking at the display.

"Kel, I'm working at the store, and some bikers I don't recognize just pulled up. Goat called James," Anne whispered over the line.

"Can you see their club name?"

"Yeah, it says Demon Slayers, Bangor, Michigan."

"They're new friends of mine. The president's name is Renato. I'll be right there."

"I'll intercept the pending conflict," Anne giggled and disconnected.

I got off the floor and dusted down my pant legs.

"I have to go to the store for a few. I'll be back as soon as I can," I called into the War Room before leaving.

• • •

Chapter Twelve

"Renato," I called out, walking around the exterior of the building.

Anne and Lisa were standing in the front parking lot talking to Renato and a few other Demon Slayers, while an unhappy Goat was leaning up against the building with his arms crossed.

"Ms. Harrison," Renato greeted with a smile and a head nod as I approached. "I didn't mean to create a disturbance with my visit. I didn't have a number to reach you by phone and thought it would be alright to stop in."

"It's fine. It's my impression that the two clubs don't have any issues with each other, just a lack of acquaintances. Is that your opinion as well?"

"We've no problem with the Players. We aren't looking for any either."

"Good. Then consider The Changing Room to be Switzerland until the two clubs are better acquainted," I grinned. "What can I do for you today?"

Six motorcycles pulled in and parked near the store. The Players dismounted and started to approach. I raised a hand, signaling for them to stop. Everyone except Bones paused in their tracks. Bones smirked and continued approaching.

"That one's not so easily trained," Renato said in a hushed voice.

"The others weren't easy either, but for the most part, they don't mess with my personal business, and I don't mess with club business. This one," I nodded to Bones, "is always in everyone's business."

Renato and I laughed as Bones finished walking up to us.

"Renato, Bones from the Devil's Players. Bones, this is my friend Renato, President of the Demon Slayers."

Both men gave each other the 'nod' but didn't speak.

"As you were saying?" I asked Renato while rolling my eyes.

"We tracked down those assholes from the bar. They won't be bothering anyone anymore."

"Good to know. They still breathing?"

"We just warned them that retaliation of any kind would result in permanent bodily damage. It didn't take much convincing after the condition you left them in," Renato grinned.

"What? I didn't even break any bones," I laughed.

"No, just teeth," Renato chuckled.

"He was ugly before I ever crossed paths with him."

"Do I even want to know?" Bones asked with a raised eyebrow to me.

"No," I answered and turned back to Renato. "Anything else?"

"I wanted to drop off my number for when you're ready to call in that marker I owe you," he said handing me a piece of paper with his number on it. "I meant what I said. I owe you one."

"Sounds good," I said turning and pointing to James, Whiskey, and Goat, motioning the three to join us. "While you're here, it might be a good idea for you to meet some of the Players. Then the next time you visit, they won't be so overbearing."

"I wouldn't count on that," Renato chuckled watching Bones glare at me.

I introduced the other Players and bowed out of the conversation to let them all get to know each other. The Demon Slayers reminded me a lot of the Devil's Players. Both clubs were too protective and in testosterone overload.

Anne and Lisa followed me inside the store.

"So, what's the story about the guy with the missing teeth?" Anne asked.

"I sort of broke a chair on his face," I answered.

"That would do it," Anne nodded.

Lisa looked at Anne, then back at me, before shaking her head and walking away.

"I'm guessing that Lisa has never been in a bar brawl before," Anne smirked.

"We have a few things to teach her after her pregnancy."

Anne and I both grinned thinking of Princess Lisa in a bar brawl.

"While I'm here, talk me through the renovation status."

"Goat is doing a great job managing everything, and the new additions seem to be coming along at a fast pace. The painters will be in early next week to paint the main sales room, and then we will get the green light to decorate for the wedding."

"Good. Do I need to do anything to help?"

"Nope. You have enough on your plate, so we are making our own decisions and running the show without you. Take as long as you need. The store is covered."

"Anne, there is something that I've wanted to talk to you about," I said looking around and discreetly turning on a scrambler. "If anything were to happen to me, go to the safe-room in the house. There is a small metal lockbox in there. I have everything all of you will need to retain ownership of the houses, the store, and the other properties. The only thing I ask is that if Nicholas ever comes home, he will be taken care of."

"You don't have to ask us to take care of Nicholas. And, I get that you aren't trying to be melodramatic. You're a mom. You have to plan things out ten steps ahead. I did the same thing. If something happens to me, I have my documents in the bottom drawer of my dresser. You and Hattie are listed as Sara's guardians. I hope you don't mind that I put your name down without asking."

"You know me well enough to know there isn't anything I wouldn't do to ensure Sara's safety and happiness."

We shared a quick girly hug, as Bones entered the store. His eyebrow rose at the display of affection between us. We both laughed, and Anne went back to work.

"Everything ok?" Bones asked.

"Yeah. Family business. How did it go with the Slayers?" I asked as I reached down and turned off the scrambler.

Bones grinned as Goat walked up to join us.

"Did you really knock out a guy's teeth with a barstool?" Goat asked, smiled proudly at me.

"Only a few of them," I answered. "He really was ugly before I messed up his face."

Bones and Goat laughed as James and Whiskey walked in and joined us.

"Thanks for the introduction, Kelsey," James said. "We've been meaning to reach out to the Slayers for a while but couldn't get enough information to know if it would be a welcomed meeting."

"The same rule applies. I don't want to know any club business. I have enough drama to deal with. But they seem like honorable men. Time will tell."

"Well, we're going to get to know them better. I sort of invited their club officers to your weekly potluck," James grinned.

"I wasn't aware that we were having a potluck, *tomorrow*," I gritted out.

"Should I ask Hattie?" James laughed.

"More like you better let Hattie know that a dozen strangers were just invited to a potluck we hadn't officially planned on. And, I advise you to do it in person seeing as she doesn't have full access to the kitchen yet, and will have to figure out how in the hell to make that happen."

James' smile disappeared, and he bowed his head as he turned and left the store. Whiskey and Bones laughed. Goat shook his head before returning to the back room.

"You told him to tell Hattie in person so he could be properly scolded, didn't you?" Whiskey asked.

"Hell, yes. Hattie has had her hands full with Carl and needs to vent some frustration on someone. Better James than me," I grinned.

The clicking of heels distracted me, and I turned to see Penny approaching. I plastered on my best fake smile.

"Hi, Penny. Are you helping Lisa with the gowns again today?" I asked.

"Yes," she quipped as she stepped up to Bones and melted into his body, dragging his face to hers for a deep kiss.

"Kelsey, let's give these two lovebirds some privacy," Whiskey said as he wheeled me around by the elbow and hurriedly pulled me into the former menswear department and into the employee only hallway. "Shit, you okay?"

"Yeah," I answered though I wasn't sure it was true. I rubbed my stomach trying to get the summersaults to stop. "Damn."

I leaned against the wall and closed my eyes.

"Just remember that it will be worth it in the end," Whiskey reminded me.

"God, I hope so."

I returned to the War Room and worked the rest of the day and into the night on tracking all the stops Feona and Trevor made while monitoring all the audio feeds with Tech and Katie's help. By 10:00 I kicked them both out to get some sleep and continued to work solo on my research while I monitored the slower activity on the feeds. By 3:00, I finally called it a night and went to bed.

• • •

Chapter Thirteen

The alarm clock blared on high volume at 6:00 am. Startled from a deep sleep, I sat up, and pitched it across the room at the wall. Pieces of the clock projected in different directions, and it was once again silent.

Sighing, I laid back on the bed as Carl came rushing into my bedroom.

"You okay, Kelsey?" Carl asked.

"I'm good, Carl. Just tired," I answered. "I'm going to get up and make some coffee. If you want to join me, brush your teeth and put on some clothes."

"Ok," Carl said as he waddled his bare hairy ass back out of my bedroom.

This day isn't starting out well, I thought, as I got up and went to my bathroom.

Hattie was already seated in the dining room. My favorite coffee mug sat in front of my chair and a Scooby Doo mug with a caramel-latte sat ready for Carl. Hopefully, Carl's was decaf.

"Good Morning, Hattie," I greeted and kissed her cheek before sitting.

"Good Morning, Sunshine," she grinned. "Do I need to put a new alarm clock on the shopping list this morning?"

"I can fix the clock," Carl said as he entered. "I will make it better so it doesn't scare Kelsey."

I wasn't sure if this was a good idea but shrugged my indifference. I looked up from my coffee to greet Carl, and stopped mid thought. Carl had his wet and oiled hair stretched into a smooth low ponytail that sported an oversized blue ribbon at the base of his neck.

"What's up with the hair, Carl?" I asked.

"I like Sara's pink ribbons, but she said boys can't wear pink, so she found me a blue one. Do you like it? I styled it like Bones does his hair."

"Sure. Looks nice. What did you put in your hair to make it all slick?"

"Baby oil. It took the whole bottle since I have so much hair, but I think I got it all."

Carl reached up to run his hand over his hair followed by wiping his hand on the front of his matching blue shirt. A large smear of oil now covered the front of the shirt.

"Mr. Carl, you look very nice. I'll pick you up some hair gel today so you don't have to use the baby oil. How does that sound?" Hattie smirked.

Hattie really just didn't want baby oil stains all over our house.

"And maybe Anne can teach you how to use it?" I added.

"Yes, please," Carl smiled.

I looked around at the construction progress. The walls were still being finished, but the new windows glowed with the morning sun, lighting up the new seating area. The overbearing dining room table looked out of place with the rest of the changes.

"Did you find a different table?" I asked Hattie.

"No. I like the size of this one, but not how formal it is. I'm having trouble finding something I like."

"What if we strip this one and then replace the chairs with something more rustic?"

Hattie looked at the table as Whiskey came down the stairs and walked into the kitchen. He returned a moment later carrying a cup of coffee.

"I could torch-strip the table to give it a more distressed look. Then I could knock out the sharp edges and clear stain it. You could mix and match chairs and benches for it too," Whiskey said. "It won't have that snobby look you both hate."

"Henry did find a good deal on some chairs that might work. Let's give it a try, but no torch-stripping inside the house. Have some of the guys help you move the table onto the deck first," Hattie said.

There was a knock at the front door, and Whiskey went to answer it. James entered.

"You're late, Mr. James. I said we started the morning at 6:00 a.m. sharp," Hattie said to James.

Whiskey and I both raised an eyebrow but didn't say anything. Carl grinned at Hattie.

"Sorry, Hattie," James sulked.

"Start cooking up scrambled eggs and toast. Anne and Sara will be up soon, and Tech stayed the night with Katie so they will be over early too. You will want to cook about two and a half dozen eggs. Lisa will be over around 7:00 and she will want an English muffin. There is also fruit that needs to be cut up while the eggs are cooking. Sara, Tech, Kelsey and Lisa will want some fresh fruit with their breakfast. And, try to get Carl to eat some too, but he won't like it. And, then there is the coffee, be sure not to run out of coffee."

James walked back into the kitchen and started to pull everything out to start cooking.

"So, what's up?" I grinned.

"Mr. James needs to understand that I don't just sit around all day," Hattie grumbled loud enough for James to hear. She turned to me and sent me a secret wink. Whiskey had to duck his head to hide his chuckles.

"So, James is on Hattie-duty today. Nice," I said.

"Sara and Anne are coming," Hattie called out to James. "Anne will want a dash of milk and a spoon of sugar in her coffee and Sara will want a medium orange juice."

"I have a lot of work to get through today, but did you need me to do anything?" I asked.

"No dear. Mr. James and I will handle everything. Whiskey, if you can wait until tomorrow before working on the table, I think that would be best. Otherwise, we won't have enough time for the finish to dry before we have company tonight."

Anne and Sara stumbled down the stairs, and James hurried to place their drinks on the table before they got there. He slopped Anne's coffee, but Whiskey wiped it up with his shirt sleeve. Hattie moved Sara's juice in front of me while Sara climbed up onto my lap.

"Where's breakfast?" Sara asked.

"Breakfast is running a little behind schedule this morning. It seems Mr. James didn't do a proper job of setting his alarm clock," Hattie grinned.

We all looked to the kitchen as James was trying to pick an egg shell out of the hot pan. Mission accomplished, he turned back to the cantaloupe and started to cut it up as Tech and Katie entered the back slider.

"Hot chocolate and black coffee, James," Hattie said.

Flustered, James tossed the knife down and turned to make their beverages. We all grinned.

"I'm not sure what's going on, but it's fun to watch," Anne said.

"Yeah, I think I'll hang out here today," Whiskey said.

"Hey, Carl," Tech grinned. "Are the British coming?"

Carl looked puzzled, and Anne turned and finally noticed Carl sporting his all blue outfit and the big blue ribbon used to queue his oiled hair back. She broke out into a huge grin.

"I don't know anyone that's British," Carl said inbetween slurps of his latte.

Breakfast was only partially edible and not only did Carl welcome eating his fruit as he pushed his eggs aside, but Whiskey was looking pretty desperate to switch as well. Everyone seemed a bit jealous of Lisa's English muffin, but none of us said anything. Well, other than Hattie. Hattie made sure to let James know everything he messed up, including the eggs that were somehow both burnt and undercooked.

Most of us were eager to move to the basement to escape the chaos of the morning and quickly raided the War Room's cupboards for snacks.

"Thank goodness Hattie stocked the cupboards," Katie said as she ate a dry pop tart. "This is a one day only event right? Hattie will be back tomorrow?"

"That was my understanding. Until then, let's let her have her fun," I grinned.

"So what did James do to earn a punishment?" Tech asked.

"He invited another club without asking to the weekly potluck that we weren't planning on having."

"Oh man. He really doesn't get it," Tech laughed.

Chapter Fourteen

I was working in the furnace room reviewing interior pictures of Pasco's house when the burner phone rang. I checked the display and saw that it was Jackson calling.

Jackson grew up with Reggie and Wild Card and was officially now Reggie's boyfriend. Years ago, he had saved my ass once in Vegas and had convinced Wild Card and me to get married to help cover my tracks. We've been friends ever since.

"Hey, Jackson, what's up?"

"I'm going to clobber Kid next time I see her. Not only did Pops flip a lid, but Reggie has turned Shauna into some type of pet project and is playing Henry Higgins to her Eliza Doolittle. It's enough to drive me mad."

"I had nothing to do with it. I swear. It's between you and Kid," I laughed.

"Oh, payback is coming. And, it's going to be good," he said. "Really, I just wanted to check in and make sure everything is okay. Wild Card said it's been busy, but neither of us wanted to discuss anything over our regular phones. Do you need Reggie or I to come back?"

"No. We are in research mode still. If and when it's time to take action, I might need you both to head to Florida, so you'll be closer if you stay put in Texas for right now. I do have a question that maybe Shauna can answer. She around?"

"Yeah, let me get her."

I heard Reggie arguing that Shauna's hair wasn't set yet, followed by Shauna informing him that he was messing up her natural hairdo anyway.

"Girly. Tis the bomb here. D'ay got horses and shit for real here," Shauna said.

"And cows too," I chuckled. "Hey, I'm looking for some names. You happen to know anyone that runs with or is close to Pasco these days?"

"Shit, girly. You don-wanna be a messen with dat crew. Likely ta be swimmin wid' da' sharks."

"I know. But that's the direction things are turning so are you going to help me out with a name or force me to walk in blind?"

"Ariel," Shauna sighed. "She was da' big blonde ho down on the corner of 5th Street. Now she's hoity-toity with slick hair. She been workin' da' ladder and does some private shows and recruits for Pasco's parties. I would start with her. She been squirrely lately, so best be careful girly."

"Ariel have a last name?"

"Ya know da' streets. Ariel probably not even 'member her own real name. I gotta go. Reggie-doll is all on me about da' curlers being in too long."

I shook my head as Shauna disconnected.

Whiskey entered the furnace room.

"Are you staying at the house today?" I asked.

"That's the agenda. A FedEx truck just delivered a shit load of boxes. Where do you want them?"

"I need them in the new addition of the War Room."

"We'll handle it. How did Carl get my fingerprints for the scanner?"

"I have no idea. Did you have a special message?"

"Yeah," Whiskey grinned. "*Smooth as Whiskey.*"

Whiskey left, and I looked back at the wall of interior pictures. I estimated that the pictures only covered a third of the inside of the mansion. Turning to the exterior photos, most of them lined up with the satellite photos we had of the property. About every hundred feet stood an elevated security post that I knew would typically be manned with heavy firepower. Some of the other photos were of unrelated fountains and poolside pictures. Several guests lounged near the pool sipping on colorful drinks.

Frustrated, I was turning out of the room when something caught my eye. I stepped closer to look at one of the poolside photos.

There, lying in a lounge chair, was Nola, grinning at the camera.

I pulled the photo down and continued to stare at it as I walked back into the War Room.

I'm not sure how long I stood there staring at the photo until I someone was pulling it out of my hands.

I looked up to see Wild Card watching me. I consciously took a deep breath and nodded to let him know I was okay.

"What's wrong?" he asked.

"It's Nola," I said nodding to the photo.

Katie came over and looked at the photo. "It does look like her, but with the sunglasses, it's hard to be sure."

"It's her. Look at the necklace. It's a photo locket. Inside is a picture of Nicholas and I. The necklace was the only item that I noticed was missing the day that Nicholas was kidnapped."

I dragged my hands through my hair as I collected my thoughts.

"Okay, so she's closer to Pasco than I thought," I said to no one in particular. "This ups the ante, folks."

"Sara, Katie and I are still sorting through the FBI files and filling the gaps," Tech said. "You and Anne start working through your old files and pulling what we need."

"Okay," I nodded moving over to the stacks of boxes that Whiskey, Wild Card, Tyler, and Donovan were hauling in.

I was glad Tech stepped up to assign orders since I wasn't running on all cylinders at the moment.

Anne and I sorted through the boxes rearranging them by year. When the last box was delivered, we had filled half of the new space with my old case files.

By the time James delivered lunch, closely supervised by Hattie, I was in desperate need of a break. Charlie had sent all my files, ensuring that anything I worked on was copied in the boxes. Years and years of both good and bad cases were flooding my brain, but so far we hadn't come across any files related to Pasco or anything else that was useful.

I bypassed lunch and walked through the gym and out the slider doors. Tyler stepped out beside me and handed me a cigarette and a lighter.

"It's a bit cold out. Do you want me to run up and get your coat?" Tyler asked.

"No. The cold air feels good after being in a crowded storage room for so long. How's the training coming?"

"Slow," Tyler chuckled. "You make it look so easy."

I laughed at Tyler as James and Bones joined us on the patio. I turned on a scrambler, just to be safe.

"My cousin Charlie and I were taught some basic moves in the academy, but we were always such a close match against each other, that it was frustrating. I started taking private lessons so I could surprise her next time we sparred. Surprise, Surprise, she was doing the same thing. We spent years training separately, just to try and outdo the other one."

"Man," Tyler whistled. "You two are nuts."

"That's probably true. But eventually, we realized the training kept saving our asses on the streets so we started training together. Besides, a little healthy competition makes a good motivator."

"You have a point," Bones said stealing a hit off my cigarette. "Maybe I should add Sam to the training schedule. We can set up a sparring match between Tyler and Sam in six months' time to see who wins."

"Sounds good in theory, but Sam and Tyler aren't as competitive as Charlie and I. You'll need a reward," I said.

"A punishment would work better with those two," James said, talking as if Tyler wasn't standing right there. "No sex for a month to the loser."

Bones and I grinned.

"For a month?" Tyler frowned.

"Only if you lose, Tyler. Only if you lose," I grinned and left them to finish the details.

Because of the audio surveillance we had on Sam, I knew way too much information about Sam and Tyler's sexual escapades. It could be just the motivator that they both need to step up the learning curve for their training.

Chapter Fifteen

The rest of the day went by too quickly. We all made progress, but not enough. We still lacked a lot of details for Pasco's estate and couldn't find any evidence linking Nola to Pasco other than the poolside photo, though their common thread of violence was enough to make them friends for life in my book. And while we had been through more than half the boxes, we still hadn't located my old files on Pasco and his associates.

Lisa had popped her head in to let us know we needed to get ready for the party. We were shutting down when I noticed that Carl wasn't around.

"Where's Carl?"

"I haven't seen him for a couple of hours," Sara said.

"Me neither. I thought he went to the bathroom, but then he never came back. I meant to go look for him, but I was too busy," Tech said.

I searched the house and didn't find him anywhere. I clicked the app for his ankle tracker, and it showed he was in town. Corning James in the kitchen, as he was trying to 'toss' a salad unsuccessfully, I asked him if he knew where Hattie was.

"I don't know. Carl came in and was freaking about needing to go somewhere. Hattie left with him about an hour ago. I sent Sam with them in case Hattie had a problem with Carl. He was really wound up. Hey, am I doing this right?" James asked gesturing to the salad.

"No, but it's fine," I answered scooping up all the food on the counter and throwing it in the bowl and setting the bowl away from him. "You better get started on everyone's drinks. People will start arriving soon. Hattie keeps a list on the refrigerator of what everyone likes."

Figuring whatever was going on with Carl, Hattie had it handled, I went to my room to freshen up. By the time I exited my bedroom, I was relaxed enough to pretend that all was right with the world for a few hours. I walked to the kitchen and retrieved my drink from the counter. Taking a sip, I immediately ran to the sink and spit up the contents.

"James, what the hell? Are you trying to poison me?" I asked.

"What are you talking about? I did everything the book said," James said, grabbing the book and showing me the recipe.

"Well it didn't taste like it should," I complained and put the glass in the sink. I grabbed a fresh glass and made my own drink before stomping over to the table where several people had gathered.

"You didn't like your drink?" Anne asked. "Mine was perfect."

"Mine too," Katie said. "James can't cook worth a shit, but he makes one hell of a martini."

"He helps behind the bar all the time at the clubhouse," Whiskey said.

"Maybe it was intentional then, and he blames me for being assigned to Hattie's duties," I said.

"Your house has an open layout now. I'm right here listening to you, and I did not fuck with your drink," James insisted.

James seemed pretty certain that he had the drink right, and I turned to look about the room. In the living room was Bones, Penny, Tyler and Sam. On the back balcony were Goat, Chops, and Candi. Entering the door was Dave, Tammy, and Dallas. I looked back into the living room, and Bones was tense, watching me. I shrugged in answer to the unspoken question.

I couldn't say why my drink was bad, just that it didn't taste right.

Dallas called my attention away. "Darling… I'm so glad you decided to throw your weekly potluck. Not that I contribute to the food, but because I couldn't think for the life of me of anything else to do tonight. And, I have a present for you."

Dallas, one of my dearest friends, liked to live her life a little on the wild side. She's not only my favorite stress reducer, but she was the one that helped me get back on my feet when I first moved back to Michigan, and I'll always be grateful to her for that.

She dug into her oversized purse and pulled out a pile of folded papers.

"Here. Do what you want with these," Dallas said handing them to me.

I started to read them and thirty seconds later I abruptly folded the papers back up and tried to control the blush that heated my face.

"Dallas, you have to give me a little warning next time," I laughed.

"Let me see," Katie said taking the papers. "Holy shit!"

"Well, I just thought that it's been awhile since you have written a new book and maybe you needed some inspiration. So I just wrote down a few of my favorites."

Over the years I had made a significant income writing erotic romance books. For the last few weeks though, I hadn't had time to work on my writing, setting it aside to focus on finding Nicholas as clues finally started surfacing.

"Let me see those," Goat insisted entering the room and taking the papers from Katie. He read the first page and then moved them back into Dallas's purse. "Hold on to these until I have a chance to read through them later," he winked.

"Actually, why don't you draft a book for me? When you're done, I'll go through it and do a re-write, and we can co-publish it," I offered.

"Oooh. That might actually be a good job for me," Dallas smirked. "I've got lots of material to work with."

Goat shook his head as the rest of us giggled. There was no taming Dallas, and I think that's what he liked the most about her.

As Goat pulled Dallas away from the group, Dallas's son Dave, a local cop and good friend, joined us at the table, pulling his wife Tammy down onto his lap.

"Steve said to tell you that he had to work tonight and couldn't make it," Dave grinned. "He's working the winter festival downtown."

"You didn't have to work?" I asked.

"I chose not to, so I could bring Tammy over. She needs a break from dealing with Dallas on her own. You and I have been too busy lately, and Tammy has been picking up the slack."

"Thanks, Tammy," I grinned. "I know it's not your favorite task."

"It's okay. It's not as bad as it used to be. I think reading your books helped me to understand Dallas a little bit better," Tammy said absentmindedly.

When shy and proper Tammy realized that she had just admitted in front of everyone that she was reading my erotic romance books, she gasped and ducked her bright red face into Dave's shoulder. "Oh my goodness, I'm so embarrassed."

"Chill sweetheart," Katie said. "We've all read Kelsey's books and know what you're saying."

Anne and Katie clanked glasses and the guys grinned. I had my own fan club at home, that was for sure.

Tammy pulled her head up and looked around the table. Everyone greeted her with a smile, including, her husband.

"Oh my, I'm surrounded by perverts," Tammy laughed.

Everyone cheered.

With the open layout between the kitchen and the table, I saw Wild Card enter the house and stop to talk to James. They were talking quietly so I couldn't hear what they were saying, but they moved over to the sink and James pointed. Wild Card looked about the room, barely making eye contact with me before he picked up a glass and smelled inside it. I watched his body go instantly rigid, as he turned back to look at me.

So someone had put something in my drink. But, what? I nodded toward the stairs and moved that direction.

Sara and Amanda were playing on the computer in Sara's room, so I chose Anne's room and pulled out a scrambler. Whiskey, James, and Wild Card followed me into the room.

"What was it?"

"I'm not positive. It smelled pharmaceutical. Could have been Bennies. Since you spit it out quickly, the worst that would happen is you might get tired," Wild Card said.

"What the hell is a Bennie?" James asked.

"Downers: Xanax, Valium, any other type of sedative or relaxer. Mixed with alcohol it could be fatal or lead to a coma if the dosage is high enough," Wild Card said.

"Shit. I didn't see anyone messing with the drinks, Kelsey. I was watching when Penny and Sam got their drinks, but I could have missed something. It's a tough job playing Hattie," James said.

"It's fine," I said looking down at my drink. "I'll just be careful. We better get back to the party."

"Not so fast, Sunshine," Hattie said dragging Carl by the arm into the room with her. "You boys head back downstairs. The other biker club just showed up. Kelsey, we need to talk, preferably in your room."

I waited for Whiskey, James, and Wild Card to leave before I closed the door behind them. Carl was clutching several rolls of paper.

I opened the hatch from Anne's room to access the safe room and led the way down the narrow steps to the lower level. Sara would be able to hear us through the passageway from her room, but she would make something up to explain the noise to Amanda if needed.

Once at the lower level, I opened the secret entrance into my room, and we all entered. I locked the bedroom door and closed the French doors.

"What's going on?" I asked after I scanned the room.

There was a noise in the safe room, and Sara entered. Just to be safe, I scanned Sara to make sure she wasn't bugged. She giggled as she held her arms out to her sides.

"I got rid of Amanda. She went to play with the other kids," Sara said. "Can I help?"

"Yes, we might need you," Hattie said. "I swear, Kelsey, I didn't know what Carl did until we were on the way back home."

Hattie was clearly upset, and I moved her over to the desk chair to sit.

"Whatever it is, we will deal with it. What happened?"

"He insisted we go to town. He was so agitated that I just grabbed our coats, and we left. We went to the print shop, and he had these huge printouts ran. I questioned him on the way home, and he admitted that he hacked that bad man's security system and got the building layouts. I didn't know what to do so I just hit the gas and got here as quick as I could. Sam was with us, and he knows we have them. I asked Tyler to wait with Sam in the basement. Do we trust Sam yet? Oh, dear, I just didn't know what to do!"

"Relax. Breathe, Hattie," I said kneeling in front of her. "You did fine. We can fix this," I assured her.

"Carl, what computer did you use?" Sara asked.

"The one in your bedroom," Carl pouted.

Sara asked me to send Tech up, took the printouts from Carl's hands and passed them to me. Then she dragged Carl by the hand back up the hidden passageway.

"Hattie, it's all going to be fine. Are you better now?" I asked.

"I prefer to run the kitchen than handle all this spy crap," she sighed.

"Well then, I think James is ready to admit defeat and relinquish your throne. Something you should be aware of, though. Someone tried to spike my drink tonight, so if you can help me keep an eye out, I would appreciate it," I grinned.

"How dare anyone try to hurt you in our home! For the rest of the night, only drink what I hand you and don't let it out of your sight," Hattie said, stomping out of the room.

I stuffed the rolled architectural specs in with my own drafting layouts and followed her down the hall.

As I passed Tech at the entrance to the dining room, I motioned with my eyes upstairs, and he moved in that direction.

"James, you're officially off duty. Get the hell out of my kitchen," Hattie yelled.

Surround sound cheers erupted, and James hugged Hattie before surrendering his apron.

"I swear, Hattie, I'll never take you for granted again," James insisted.

I reclaimed my chair at the table, but realized somewhere along the way, I had lost my drink. I pouted for all of about 10 seconds before Hattie set a fresh glass in front of me.

"Thank you, Hattie," I grinned.

"You are most welcome, Sunshine," Hattie replied returning to her roost.

Chapter Sixteen

"Sunshine?" Renato grinned.

I looked up, surprised to realize that Renato and several of his club members sat across from me at the table.

"Don't sweat it if you didn't meet that side of her either. She's only that nice and sweet to Hattie, so the rest of us compare her closer to a summer thunderstorm," Katie grinned.

I flipped Katie off, and Renato laughed.

"How are the girls?" I asked Renato.

"On short leashes," Renato answered. "We've been trying to teach them to fight, but they aren't paying much attention."

"You should try a competition," James said. "We have two prospects in training right now, and they have a bet going. Loser has to go a month without sex. We set a date six months from now for them to fight against each other."

"The parameters set for Tyler and Sam may not be the best example to use when describing Renato's *daughter*, James," I said.

"Ah, shit, sorry," James stammered. "Maybe a shopping trip or something?"

Renato laughed. "I'm not naïve when it comes to my daughter and her friend. It might be the no sex restriction that does the trick for them as well."

• • •

"Unless you want to become known as the creepy dad, you might want to pick something easier to enforce. What about the loser has to scrub the clubhouse down from top to bottom? Neither of those girls is the type to get dirt under their manicures," I grinned.

"I would pay good money to see either one of them scrubbing a floor," one of Renato's men admitted.

"Me too," another one chuckled.

"That might work. The only problem is that we don't seem to have a good handle on teaching them how to fight a man twice their size," Renato said.

I turned to Katie. She grinned and nodded.

"Kelsey doesn't have time to help right now, but I can spare an hour or two. Our store is shut down for a few weeks. I'll come out a couple times a week and teach them new moves. It's up to them to practice and work out, though," Katie said.

"I would appreciate it. I can pay you," Renato said.

"No need. I'm more than willing to volunteer the time if they put in the effort," Katie said.

"You're not traveling out of town by yourself right now," Tech ordered, coming back down the stairs.

"Whiskey or I can escort her," Wild Card said. "We'll make sure she gets there and back just fine."

Renato was about to question why she would need an escort, but I discretely shook my head at him. He raised an eyebrow, and I sighed nodding for him to follow me.

"Excuse us boys," I said getting up and carrying my drink with me. Renato and one of his men followed me down the hall and into my room. I pulled out a scrambler, turning it on and laying it on top of the dresser.

"Trouble?" Renato asked.

"Cautious. We are in the middle of some things that I'm not willing to discuss with someone I just met. So far, we are flying under the radar, but that can change at any moment," I answered.

"Do you need extra protection?"

"No. If a war hits, it will most likely happen outside of Michigan, further South."

Renato nodded and glanced back at the scrambler. "We have club charters in most of the Southern states. You drop my name at any one of them if needed. Until then I'll make sure there are plenty of Slayers guarding Katie during her visits, and I can provide additional escorts."

"Not necessary. Both Whiskey and Wild Card are on the injured list, so their roles are more along the line of having an extra set of eyes if needed. Katie is more than capable of handling herself."

The man that accompanied Renato snorted.

"You don't think a woman can handle a man?" I questioned.

"Not unless he's drunk or a pussy," he offered freely.

"Well then, let me enlighten you," I grinned.

I led them back through the bedroom, down the hall, and down the basement stairs. Several members from both clubs followed us down to the gym. The Players all had plastered grins on their faces, and the Slayers looked confused but curious.

"Pull your weapons," I instructed pulling my own gun and knives and setting them on the bar top. The Slayer in question did the same and followed me to the mat.

I motioned him to come at me, and when he did, I flipped his body head-over-heels, slamming his weight into the mat.

"The training that Katie will be providing Trinity and her friend will be focused on the fact that they *are* smaller, and teaching them how to use that to their advantage," I said as the Slayer got up.

He came at me again, throwing a fist this time. I easily ducked the punch, and side kicked him, knocking the wind out of him with enough force to bring him to his knees.

"That's two moves out of hundreds. Do you want to continue or can you admit now that they may have something to learn to fight off an attack by a man?" I asked.

"I'm good. Just don't show my girlfriend that shit," the Slayer said.

I laughed and helped him up.

"Kelsey Harrison," I said offering my hand to shake his.

"Nightcrawler," he smirked and returned the handshake.

Players and Slayers took turns throwing each other around the mats all in good fun as James, Renato and I oversaw the camaraderie to make sure no one lost their temper. Feeling eyes on me, I turned to see Penny standing on the staircase. She quickly averted her eyes to where Bones faced off with Wild Card. Bones was going easy on Wild Card since he wasn't healed yet, but still, the dominance level was obvious.

"Kelsey," Penny asked. "Why does that door have a security access?"

"Because I do my writing in there," I answered and turned back to the fights.

"What kind of writing do you do?" Renato asked.

"She writes porn," James answered on my behalf.

"What?" Renato laughed.

"She writes erotica under the pen name of Kaylie Hunter," James answered.

Nightcrawler and one of the other men turned dramatically and stared at me in silence.

"What the hell? I thought the stereotype of a biker is that they didn't read?" I laughed and made a fast exit back upstairs.

Penny watched me a little too closely the rest of the night and all of my crew seemed to sense it. Even Lisa couldn't distract Penny into idle conversation, and I finally called it an early night and moved into my suite.

About twenty minutes later, Hattie snuck in my room.

"I saw Penny trying to spike your drink. I dumped it and gave you a fresh one, but I think that's why she was watching you so closely," Hattie said.

"Shit." I paced back and forth. "It doesn't make any sense. If Nola wanted me dead, she would have sent someone after me a long time ago. Penny must be acting on her own instincts. Nola likes the game too much to order my execution."

"All I know is that I had Wild Card do his sniffer thing, and he said it was enough drugs to knock out a horse. I can't wait until that bitch is gone," Hattie sputtered.

I grinned at Hattie. Typically, Hattie swore about every three months but lately she was turning into a regular drunken sailor.

"Don't you grin at me! I don't care how many swear words I use. You get that bitch out of our house soon, or I'll take her down myself."

"Ok, Ok. She's leaving soon. I should check to see if she updated her message and then we will have a better idea of when. Until then, I'll be careful, promise," I said while hugging Hattie.

"You better be, or I'll never forgive you. And, another thing," she added. "Sara let me know that everything was fine with the computers and information that Carl hacked. She couldn't find any tracks. Whatever the hell that means," Hattie said as she stomped out.

I grinned, staring at the door. Poor Hattie. She's had a rough week.

Chapter Seventeen

Sunday morning, I awoke earlier than normal. I sat up in bed and listened for unfamiliar noises. Nothing. My spidey senses weren't freaking out either, so I must have woken early just because I had too many stressful thoughts streaming through my brain.

I wrapped a robe around me and checked the time. It was 5:00 am. Ugh.

I moved out to the atrium and opened one of the electric skylight windows. Pulling a pack of cigarettes and an ashtray from the drawer of a side table, I lit a cigarette and slowly inhaled.

Normally, I didn't smoke inside the house, but it was rare for anyone, especially Sara, to be in my atrium so I wasn't overly worried about it.

A light knock on my door interrupted my thoughts. I called out to enter, knowing it was Hattie. She was the only one other than me that was insane enough to be up this early.

Hattie entered carrying a tray, and she asked if she could join me. I stood to help her set the tray down which was loaded with a coffee carafe, cups, and all the usual fixings.

"Sure. As long as the cigarette smoke doesn't bother you," I answered.

"Simon used to smoke, usually when he had a lot on his mind. I find it comforting sometimes, but let's not forget that Simon died of cancer," she scolded.

I smirked and put the cigarette out.

I accepted the cup of coffee Hattie offered, and we exchanged our normal morning good manners.

"Are we safe, Kelsey?" Hattie asked.

"Yes, for now," I assured her. "But I need to leave soon."

"I know. You just do your damnedest to get back to us in one piece. That's all I ask. I won't try to stop you from leaving because I know you have to go."

We sat in silence for the next half an hour, watching the sky slowly illuminate in the early morning light while sipping our coffees. I saw Donovan exit his front door, and stop to put on his shoes. Before he made it down the walkway, I knocked on the atrium window to get his attention. He crossed the yard, and I unlocked the atrium side door for him to enter.

"Please tell me you guys have coffee," Donovan grinned. "Lisa has insisted that caffeine is bad, and removed it from the house. I got up early in hopes of sneaking over here for some before she woke."

"Help yourself, Donovan," Hattie gestured to the coffee carafe and cups. "I'm not in the mood to wait on anyone yet this morning," she grinned.

"Sounds perfect to me," Donovan said filling up a cup.

"Man, it's nice in here," he said leaning back into the loveseat and looking out the atrium windows.

"Peaceful," I added.

"The quiet before the storm," Hattie added.

Donovan and I both grinned and looked back at Hattie.

"What? I'm not stupid. I might choose not to hear the dirty details, but that doesn't mean I don't always have a good idea of what's going on," Hattie said.

"Anything new?" Donovan asked.

I got up and scanned the room and turned on a scrambler. I had removed the bugs from my bedroom the night before, but I was still paranoid.

"Lots of little stuff," I answered Donovan. "Any chance you can stay closer to home for the time being while I head out to take care of some things?"

He sighed and rubbed a hand over his face. "I'm trying. My partners have agreed to relocate here if I can find a good location for a good price. None of us have family in Chicago, so it doesn't matter if that's our headquarters or not. But I'm having trouble finding somewhere that works."

I snorted and walked over to my drafting table. Selecting one of the blueprints, I walked back and handed it to Donovan along with a folder I retrieved from my desk.

"What's this?" he asked taking the rolled print and folder.

"Your wedding present," I answered, curling back up on the couch.

Donovan looked first in the folder where he would find a deed of sale for a large section of the property across the street from the store. Then he opened the print that would show a layout of the buildings and barracks that they would need to relocate the business.

"Shit. Are you serious? I know how much money you've had offered for that property. It's not cheap."

"She's serious, Donovan," Hattie said. "She wants you and Lisa to be happy, and Lisa will be happier if you're home more often."

"I don't know what to say."

"Say you accept the land and will build your business there," I said.

"I accept," Donovan grinned while jumping up. "I'll go call my partners and tell them the good news."

"It's not even 5:00 in Chicago yet," Hattie said, reminding Donovan of the time zone difference.

"I don't care," Donovan laughed as he jogged out of the room.

A little after 6:00 Anne joined us, closely followed by Katie. Alex was walking by the house when he noticed us in the atrium and turned to enter the side door. Lisa entered minutes later following the same path. Hattie brought in another carafe and more cups, and we all lounged about enjoying the peaceful morning.

"When are you leaving?" Katie asked, not turning to look at me but holding her gaze out the window.

"Tomorrow afternoon. No one outside of our circle is to know, though. The story will be that Dallas and I are at a spa for a few days," I answered honestly.

"I should go with you," Katie said.

"No. I need you here, and you know it."

She nodded, still looking out the window. Katie always knew that her priority was to protect home base if I ever needed to leave.

"Will you be back for Christmas?" Alex asked.

"No. I have presents in the closet ready to go under the tree on Christmas Eve."

"Will you be back for the wedding?" Lisa asked.

"That's the plan. You'll need to find something for me to wear though," I grinned.

"Maybe something fluffy and pink," Lisa grinned back.

"Or big gaudy rhinestones," Alex added.

They all came up with horror story outfits, meant to scare me, but it was nice to hear them laughing and joking around.

"This room really is the best room in the house," Hattie sighed.

"I know. Feel free to share it until I'm back. But after that, it's all mine again," I grinned.

Hattie, Lisa, Anne, Alex and Katie grinned back at me.

Sara entered and curled up on my lap. We discontinued talking about anything serious and rambled about the store or gossip from the party.

Tech and Whiskey arrived carrying several boxes of donuts, and Donovan returned to enjoy the festivities. Lisa was ecstatic when she heard that they would be building their new headquarters across the street from the store and that Donovan would be home more often.

"Why is everyone in here?" Carl asked from the doorway.

"Because this is where we ended up," I answered without turning. "Are you dressed, Carl?"

"Sorry," he hollered as he ran back to his room and slammed the door.

We all laughed and waited for him to return.

"Who's in charge of Carl while I'm away for my spa trip?" I asked.

"I think that's a full team effort. I'll create a schedule so we can share the responsibility," Hattie giggled.

"Tech and I password protected all the computers in the house, so let us know if you need help signing in to your personal computers," Sara said.

"What's the password?" I asked.

"I can't tell you," she giggled. "Carl still has the sound magnifier hooked up to your room so he can hear us right now."

"I do not," Carl yelled from his room.

I rolled my eyes. He had promised to remove it.

"He definitely keeps us on our toes. I don't know how one person used to keep track of him," Katie said.

"Scott's nice, but he lost me all the time," Carl explained joining us in the atrium. "Kelsey used to have to find me and bring me home. I like it better here because I don't get lost anymore."

He was dressed in orange stretch pants that were a little too form-fitting and a neon green sweatshirt. I wasn't sure what the outfit was all about but knew better than to ask.

"We like having you here too," Hattie chuckled, looking at his outfit.

Chapter Eighteen

It was mid-morning before we all had our fill of coffee and sweets and decided to start the day. I had a lot of work to get through if I was going to leave tomorrow. Everyone except Hattie joined me in the War Room, and we dug in.

Lisa, Anne, and Katie caught up on audio feeds. Sara worked on the cloned phone data and Tech, well, I wasn't sure what Tech was doing, but he looked busy. Alex and Whiskey picked up where I left off digging through all my old boxes looking for the Pasco file. Carl and Donovan hung the building designs of Pasco's mansion in the hallway, and I was studying them, floor by floor, committing them to memory.

I was working my mind through the second-floor plans when I was called back into the War Room by Whiskey.

"Found the Pasco file," Whiskey said handing it over to me. "It was buried under some files marked prostitution."

Holding the file in my hand, I paused and looked back at Whiskey. The wheels in my brain were turning at warp speed. "What prostitution files?"

"I don't know. Some high-end call girls it looks like," he said pulling the rest of the stack out and setting them on the nearby table.

I set the Pasco file down and placed my hand on the other files. I was looking off in space, allowing my mind to drift back to the last time I would have had the Pasco file out, back when I was a cop. Shauna said that Ariel moved up the ladder and was a high-end prostitute now. Back then, I was working a new call-girl ring operating out of Southside. Why did I pull the Pasco file, though?

"There is a whole lot of shit floating around in that head of yours, isn't there?" Alex asked. "Will it help to talk it out?"

"Maybe," I answered. "I'm missing something."

I walked over and retrieve one of the new burner phones that hadn't been used. Looking up a number from my little black book, I dialed and waited for the other line to answer. The War Room was quiet as we waited together.

"Hello," the older woman's voice answered.

"Mrs. Nannington? My name is Cecil Harrison, and I am so worried about my daughter," I rambled in my best impersonation of a concerned mother. "Charlotte lives in your building, and I haven't heard from her in days. I've called, and called, but I can't get her to pick up her phone. I have your number written down as her landlady. Can you check to see if she is okay for me? Oh, I just keep thinking of all the horrible things that might have happened, and I'm just so worried about her. Please. Could you check on her?"

"Who did you say this was?" the woman asked.

"Cecil Harrison, I'm Charlotte Harrison's mother," I answered.

"Charlie's mum?" the woman asked.

"Yes, yes. She does go by Charlie now. Please, if you could check on her, I would so appreciate it," I said.

"Hold on. I got to put on some slippers," the woman moaned, and I could hear a door opening, followed by stomping up the stairs. For a little old lady, she pounded the hell out of Charlie's door before Charlie answered.

"What?" I heard Charlie's voice in the background.

"Your mum is worried you were dead or something," the old lady blasted in the phone while talking to Charlie.

"My mum? Oh, yes, my mom! Tell her that I need to finish my shower and I'll call her back in about fifteen minutes. So sorry she disturbed you, Mrs. Nannington."

"Did you get all that, Charlie's mum?"

"Yes, thank you. I so appreciate you taking the time—,"

Apparently, Mrs. Nannington had had enough and disconnected the call. I sighed in relief.

"How does Charlie know to contact you and not her mom?" Anne asked.

"Because her mother is a real bitch that would never dare to contact Charlie, not even on her death bed," I said.

I got the red laptop down and paced, waiting for it to ring. I knew that it would take Charlie at least 10 to 20 minutes before she called back because her connection was kept in the backroom of a seedy bar in uptown. The owner was a mutual friend of ours and offered up his office and a secure location to store her laptop. I continued to pace.

Eleven and a half minutes later, the laptop rang, and I jumped to answer it.

"This must be pretty damn important if you're pulling out the Mommy Dearest card," Charlie said as a means of greeting.

"I think so, but I just don't fucking know!" I paced.

"Whoa. Settle down, Cuz. Whatever is going on, getting all stressed about it is not going to help. That's how I work, not how you work. You're the logical one, remember. Stop pacing. Focus. Tell me what's going on."

I stopped pacing and pulled a stool up to the laptop. I took a few deep breaths. Charlie was right. I worked best when I focused my thoughts and kept them logical.

"Do you remember what I was working on before Nicholas disappeared?" I asked.

"Wow. Umm. Let me think. You were working long hours. You weren't undercover, but you were deep into something. Let's see. You met up with Trevor, Feona, and I at the bar. You said the ring you were working on bringing down, wasn't adding up. You said you kept running into missing person files and that you needed more help. Trevor said he would take a look at the files and see if he could lend a hand. I don't think you said anything more than that, though. You got kind of quiet and went home."

Charlie and I worked in different divisions so it was common that she didn't know any of the details of my cases and vice versa. It wasn't that we didn't trust each other, but when we usually got together, we didn't discuss work because Nicholas was around.

"Wait, you mentioned a club. The Highlander. You said you needed to get someone undercover to check it out. But I don't remember what that was about. Does this have to do with Nicholas?" Charlie jumped up off the chair she was sitting on and leaned into the computer monitor. "*Damn, Kelsey*. The next day he was kidnapped!"

"The Highlander! That's it!" I said tearing into the folders beside me. "Pasco owns a shell company that owns the Highlander. I suspected the prostitutes were being managed out of the club."

"Shit. We're back to Pasco, again," Charlie sighed.

"No, it's always been Pasco," I said. "Who else could afford to keep Trevor, Feona, Internal Affairs and the DA's office on the payroll? Nola and Max make good money, but they would rather flee than bankroll that kind of protection. Pasco is the one that pays for the protection, and he called in the kidnapping when he heard I was on his trail. *Son of a bitch*! I blanked out that whole day of work after Nicholas was taken. I forgot that the owner of the bar came back as Pasco, so I had pulled his file."

I stood and resumed pacing.

"It's my fault. It really is all my fault. They took Nicholas to distract me."

My son was kidnapped because I got too close to Pasco and those that protected him. Nicholas's crazy biological mother was just another sick pawn in the game, and I had been looking in the wrong direction for years.

How could I have been so blind?

I cried as I dug through the files, remembering the case. I was in my own world, not hearing or seeing anyone around me as my emotions overwhelmed me.

It wasn't until I was picked up and sat down to straddle another body that I felt reconnected. I didn't have to look up to know it was Bones that held me. I clutched my arms around him as he stroked my back.

After a few minutes, he wiped my tears and turned my head to face him.

"You can't blame yourself, Babe. We just have to move forward with the cards were dealt."

• • •

I pulled my head back and nodded while he wiped more tears with his shirt cuff.

I looked into his eyes and nodded again. Taking a deep breath.

"Sorry," I said the room at large, as I stood and stepped away from Bones.

I took a few more deep breaths as I pushed my emotions back and focused.

"I'm back now," I assured everyone.

I pulled the stool back out and sat in front of the red laptop. "So, Pasco runs the high-end call girls and sometimes picks from the litter for his personal use," I said, accepting the tissue that Whiskey passed to me and blew my nose. "I got too close, and he had Nicholas taken to throw me off my game. Maybe even ordered it as a hit. But, Nola knows how valuable Nicholas is and faked his murder. Pasco might not have even known at the time that it was fake, but Feona or Trevor would have eventually told him. So then what? Does he order Nola to turn Nicholas over to him or does he allow her to keep him?"

"Both, I think," Tech said. "I think he requires proof of life occassionally but other than that Nola has possession of Nicholas." Tech turned the screen on his laptop to face me.

On the screen, staring back at me was Nicholas.

He was being escorted out of the mansion by Nola.

Nicholas stared directly at the security camera on his way out the door. He looked taller, wiser, thinner, and pissed at the world.

I felt Bones pull me back against his body to help support me. I shook my head and stood on my own.

"How old is that photo Tech?" I asked, stepping closer to the display.

"What photo? What are you guys looking at?" Charlie asked.

"A picture of Nicholas on Pasco's security system," Donovan answered.

"It was three months ago," Tech answered.

I heard Charlie gasp and looked to see her cover her mouth as the tears streamed down her cheeks unchecked.

"I need to talk to Charlie alone. Please, everyone, give us a minute," I asked.

Bones pulled my chin to face him. He saw the resolve in my eyes and nodded, leaving the room along with everyone else.

"Oh, Kelsey. Is it really him?" Charlie asked.

"It's him," I answered and lifted Tech's laptop up so Charlie could see the screen.

"I never gave up hope. I just kept praying. But as time passed…"

"I know. Me too," I interrupted her.

"What now?" she asked wiping her face.

"Keep a low profile. Make up an excuse and an airtight cover story and meet me at the safe-house on Tuesday. I'm coming to get my son back."

Chapter Nineteen

After utilizing several meditation exercises, I went out to the gym to let everyone know they could come back. They entered, waiting quietly to hear what I had to say.

"I know I'm asking a lot of everyone, and you will never know how grateful I truly am for everything you're doing for my family and me, but if I can ask for one more day. I need every detail possible in the next twenty-four hours dialed in. I'll be leaving soon, and hopefully, when I return, it will be with my son."

"You don't have to ask, Kelsey. Just point us in the right direction," Anne said.

"Bones – I need you to get Penny out of town. We can't afford to be watching over our shoulder for her, and I can't have her see me leave. Can you go to Pittsburgh?"

"Does it have to be today?"

"Yes," Wild Card answered. "Penny tried to drug Kelsey at the party last night, twice. It's safer to get her the hell away from here as soon as possible."

"What?" Bones yelled.

"I'm fine. But I'll be free to move about if she's out of the picture," I said.

"I'll get flights out this afternoon," Bones grumbled walking out of the room.

"Sara, keep close tabs on that cloned phone. As soon as travel arrangements are booked and the cover story is set-up, Penny will be sending a message to Nola."

Sara nodded, not looking up from her laptop.

"Katie, reach out to Maggie and tell her we might need some warrants issued later this week around the Southern Florida area. More details to come, when available."

Katie nodded and grabbed a burner, crossing over to the furnace room to make the call.

"Wild Card and Donovan, I need help going through the mansion plans. Work with Tech to find the security checkpoints and camera locations. I need to know everything possible about that site for a covert or assault attack. I need every entrance and exit documented and marked, and every option of accessing the island itself."

They turned back into the hallway, grabbing some markers and a notepad on their way.

"Anne, you and Whiskey go through the files on the prostitutes and Pasco and shorthand everything out for me: names, dates, times. I need a reference guide. Lisa and Alex, start doing the same with the file the FBI sent on Pasco."

"Tech, I need you to bounce between the groups, beginning with loading a copy of Pasco's security feeds on a computer for me so I can scan through as much as possible."

"Carl, I need you to design your audio bugs and trackers into some jewelry. I need to have several pieces that I can wear so someone can monitor me if I have to go undercover."

"Yes, ma'am," Carl said saluting me.

• • •

"What do you need me to do?" Hattie asked from the doorway.

"Help Carl pull some jewelry to use for his devices and then help Tyler monitor the house."

Katie walked back into the room and handed me the burner she was using. I took it and answered.

"Kelsey."

"What's your ETA for Florida?" Maggie asked.

"Tuesday."

"Where?"

"If your computer genie is as good as you say, she'll know where to find me," I grinned.

"I'll tell her you said that. See you on Tuesday," Maggie laughed, disconnecting the call.

"Katie, can you help Tech with the security feeds?" I asked.

Bones returned and said he had flights booked and that he was heading back to the clubhouse to let Penny know. I nodded but didn't say anything. Now was not the time to think of Bones and the complexity of our relationship. Bones sighed and left without saying anything else.

I called Dave and Steve and told them I could use their help if they could spare it. They both arrived within a half an hour and jumped in to sort through the police and FBI files to help make sense of it all. With their law enforcement background, they were able to move through the folders faster. They never questioned why, or if anything we were working on was legal, which luckily, at least half of it was.

I was reviewing security feeds on three monitors when the red laptop rang, and I answered Charlie's call.

"What's up?"

"Good, you're still there. I can't come up with a cover story. I've discarded everything I could think of, and I'm out of vacation for the rest of the year. I know – lame right? But you're the one that always thinks of these crazy stories that nobody ever questions."

I grinned at Charlie. "Not all my cover stories were crazy!"

"Yeah, sure. Like you didn't go undercover once as a candy striper and take down a seven-figure drug ring. Or how about the time you pretended to be a hot dog vendor to get that video recording of that con artist."

"Okay, so I know how to think outside the box," I said leaning over and grabbing a burner phone. I dialed a number I knew by heart and hit speaker so Charlie could hear.

"Hellllllooooo," the elderly woman's voice on the other end of the line answered.

"Hey, Nana!" I said.

"Kelsey, Sweetheart. How are you, Dear? Your brothers told me you were back in Michigan, but when I visited in August, they said you weren't up to socializing. I've been trying to give you some space, but shame on you for worrying your grandma so," Nana scolded.

"Sorry about that, Nana. Am I still your favorite granddaughter?" I grinned.

"Ha. You can't fool me, Kelsey, Dear. I have two of the best granddaughters in the world, and you'll never catch me calling favorites!"

"You tell her, Nana!" Charlie called over the laptop speaker.

"Oh, and Charlie's on the phone too! This is a good day. I never believed that hogwash about Charlie locking you up, but never told a soul it was bogus. Not a soul."

"Appreciate that. It needs to stay a secret for a little while longer," I said.

"Of course, Dear. I assume it all has to do with the people that took our sweet Nicholas from us. And, if you're calling me now, you need a favor. What can I do to help?"

"Well," I stalled trying to think of the best way to ask.

"Spit it out, Kelsey Harrison. I'm sure it's something crazy, but if it helps my girls, I'm in," Nana said.

"I need you to die for a couple days so Charlie can pretend that she is flying to North Carolina for your burial," I laughed.

The War Room went silent as everyone turned to look at me with huge eyes. Nana was laughing loudly over the phone, and Charlie snorted.

"Of course, Dear. Would it help if I overdosed a bit on some of my prescriptions?" Nana asked.

"Don't you dare!" I said. "No, I can arrange for someone with the FBI to plant some fake reports. I just need you to go hide out at Gwen's house and not be seen by anyone. The family will have to be dazed and confused for a few days running around in circles. And, you might miss Christmas."

"Oh darn. I was so looking forward to flying to Michigan for the holidays to eat for your mother's dry chicken and Cecil's burnt pies!"

"Seriously, Nana?" Charlie said. "Kelsey calls you and asks you to die for a few days, and you're good with that?"

"Well, of course, Dear. It will be fun to have my horrible daughters all excited about getting their inheritance and then pulling the rug out from under them. Sounds like the best Christmas I've had in years. Plus, Gwen and I like to mix our meds with alcohol so the time will fly right by. Maybe we will even take a road trip up to Atlantic City for the week."

"Okay, sounds like a plan. I'll have the FBI call you when they have it all setup, and they can give you your drop dead date and time, but it might even be today, so you should pack a bag and have Gwen come get you."

"I'll get started now. When you're done with whatever you're currently scheming, I expect an invite to catch up with both of you!" Nana scolded.

"Yes, ma'am," we promised as Nana hung up on me.

"I can't believe your Nana just agreed to play dead," Katie said shaking her head. "I'll call Maggie and see if she can get it set up."

"Anything I can do to help until I get my bereavement call?" Charlie said rolling her eyes.

"Yes, actually. We need to find a high-end hooker that goes by the name Ariel. She used to be low end hooker down on the corner of 5th. Sounds like she's in the system somewhere, but she may be monitored so I haven't wanted to go that route. Can you reach out and try to get a bead on her? But, don't make contact. I'll need to surprise her when I get to town."

"A hooker named Ariel. Got it. I'll find her," Charlie said disconnecting the call.

Alex snorted but by the time I looked up, everyone was at least pretending to work. Even Anne was discreetly leaning into Whiskey, both turned away from me, as they were silently laughing so hard their bodies looked like they were sharing a seizure. I hit play on the security feed and resumed studying the rooms and the guards.

Chapter Twenty

Hattie dropped off food several times during the day and evening. By 11:00, we sent her, Carl, Lisa and Sara to bed and James, Tyler, and Sam joined the working group.

By 3:00, Anne fell asleep on the floor. The rest of us kept pushing through the data and linking all the pieces together. By 5:00, Dave and Steve both called in sick to work, claiming they must have gotten food poisoning. I wasn't sure which restaurant they were blaming it on, but suspected whichever restaurant they blamed was going to have an unexpected dip in their business.

Between the photos, the security feeds, and the construction layouts, we had a good idea of the interior of the mansion. I was staring at the architect prints while Donovan and Wild Card tried to drill all the exits into my head.

Around sunrise, Hattie arrived with several carafes of coffee followed by Carl, who stopped to look at the layouts in the hallway with us.

"Carl, I need your mathematical skills."

"Okay, Kelsey," Carl said.

"The man that owns this house is a bad man with a lot of money. He would have built secret passages. He also uses one of the rooms to hurt people so he might have a passageway off from his bad room where he hides his prisoners. Can you find the hiding spots?"

"Yes."

Carl went into the War Room and quickly returned with a felt pen. He started marking off areas on the layouts, showing all the spaces not accounted for on the drawings.

"Holy shit," Donovan said.

"I can't believe we have been studying these for almost twenty-four hours and never noticed any of this," Wild Card said as Carl continued to find more gaps in the square footage.

I walked away grinning. I would give Carl some time to finish and then the boys some time to make sense of it before I went back to the layouts again.

I retrieved a cup of coffee and went to the back porch to smoke a cigarette.

Dave came out and handed me a burner phone.

"Kelsey," I said into the receiver.

"It's Haley. I'm on a payphone at a rest stop in Georgia. We picked up the drop vehicle and should be in Kalamazoo by noon tomorrow."

"Any chance you both are willing to double back?" I asked.

"Just tell me what you need."

"Thanks. I have an address for you to write down," I said.

I gave Haley the address and let her know that they would be almost a day ahead of me so to take their time.

Dave pulled a cigarette from my pack and lit up. He usually gave me crap about smoking, so I knew he was tired.

"I hear my mom and you are going to a spa for a couple days. Since I know that's not true, promise me that my mom will be kept on a tight leash and not end up in a body bag."

"I wouldn't let anything happen to Dallas. She'll be around to meet the grandkids when you and Tammy are ready."

Dave snorted. "That's not far off. I'm pretty sure Tammy's pregnant but I'm not saying anything because she's not allowed to think about anything baby related per your orders."

I grinned and chucked him on the shoulder. "Keep enjoying the quality time. Pretty soon she's going to go crazy without any fertility meds involved."

Dave grinned and chucked me back.

Steve joined us on the patio.

"You know, you confided to us a long time ago that you used to be a cop. But until I started going through your files, I had no idea. You took down some monster drug dealers. I can't imagine working some of the undercover jobs you worked," Steve said.

"Most of it was before Nicholas came along. After that, I had to settle down a bit, so I quit doing the undercover work. My face was pretty popular by then in the underbelly of the city anyway," I shrugged.

"Seeing you manage this case, family or not, it's impressive. Will you return to law enforcement when this is all over?" Dave asked.

"I have no idea. I can't think of anything beyond getting my son back. Nothing else matters."

I chain smoked three cigarettes and downed two grande coffees before returning to the hallway where the mansion layouts were taped to the walls. Wild Card and Donovan looked bewildered. I hollered for Whiskey to bring a stapler. When he came out, I took the second and third-floor prints down and asked Carl to move the first-floor print to where it should be on top of the island drawing on the opposite wall.

Carl stapled the first-floor layout to the wall, and I handed him the second floor, followed by the third floor. He layered them with the second floor sitting further to the South than the first and third. Whiskey and I shared a grin.

"Holy shit," Donovan said flipping through the different stories. "It's a maze of hidden access points."

"And, look, this appears to be an exit right into the cliff side. He must have a tunnel that goes through!" Wild Card added.

"There's another tunnel on this side too," Donovan said.

"Tech," I called out.

Tech came around the corner and joined us.

"How do we send this to Maggie in a way that makes sense and shows these passageways overlapping? I'm going to need her and her team to understand them."

"Digital image, overlaid, turned 3D," Tech nodded to himself and walked off.

I was assuming that meant he would take care of it, but I had realized hours ago that the less sleep Tech got, the fewer words he actually spoke aloud. So, I wasn't positive.

"Breakfast," Hattie called down the stairs.

Wild Card was the only one that moved toward the stairs, and when he realized no one else was following, he stopped to look back at me.

"Go. I'll send everyone else up and make them take a break," I laughed.

"Good, because I'm starving. If I go without food for much longer I'm going to wilt away," he grinned.

I pushed everyone else to take a break and followed the last of them to the kitchen. Upon entering, I was surprised to see the large table had been stripped and sealed. The torch stripping had brought out the simple grain pattern of the wood and the clear seal coat gave it a rustic appearance. The table looked pleasantly worn and homey in the new space.

"This is great! When did someone have time to do this?" I asked, running my hand across the table.

"Saturday night after you went to bed the Slayers helped us haul the table out and torch the finish off. Nightcrawler did most of the work," Whiskey grinned.

"He's also going to strip down the chairs and benches that Henry found to match the table. He likes doing woodworking projects and volunteered his time as long as you keep your promise and not teach his girlfriend how you do your Kung-foo shit," James grinned.

Goat came in through the garage door and settled in at the table. "Bones called this morning. They're at Penny's parent's house in Pittsburgh. That bitch is finally gone. Let's hope for her sake she stays gone."

"Language at the table, Mr. Goat," Hattie said as Sara tromped down the stairs.

"Sorry, Hattie. Sorry, Sara," Goat grinned.

"I didn't say I disagreed with you, Mr. Goat," Hattie grinned.

I suddenly realized we didn't have a scrambler going and stood in a panic.

"Relax, Kelsey. Carl modified some scramblers to feed blank noise over the bugs. They will still show as active, but they won't receive any audio, and there's no static like when a scrambler is running. They'll think something is interfering with the signal and not think anything of it. He hooked them up to his amplifiers, and the whole house is covered," Tech updated me.

I sighed and sat back down.

"You need some sleep. Your reactions are slower," Wild Card said.

"I'll be able to catch up on my sleep later. I'll be ready when I need to be," I said.

"Okay, I need some sleep," Wild Card chuckled. "I need to find a spot to catch a few winks."

"Completely understand. I'll be sneaking out early-afternoon, so for those who don't see me before I leave, don't contact me on anything other than a burner and only when it's important. I'll be officially at a spa until at least the day after Christmas."

Everyone nodded and dug into their breakfast. I appreciated that no one was trying to pressure me to change my plans, but there was one more thing that I needed to say.

"While I'm gone, everyone is at risk. I need the club to help monitor the house and store. I also have a marker with the Slayers that can be called in if needed. I need everyone protected. They could try to grab someone from here to use as a negotiating tactic against me."

"We already have it covered," James said. "We had a meeting last night and went on yellow alert. The wagons are circling, and we have security shifts set up."

"I have my partners and some of my top guys coming to spend the week with us. We are splitting up sleeping quarters between the three houses and have some of the bunk beds being set back up," Donovan added.

"We'll put the word out with the police and airport security to watch for city slickers and muscle," Steve added.

"Hold off on that broadcast until my guys get in late tonight," Donovan grinned at Steve.

"Sure," Steve grinned back. "Just give me the green light when they're settled."

Chapter Twenty-One

We worked the rest of the morning and through lunch, and by 1:00 I was as ready as I was going to be. Most of the information was stored in my head, but Tech had downloaded everything onto a spare laptop and loaded me up with all the surveillance supplies he could think of in a duffle bag.

"Do you need a ride?" Alex asked.

"No. I'm leaving through the tunnels to your house, then I'll climb in the back of Henry's freight truck. He will drive me out of here."

"I still can't believe you never told me there were secret tunnels to my house. Do you know how convenient that would have been to steal food or booze in the middle of the night?" Alex grinned.

"And, get shot when Donovan heard you sneaking through our basement at 3:00 a.m.?" Lisa asked.

"Okay, so it's not a perfect design. Maybe we can modify the tunnels to go around Donovan's house," Alex laughed.

I grinned back and looked about the room. I was so grateful, words failed me.

"Don't start. You got shit to do, Luv. Stay focused and bring your boy back," Alex kissed my cheek.

Quick hugs were exchanged before I bailed. I entered the tunnels through the furnace room and made quick progress to Alex's house.

Once in Alex's house, I ran upstairs, through the kitchen door into the garage and climbed into the back of the truck, closing the overhead truck door, which was Henry's signal to pull out. Ten minutes later, the truck stopped, and the overhead door opened.

"I didn't see anyone following, but this shit's not my normal shit, so can't be sure," Henry said looking around.

"Relax. I don't think anyone was watching me. This was just an extra precaution, and I'll watch for spotters on the rest of my journey," I said as I lowered my crotch rocket down the freight truck ramps.

Henry helped me steady the bike while I put on my helmet and adjusted the duffle bag's weight on my back.

"Now, you come home in one piece, hear me? Hattie would be inconsolable any other way," Henry said.

"I'll do what I can to make that happen, Henry," I said, lowering the visor on my helmet and starting the bike.

Twenty minutes later, confident that I wasn't followed, I cut the engine at the entrance of the dirt alley that led to Dallas's backyard. I walked the bike the rest of the way and stored it in her back shed, before jogging across the yard and entering through her back garage door.

There stood Tech and Wild Card, arms crossed waiting with Dallas to greet me.

"Oh, no. You two are staying here," I said.

"Not happening. We voted on it. Tech and I go, or you stay here, and we go without you. You're call," Wild Card grinned.

I turned my glaring eyes to Dallas.

"Oh please. Save it. Goat promised me a whole lot of sexual favors if I made sure Tech and Wild Card were invited on our spa trip," Dallas grinned.

I threw my helmet across the room.

"Do you even understand how dangerous this shit is?" I screamed.

"Yeah, I fucking do!" Wild Card yelled back. "But it's a hell of a lot safer if I'm around to watch your back and Tech's close by to do his computer shit, so for once in your life, accept that someone else is willing risk it all to protect *your ass* and get in the damn car."

I paced trying to calm myself and think of a good enough excuse to use to get them to stay in Michigan. The reality though was that if I was going to pull this off, I would need all the help I could get.

"Kelsey," Tech said. "Let's go find Nicholas."

Exhaustion was setting in and before they could see the tears rolling down my cheeks, I climbed in the backseat of the SUV. Dallas got behind the wheel, Wild Card taking the passenger seat and Tech joined me in the backseat.

Tech pulled me over to lean against him.

"You need to sleep. You've done everything you can for right now. We'll split the driving and get you to Florida in record time," he whispered.

"Watch the billboards for the sex toy stores. Dallas will want to stop," I said as my body finally crashed into never-never-land.

Chapter Twenty-Two

When I woke, it was 3:00 am and Wild Card was snoring loudly beside me in the backseat. In the front, Dallas had her head propped at an awkward angle on the center console and was also snoring. Tech was driving.

"How far are we?" I asked rubbing my eyes.

"Somewhere in Georgia, that's all I know," Tech sighed.

"Pull in at the next rest stop. I have to pee and then I can take over driving until breakfast."

"I won't argue. I'm beat," Tech said as he watched for the next rest stop. "You weren't kidding about the sex store shit with Dallas either. We had a hell of a time keeping her from exiting. I didn't know there were so many billboards advertising adult toys," Tech grinned.

"Yeah, well, this isn't my first road trip with Dallas. I promised her if I survived the job I needed to do I would take her to The Other Layer. It's a S&M dance club in Miami."

Tech laughed as he exited at a rest stop. I ran inside to relieve my bladder. By the time I returned, Tech was already asleep in the backseat.

I knew the route well, and even a few shortcuts, so I was well into Florida by the time anyone stirred again.

"What time is it?" Wild Card asked after the sun rose enough to prevent him from sleeping anymore.

"About 9:00, sleeping beauty," I answered.

"Where are we?"

"Near the Everglades."

"And, where is that?" Wild Card asked sitting up a little straighter and looking out the windows.

"We are on the west side of Florida, across the state from Miami. We'll be cutting over in about ten miles, but I need to make a stop first, and we can eat breakfast too. Dig out a burner and give Haley a call at this number." I passed a piece of paper back to Wild Card that had a phone number written on it. "Let her know we will be another couple hours."

"Where the hell are we going to eat? There's nothing around," Wild Card asked.

Dallas and Tech started to stir and sat up trying to gain their bearings.

Dallas' hair was flat against her head on one side and pitched at a strange angle on the other, peaked out above her ear, sort of in some funky trapezoid shape. If I were a better friend, I would tell her. Instead, I just giggled and looked at Tech in the rearview mirror. He raised an eyebrow and then peeked around the seat to get a better view. He grinned wide, but also didn't say a word.

Dallas dished enough shit out to others that I never worried about throwing a bit back at her. And, her being the type not to take life too seriously, I wasn't worried about offending her with my silence.

"I know a restaurant up around the next turn off that we can stop and get a decent cup of coffee and some mystery mixed eggs. It's home cooked grub, and I know the owners, so it's all good."

• • •

Three sets of eyes looked at me questioningly but never said a word as I exited on a two-track lane that wound into the swamps.

Wild Card was just finishing the call to Haley when I made the last turn into the restaurant parking lot. I had to hit the brakes and lay on the horn to get a gator moving that was blocking the truck's path. The gator hissed and snarled a bit before snapping its tail and sliding off into the swamp that edged the parking lot.

"Shit," Tech cursed from the backseat.

Dallas giggled.

Wild Card shook his head as he tucked the phone away and pulled his glock.

"Put the gun away, it's not gator season," I said exiting the truck and heading up the stairs to the raised shack of a restaurant.

"As I live 'n breathe," exclaimed Carly exiting the restaurant. "Tobias, you aren't going to believe who's out here on our stoop!" she yelled.

"Holy Moses, is that Miss Kelsey gracing us with her presence?" Tobias hollered, flying through the screen door and pushing Carly out of the way to claim first hugs.

"Tis me alright and damn, I'm hungry!" I laughed.

"Well let's get some gator on those ribs girl. And, tell your city folk friends to get their spooked asses out of that truck and join us," Carly said.

I looked back to see that Tech, Dallas, and Wild Card were still sitting in the SUV looking for gators.

"You wait much longer, and that momma gator will come back. Then y'all be stuck," I yelled.

Three doors opened in a flash, and three sets of legs ran across the parking lot and passed us into the shack building.

"Northerners?" Tobias asked.

"Two are, the third is Texas bred," I answered.

Tobias and Carly snorted as they followed me inside.

There wasn't anyone else in the restaurant which was typical before two in the afternoon.

"Two regular black coffees, a coffee filled halfway with Bailey's, and a hot chocolate with whip cream," I told Carly as I tossed my bag into a nearby chair and we all settled in at the largest table.

"What to eat?" Tobias asked as Carly gathered our drinks.

"Three specials and my usual," I grinned back.

Tobias shook his head and went into the kitchen.

Carly came over setting our drinks down along with ice waters.

"How did you know the boozy coffee was mine?" Dallas asked.

"Honey, with that hair, you need it," Carly laughed.

Dallas reached up to feel her hair and shrieked. She ran off to find the bathroom as the rest of us laughed.

"What about me? How did you know the hot cocoa was mine?" Tech asked.

"Those tattoos aren't fooling anyone, Dumpling," Carly grinned.

Tech grinned back as he drank his cocoa.

"So, where's Lenny? I expected he would be here cracking open his first beer by now," I said.

"He hasn't been in for a while," Carly hedged.

"How long is a while?"

"Bit over a week," she admitted.

"I checked his boats," Tobias said carrying the breakfast plates out. "They're all there except the old flat bottom. We sent the Sheriff out to his hunting shack, and he said the boat is there, but he couldn't get up to the shack. Too many gators."

"That's not good. Only one thing I can think of that would keep them from moving off when humans are about."

Tobias nodded and looked down at the floor.

I ate some of my breakfast but lost my appetite thinking of Lenny possibly trapped and hurt inside his shack, or worse, dead.

"Call the Sheriff. Have him pick me up at the back dock, but tell him it's not public knowledge that I'm in Florida."

Carly nodded and ran off to make the call.

"I'll gather your canisters," Tobias offered, going into the back room.

I sighed.

"What's going on?" Wild Card asked while he feverishly ate his breakfast. I looked up to see Tech and Dallas were also devouring their food.

"I need to make a run out into the swamp. Did you bring your glock in?" I asked.

"Yeah. Why?" Wild Card asked.

"Because gator season or not, I might need you to cover my six as I attempt a rescue mission," I answered getting up. "Tech and Dallas, you two stay here with Carly and Tobias. We'll be back as soon as we can."

Wild Card quickly scarfed down the rest of his food and followed me into the back room. My name was still posted on the middle coat cubby, and I pulled my gear out. I put on my lightweight hip waders and strapped some pressure bottles that Tobias handed to me to the sides. Tobias then loaded up a canvas bag with a shoulder strap and handed it over.

"That's all we have in stock," Tobias said.

"It will have to be enough then," I sighed.

"Do I need waders?" Wild Card asked.

"No. You'll stay in the boat with the Sheriff. Follow his lead. We've done this before," I answered exiting out the back door.

I crossed the backyard and down the dock with Wild Card close on my heels. The sheriff's boat pulled up, and the Sheriff nodded at me as I stepped in and pulled the boat up closer to the dock for Wild Card to step in after me.

"Better hang on. The sheriff isn't so good at driving a boat," I warned Wild Card.

Before Wild Card had a chance to find a spot, the throttle was opened and the boat spun a quick circle. I barely had time to pull Wild Card to the floor, before he would have toppled over the side.

"What the hell is his problem?" Wild Card yelled.

"We used to date," I grinned.

Wild Card laid back on the boat floor and laughed. "That makes sense."

When the boat slowed, I pulled myself up to get the lay of the land. Lenny's shack had a large clearing between the dock where his boat was parked and the front door. In that clearing, about twenty gators sunned themselves, occasionally snapping and hissing at each other.

"Shit," Wild Card said, standing beside me.

"Yup. Turn the safety off on your glock but don't shoot until it's necessary."

"Why are they all here?"

"Most likely they smell blood or a dead body," the Sheriff answered taking his own gun out. "You sure this is worth it?"

"Lenny's a friend," I answered stepping off the boat and onto the dock. I went first to Lenny's boat and untied it, throwing the sheriff the rope. He'd move it around so we could tow it out with us. I then moved to the end of the dock where several gators turned to hiss at me. I unhooked a pressure bottle from my side, activated it and tossed it in their direction. The pressure bottles were the equivalent of a stink bomb but mixed with an odor that offended the gators, rather than humans. They did the trick, and the gators moved back away from the smelly smoke.

I continued to toss the bottles making my way quickly to the door. As I stepped onto the porch, Lenny stepped out with his leg wrapped in garbage bags and sealed with duct tape. He was using a bar stool as a makeshift crutch.

"About damn time someone came to rescue my ass," he grinned, trying to make his way down the stairs.

"You can bitch later. These stink bombs won't last long," I said.

Several gators moved closer to the pressure bottles, smelling what I assumed was Lenny's injured leg. I threw the last one and pulled out the fireworks from my bag. They weren't as effective, but they were all I had left. I lit the first one and carefully set it down. It burst up in a four-foot waterfall of colors and loud pitching noises. The gators backed off again, and we continued to make our way to the dock. I set off the remaining two along the way before tossing the bag aside.

"That was the last of my bag of tricks, Lenny. Get ready to haul ass," I warned as we were still twenty feet from the docks. "Get ready to shoot when needed Wild Card."

"Just tell me when—," Wild Card started to say when he opened fire and shot behind me.

I turned to see a gator had crossed the line and was two feet away from me with a hole in his head. The other gators moved in as they smelled the blood.

"Run, Lenny!" I yelled pulling my gun.

Wild Card and the Sheriff shot around us as I shot at the gators in front of us.

"Shit!" I yelled as a gator ran in front of my path, separating Lenny and myself. I was running too fast and couldn't stop. I jumped over it as I continued firing behind me, hoping that I hit it so it wouldn't spin and bite me.

Hearing Lenny's feet pounding ahead of me on the dock, I didn't look back but rushed for the boat. The sheriff pulled Lenny over the side, and Wild Card pulled me in afterward, still shooting behind me.

The Sheriff gunned the accelerator and moved us away from the dock as another gator came hissing at us.

"Holy Mother," Wild Card gasped as he fell to the floor of the boat next to me. "You've done this before? Are you nuts?"

"It's usually not that hard," I panted back. "Lenny's leg must be really messed up for them to be that feisty."

Fifteen minutes later, we were back at Tobias's dock. As Tobias and Wild Card helped Lenny into the restaurant, I tied down Lenny's flat bottom boat. Once secure, I started toward the restaurant as well.

"You even going to say 'Hello' Kelsey?" the Sheriff said.

"I'm not the one that has my panties in a bunch about our past, Eric. If you can accept that, then Hello. If not, then Goodbye."

I walked through the back door without checking to see if Eric followed or not. Entering the main room, I made a beeline to the bar, and Carly handed me a rum and coke. I downed it and slid my glass back for another.

Lenny and Tobias were arguing about whether to go straight to the hospital or wait until Lenny drank a beer or two. When Tobias removed the garbage-bag-bandage from Lenny's leg, Wild Card took the decision away by helping Tobias move him out to the truck. Carly ran over and gave him a beer for the road.

Dang. That was nasty. I walked over and opened some windows and turned on the ceiling fans to move the smell out.

"I was kind of hoping Lenny would make himself and his boats available later in the week in case I needed him," I sighed.

"I've got copies of all his boat keys. Call me if you need a ride," Eric said taking the stool next to me.

"Problem is I don't know if what I'll be up to is legal or illegal," I said.

Eric snorted. "That's a given with you."

Carly laughed as Wild Card, Tech, and Dallas joined us.

"What's the plan?" Wild Card asked.

"We need to hit the road," I answered, downing my drink and throwing some cash on the bar. "We weren't here," I said looking at Carly and Eric.

"That's also a given," Eric grinned.

Carly came around the bar and handed me a to-go bag and gave me a hug.

"Whatever you're up to, stay safe," she said.

Eric snorted.

Chapter Twenty-Three

Two hours later I pulled into the driveway of the safehouse and pulled around to the back parking lot. I grinned when I saw three cars were already there. We gathered our gear.

Walking across the back porch, Charlie flew out of the door and threw herself at me, knocking me backward into the railing.

"Damn, Cuz, it's so good to see you!" she squealed.

"Right back at you, Kid. But you're going to break me," I laughed.

She laughed and grabbed some of the bags, leading the way into the house. In the living room stacks of everyone else's bags sat, so we piled ours there as well.

Dallas went in search of an adult beverage, and Tech looked for a place to set up his computer equipment.

A woman I recognized from the hospital that had been with Maggie and Agent Kierson occupied half the dining room table with three laptops in front of her.

"You must be the genie," I grinned.

"Welcome to my magical realm where I strive to grant all your wishes," she grinned back. She was young, dark skinned with short cropped hair and a bright white smile. The nickname suited her well, with her small frame and happy demeanor.

"Do you have a real name?"

"I do, but everyone calls me Genie, so feel free to stick with what you know," she winked as her laptop pinged, pulling her focus away. "That was confirmation that the blanket warrants were signed for the corrupt Miami public services employees. We are ready to roll on them whenever you give us the green light."

Tech grinned and set up his gear on the other side of the dining room table.

I went back to the kitchen where everyone else was waiting. Haley slid me a black coffee, but I pulled a bottled water instead. I had a lot to get done and didn't need the coffee shakes.

"Anyone hungry?" Bridget asked.

"No, I'm full," Wild Card said. "We had an amazing breakfast scramble this morning that had incredible strips of steak. Man was that good. Tech and I were fighting over Dallas's leftovers."

"Ah, what kind of steak?" Charlie asked, looking back at me.

"I don't know. It was cut narrow like jerky, but I assumed it was some special cut of beef," Wild Card shrugged.

"And, let me guess, Kelsey didn't eat any?" Charlie grinned.

"No, she just had eggs and toast. Why?" Wild Card asked getting a little suspicious now.

"What did we eat?" Tech asked coming into the room followed by Genie.

"Gator," I answered truthfully.

"You're shitten me," Tech said.

"Well, it was good," Wild Card shrugged trying to decide how he really felt about it.

"It's okay, I guess. But there's a reason that a lot of people don't eat gator around here," Charlie smiled.

"Why?" Dallas asked as she sipped her martini.

"Because we know the things gators eat for dinner," Charlie answered.

"Yeah, like half of Lenny's foot," I added.

Wild Card went flying out the back door as Tech went rushing down the hall toward the bathroom. Both of them hurled loudly as we all laughed. Dallas grinned and drank her martini, unfazed.

The screen door slammed, and I looked up.

"Hey, Sis. You didn't think we were going to miss this party, did you?" Reggie grinned.

Jackson trailed through the door behind Reggie.

"Damn," I laughed, running over to greet them.

They took turns hugging me and spinning me around.

"What is it with her always having hot men clinging to her?" Maggie chuckled.

"That's my favorite part about her," Dallas said.

"Well if it isn't the Fairy and his better half," Charlie grinned.

Jackson and Reggie both took turns hugging Charlie. Afterward, introductions were made all around, and Wild Card and Tech returned.

"Something you ate?" Jackson asked.

Wild Card went running back outside again.

"So what's the plan?" Maggie asked.

"Haley and Dallas are heading up the coast and taking a spa vacation in the Palms area. If we need them, they'll be close enough to drive back down, but will still also have alibis. Haley, you're in charge. If Dallas strays, reel her ass in," I said.

Haley grinned and dragged Dallas off her stool. "That's our queue, let's pack up. We'll take your car."

"What kind of spa is this we are going to?" Dallas asked, unsure if she really wanted to go.

I pulled the brochures and reservation information from my shoulder bag and handed the information to her. On the cover of one of the brochures were two tall, muscular men wearing speedos giving a woman a massage. She didn't need any more coaxing but was dragging Haley out the door.

"Bridget, if you can stay here and cover home base with Genie and Tech, I'd appreciate it. I might need your skill set so I need you closer to the action."

"Sure. We already got groceries, but I'll start setting up the rooms for everyone," she said bouncing off in her pixie way toward the living room.

"Charlie – did you get a bead on Ariel?" I asked.

"Found her. She's got a nest in a condominium development. The building has a doorman during the day and security at night. I didn't have enough time to determine what her daily routine is."

"That's fine. I can get in unseen. Can you call our favorite Aunt and arrange a private breakfast with her and our Uncle in the morning? Let her know to keep the guest list private, but to expect three of us."

Charlie nodded and pulled a burner phone, stepping on the back porch to make the call.

"Jackson, we have a tactical op planned for tonight in the warehouse district. Sort out the supplies and make sure we have everything packed and ready. We'll be moving in around dusk and be sitting in wait for maybe an hour or two. Plan for a four-man team.

"Reggie, I need you to come with me to meet Miss Ariel. It's time to even the playing field," I grinned.

"Oh, no, you don't," Wild Card argued coming in the back door. "The last time I heard you say something like that, you both were arrested three times in one day and still didn't come home until after three in the morning."

"Yes, but it didn't matter that day if we were caught or not. Today it does so we won't get caught. I need you to go over the layout for the warehouse and surrounding grounds. Tech has all the information. Maggie and Genie, Tech can also update both of you on all the bad guys."

I watched Bridget come back out and look at the living room wall, then walk back down the hallway. I waited for her to return again a few minutes later.

"What the hell, Kelsey?" she asked pointing at the wall.

"She's good," Charlie grinned having returned from the back porch. "Auntie expects us at 9:00 and won't tell a soul," she said as she walked past me and joined Bridget. She pulled a few books out and hit a release. The bookcase popped out away from the wall and revealed a hidden doorway.

"Sweet," Bridget said as she walked inside. "This is so cool."

"Now this is better," Genie grinned, as she and Tech followed Bridget inside.

"Wifi, yes," Tech agreed. "And, wall to wall touch screens."

I shook my head and gathered my gear as everyone was checking out the safe house's War Room. Charlie walked over and handed me the address for Ariel's condo.

"Charlie, I need you to get up to speed on everything as quick as you can. This is going to go down fast."

"I'll be ready," she nodded and walked into the living room.

Reggie and I snuck out the back door while everyone was pre-occupied.

Chapter Twenty-Four

"How are you holding up, Sis?" Reggie asked.

"Good," I answered honestly. "I feel like for the first time in a long time, I have a chance of finding my son. And, if I don't find him, at least we will take down Nola's safety nets. It will be easier to find her without her hiding behind everyone else."

"You have a plan then?"

"No. But I'll have one after I talk to Ariel and after we check out that warehouse tonight."

"So we're winging it?" Reggie grinned.

I winked at him as I made another turn and slid into a parking space one block past the condominiums. We put on our sunglasses, and I clipped my hair up before we started strolling down the public beach toward the private condo entrance.

"Are we visitors or do we live here?" Reggie asked as we approached the doorman.

"Timeshare rental," I answered checking my phone. The text from Tech came in telling me 3B had regular rentals. I smiled as we entered.

"What floor?" the elevator attendant asked.

"Third, please," I answered with my best smile as I wrapped my arm through Reggie's.

"Ah, you must be the Websters. I thought you weren't going to be in until later in the week," the man said as he pressed the three button.

"My husband's meetings were rescheduled, and we were able to come sooner."

"It's a good thing then," the attendant said. "We haven't had weather as nice as today in weeks. Another cold front moves in this weekend and it's supposed to get down into the 60's."

We wished him a good day as we stepped out of the elevator. After the doors closed, we turned to the stairs to jog up two more floors.

"How are we getting in the apartment door if she's not home?" Reggie asked.

I held up the elevator attendant's security pass and grinned.

"Damn. You've been spending time with Bridget," he grinned back.

"She has a skill that I thought would come in handy. She's taught me the basics, but I'll never be as smooth as her," I said as I opened the entry door and we slid inside.

I could hear someone in the back bedroom. Reggie stayed in the living room while I moved forward and slowly stepped behind Ariel with a gun to the back of her head.

She froze.

"If you behave, I won't hurt you. But you will need to do what I say and not create a disturbance. Do you understand?" I asked.

She nodded slowly.

"Good. Tie your robe shut and let's go into the living room and have a little chat."

She did as she was told and when I directed her to the couch, she saw me for the first time.

"It's you! Officer Harrison!" she cried and threw herself at me in an embrace.

I looked at Reggie in absolute confusion, and he started laughing.

"Only you could make a friend while threatening to kill them," he shook his head.

He turned down the hall to check the other rooms, and I separated Ariel from me and pulled out a scrambler.

"Is your house bugged?" I asked.

"I don't know," she answered as I pushed her gently onto the couch. I ran a scanner through the room but didn't find anything. I went back and sat next to her as Reggie came back out and handed me a framed photo.

"Please, you have to help me," Ariel cried.

The picture I held was of Ariel and a little girl playing at a park.

"They took her," Ariel cried, leaning forward into my lap.

"Son of a bitch," I sighed.

It took a long time to get Ariel to calm down enough to explain what was going on. She was planning on skipping out of town with her daughter and trusted the wrong John with the information. He was worried that she would talk about her customers, so he turned over the information to Max, and Max turned the problem over to Nola.

Nola kidnapped Ariel's daughter and was holding her as blackmail to make Ariel do her bidding. Ariel remembered me from when she worked the streets and asked how to contact me, but nobody knew. She was even more freaked out because she was supposed to go to Pasco's Christmas Eve party tomorrow night and take at least one other girl with her. She knew she wouldn't make it out alive and neither would anyone else that was dumb enough to go with her.

"Are you and your guest supposed to be escorts, strippers, or open season prostitutes?" I asked.

"Strippers and arm candy, but you know how it really goes down," Ariel sniffled.

"We can work with that. What time do you leave and what's the transportation arrangement?"

"Pasco rented boats to ferry his guests every half-hour to and from the island. I'm to be there by 10:00."

"Good. I'll have a car pick you up at 8:30 tomorrow night in front of the building. I can't promise you'll live through tomorrow night, but if I'm with you, your odds improve and so do your daughter's. If you tell anyone, though, trust anyone, mention my name to anyone, we're all dead. Do you understand?"

"Yes. I won't tell anyone," she cried.

Reggie and I left her to her tears.

"Where to?" Reggie asked when we were back in the car. I knew the roads better, but where I had parked, the lot was congested, and our odds of leaving without unwanted attention increased if Reggie drove us out.

"North past the highway, then West," I answered as I pulled my bag onto my lap. "We have one more stop to make, and I'll need you to wait in the car."

Using the visor mirror, I applied heavy layers of makeup. I then used powdered hair coloring to dust my hair to a dark brown. I grinned knowing Reggie was itching to pull over and fix my hair for me.

"More on the left-side," Reggie sighed.

"Turn right at the second light and drive to the end."

Reggie made the turn, and I saw him tense up. We weren't in a good neighborhood. In fact, we were in one of the worst neighborhoods. But I needed some information, and I needed it quickly.

"You're going to leave me waiting in the car in this neighborhood?" Reggie complained as he eyed the gang colors and open drug deals.

"Either that or we'll have a long walk to the bus station when I get done with my meeting. Cars don't last long unattended on this block."

"I can imagine."

"Pull over in front of the next building. I should be about five minutes. If I'm not out in ten, drive away and call home base and let Charlie know. She can get me out."

"That sounds promising," Reggie grumbled.

I didn't wait for him to argue with me but exited the car after donning my sunglasses. I walked straight and with a purpose past the gang bangers and into the building. Up two flights of stairs, I turned and greeted the spotter standing outside Chills' door.

"Message for Chills. He home?"

"Who's asking?" the kid asked with attitude, stepping into my space.

"An old friend," I answered, stepping into his space. "Tell him I need a private visit or I'm calling Irene."

"Wait here," the kid ordered and stepped inside.

A few minutes later, a head popped out and looked at me. I hid my grin as he ordered everyone out of the apartment and let me inside. As soon as the coast was clear, Chills smiled and offered me double fist bumps.

"Damn girl. What the hell you doin' back here? You know they got bullets and knives and shit with your name carved in them if you step back in the city."

"I didn't have a choice. But only a handful of people will know I'm here, so it will be easy to track back if someone snitches on me. Hear me?"

"It's cool. It's cool. Not a word from me. You coming back for good?"

"No. Your drug trade is safe from me for a little while longer," I grinned. "I need a quick update on what talk can be heard on the streets. I'm on a tight schedule and don't have the time to reach out to multiple contacts."

Chills dropped into a sofa and motioned for me to sit on the one across from him.

"Hearing dirty cops are covering for something down in the warehouse district. Not sure who all or what all, but heard Max's name dropped. Also hearing that more and more white girls are disappearing from the streets these days. It's finally safer to be dark skinned."

"That lines up with what I know too. Anything else?"

"Saw your nemesis."

"When?" I asked, leaning forward.

"About two weeks ago," he answered. "I cleaned up for the day and snuck down to Grandma Irene's to check on her. I was inside and heard a car pull up three doors down Nola came out of the house in a hurry and got in the car. Fancy town car. Heard on the news that a body was found a few days later. Throat slit – just her style."

"Did Nola see you?"

"Hells no. I never stepped outside."

"Good. Keep that to yourself or Irene could be in danger. I have to go. A friend is keeping the car running."

"White dude? In this neighborhood? The brothers are probably having fun with him by now. I better escort you out," Chills grinned.

I opened the door and walked back the way I came. I tried not to grin as Chills did his gangster sway of acting all big-man and his posse trailed after him following suit.

We stepped outside and with a hand signal from Chills, the boys that were rocking the shit out of our car all stepped away and wandered in different directions.

I got in the car, and Reggie jammed both feet on the accelerator and launched us down the street.

"Next time, I'll go in, and you wait in the car," Reggie said, choking the life out of the steering wheel.

"Sorry, white boy, but you wouldn't have made it into the building," I grinned.

Reggie sighed. "Okay, so what was that all about?"

"I was checking in with Chills for any current street news. White girls disappearing like hot cakes, and Nola executed someone downtown two weeks ago. Also hearing a lot of traffic about dirty cops and the warehouse district."

"And, why would a gang banger tell you anything?"

"Because his grandma and I are friends," I grinned.

Reggie shook his head, and I gave him directions to get us back to the safe house.

Chapter Twenty-Five

On the back porch of the safe house, a tall, very muscular man wearing a cowboy hat and an apron was flipping burgers on the grill.

"Who the hell are you?" I asked, getting out of the car.

"Don't see where that's any of your business, little lady," the cowboy said, tipping his hat at me.

I stepped up onto the back porch, pulled my glock, and pointed it at his chest.

"I'll ask one more time, who the hell are you?"

"Grady, what the hell are you doing here?" Reggie asked, jogging up to stand beside me.

"He's with me," Bones said coming out of the house with a platter.

"Damn it, Bones," I bitched, holstering my gun. "You're supposed to be in Pittsburgh!"

"It's fine. I said I had to go on a mission in Mexico," Bones said. "Penny is at her parents' house until I get back."

"*Why are you so naïve when it comes to that woman?*" I yelled, pacing back and forth. "If she finds out you're in Florida, we could all end up dead."

"Relax, Kelsey," Bones said, placing his hands on my shoulders. "I covered my tracks."

"You better hope that she believed your bullshit story," I said, shrugging away from his touch. "And, how in the hell did you find out where we were?"

"He flew to Miami before he called me," Wild Card sighed, stepping outside. "I figured it was safer to tell him where we were at rather than have him stumbling around asking anyone and everyone where to find us."

"Great. Just fucking great," I paced. "Shit!"

I stormed into the house and into the War Room. Tech was simultaneously running two laptops, and I threw myself into the chair next to him and crossed my arms.

"I know," Tech nodded. "Pissed me off too."

"She on the move yet?" I asked.

"No, not yet. I have her tracker on that screen." He pointed to the far left wall TV screen.

"Keep an eye on it. She'll make her move earlier than we planned. I just hope we have time to fit it all into the schedule."

"I'll let you know as soon as it blinks. I also got an update from Sara and Katie. Trevor and Feona's trackers landed in the warehouse district last night for about an hour. The same location you had me pull the building designs on. How'd you know?"

"It was one of the properties owned by a shell company that sent Sam funds for all the spy equipment. Max likes to use boats to move his cargo, and the warehouse district is his old stomping ground. I checked in with a source today that confirmed that he has some action taking place down there."

"Reliable source?"

"No," Reggie answered, walking in and pulling up a chair. "Unless you count a gang-banger as a reliable source."

"Ah. How's Chills doing?" Charlie grinned, joining us. "I haven't seen him around much lately."

"He's good," I answered Charlie. "And, he's reliable," I answered Tech.

"Of course, he is. He wouldn't dare lie to Kelsey, or Grandma Irene would kick his ass," Charlie grinned.

Tech shook his head and continued with his update.

"Katie said the only other update was that Donovan had overdone the security order, and they each had a bodyguard. She's not happy," Tech grinned.

"This is one time I'm not going to argue with Donovan. I don't have enough energy to focus on them with everything going on here."

"Lunch time," Bridget called out.

We moved to the kitchen and fixed our burgers.

"So where are we at?" Maggie asked as we sat at the kitchen table.

"Some of us are doing a recon job tonight, but the less you know about that, the better off you'll be. Tomorrow night is the big night. Pasco's throwing a Christmas Eve party, and I was invited. I'm going to need you to be my backup plan with teams ready to go in if I give the signal."

"If you live long enough to signal," Charlie griped.

"Kid, I have to do this," I said.

"And, tell me, Kelsey, what kind of invitation are you using to get inside?" Charlie fumed.

"You already know the answer to that, and either you support my decision and agree to have my back, or you bail

176

now. I can't have any doubts about what I'm doing. You know how dangerous it can be undercover if you go in scared."

"You would be a fool not to be scared going in that mad man's house. Damn it. You and Nicholas are the only family I have. I can't lose you."

"Then track my ass the best you can and cross your fingers for the rest. And, if I don't make it out, find Nicholas. Finish it," I snapped back.

Charlie got up and stormed down the hall. Jackson sighed and followed after her.

"Bridget, I'm going to need supplies for tomorrow night. Can you help Reggie go through whatever Anne packed for me and buy whatever else I'll need?"

"Sure."

"What's the op?" Wild Card asked.

"Destiny is going to be working a party," I sighed, waiting for the explosion.

"You're shitting me," Wild Card yelled, standing up from the table. "No way. No wonder Charlie is pissed at you. Have you lost your fucking mind?"

"What the hell is everyone talking about?" Bones asked.

"Destiny is her stripper name. She's going in as a call girl," Wild Card said.

"Like hell you are," Bones said.

"Everyone needs to calm the fuck down," the Cowboy said, setting his hat on the deep window sill as he sat at the kitchen table. He turned to me and grinned, holding out his hand, "Grady."

"Kelsey," I answered, shaking his hand.

"You trained for this op?" he asked.

"Yes. I have years of undercover experience, extensive fighting skills, and I'm a damn good shot with any gun. My mission is clear. Save the prisoners, get enough intel to lock up Pasco, and if possible, find my son and Nola."

"You're forgetting the part about getting out alive," he grinned.

"Well duh, that's in the plan somewhere too," I grinned back.

Reggie snorted, and Bridget started giggling.

"We've sent agents in before that we never heard from again. How is what you're doing any different?" Maggie asked.

"Because I have done the research. I know the people involved, the island, the house, my cover story is solid, and because the other agents weren't me. You know I can make it in and out, Maggie."

"I believe you," she nodded. "I might have trouble getting a task force to back up the op though seeing that you're no longer in law enforcement."

"And, if come tomorrow, I'm wearing a Miami PD badge, will that make things easier?"

"Yes, but how are you going to pull that off without tipping your hand?"

I just grinned.

Tech walked into the kitchen and slammed his plate on the counter with enough force that shards of the plate scattered along the counter. .

"You're an idiot!" he yelled at Bones, before turning back to the War Room.

None of us had ever seen Tech yell at someone before, so it stunned me for a minute until I realized that the tracker must be showing that Penny was in motion.

"Damn it, Bones," I whispered, running off to the War Room.

Sure enough, the left TV screen showed Penny traveling south at a little more than 500 miles per hour. She was on her way to Miami.

"She's on a private jet. She'll be here mid-afternoon," Genie said.

My burner phone rang.

"Kelsey."

"It's Sara. We are showing Penny is on her way. She's scheduled to check in this afternoon at the downtown Hilton. She's traveling alone, but she has a new draft message on her email account. It says 'Can meet tonight. Time and place.'"

"We'll put eyes on her, but let me know when Nola answers the email," I said. "Thanks, little-bug."

"Be safe, Aunt Kelsey," she said before hanging up.

"Penny has a room reserved at the downtown Hilton. And, she contacted Nola to schedule a meeting for tonight."

"Damn. Maggie told me the little girl was good, but that was fast."

"She's a whole lot of special," I nodded.

"What can we do?" Jackson asked from behind me.

I turned to see everyone had followed me in, and they were standing there absorbing the intel.

"I have to figure out surveillance teams for when Penny lands. She'll recognize most of us, and Nola will recognize the rest of us," I sighed. "I hadn't planned on her being in Miami for at least a few more days."

"They won't recognize me," Maggie said. "I wasn't part of the FBI team that held her for questioning in Texas, and I made myself scarce when I was in Michigan."

"I'm a nobody around these parts too," Grady added.

"I doubt I've ever hit Nola's radar, so count me in," Jackson said.

I looked at Maggie in her black business suit and pressed white blouse. Then to Grady in his worn jeans, cowboy boots and hat. Then to Jackson, with his plaid button-down and rodeo belt buckle. *Shit.*

Bridget giggled. "Unfortunately, Penny has met me, but how about I steal Reggie, and we turn these three into Miami locals so they don't stand out so much?"

"Do you think it's even possible?" I sighed.

She giggled again and pushed the three of them out of the room and down the hall.

Charlie looked up expectantly.

"I need a backup plan if Bridget can't fix them. Can you find me a good wig and some street wear?"

"I'm on it," she chuckled.

"Kelsey, how the hell are you going to watch Penny and get through the warehouse tonight?" Tech asked.

"This is my fault. I'll take the warehouse with Wild Card," Bones said.

"No, you won't. You're officially grounded until tomorrow night's operation. I can't afford for you to be spotted. I'll juggle the rest of it with the team I have."

"She's right. If you're spotted, it's game over. Nola will know that everyone is here waiting and watching," Wild Card supported me.

"I can't just sit here and do nothing," Bones said.

"When are you going to get it through that thick skull of yours that you're going to get us killed!" I yelled in his face.

Wild Card pulled me back, pivoting me back to the work stations. I caved, placing my palms on the table, trying to calm myself.

"There is something you can do," Wild Card said. "Not everyone will have time to go through the island and mansion layout for tomorrow night's op. Kelsey and I are the only ones that will be on the ground that will know it well. You can memorize the plans and get ready."

"That's not going to take me a day and a half."

"Brother, you'll be surprised. That place is a freaky maze," Wild Card said.

Tech handed Bones a pile of blueprints and a laptop. "The file you want is named 'Rat Bastard' on the desktop."

Bones left with the plans and laptop.

I was reviewing the designs for the warehouse with Wild Card when Reggie yelled for me to step out into the living room. I walked out and laughed.

Bridget and Reggie were staring in distress at Maggie, Grady, and Jackson. They had dressed them in casual shorts and t-shirts but their white vampire-like legs advertised that there was no way they were Miami born and bred.

"Charlie!" I hollered.

"Yeah," she answered, coming out of my bedroom.

"Can you get them to a spray tanner?"

"Yeah, that would be a good idea," she laughed, checking out Jackson's white legs.

"I'll go with you. None of them have sneakers or sandals so we can stop at a shoe store," Bridget said.

After they left, I asked Reggie if he had everything I would need for tomorrow night and he assured me that he found a dress that would work. I trusted his opinion so while he joined forces with Bones to review the Pasco site plans, I returned to the War Room to work with Tech and Genie.

"This is the oddest assignment I have ever been on," Genie giggled.

"I wish I could say the same," I grinned. "I was tasked once with infiltrating a carnival crew to bring down a drug ring."

"What was your cover?" Genie laughed.

"The fortune teller, of course," I grinned. "Six weeks later, I gave a dozen of the men a free reading. Told them I saw small cells, iron bars, and same-sex marriage in their future, as I slapped the cuffs on them."

Chapter Twenty-Six

"What's next?" Tech asked.

"I need you to look up a murder on Riverside a couple weeks back. A woman had her throat slit," I said.

"I can access that faster through my database. Do we think it was Nola?" Genie asked, tapping away at her keyboard.

"It was definitely Nola. I just need to know the who the victim was," I answered.

"You have a witness then?" she asked.

"Not one that would be willing to testify," I grinned. "It wouldn't be good for his image since he's a drug dealer and all."

"No, I expect that would make for a bad marketing plan," she grinned back. "Terecca Byrd, 66, divorced, lived alone, has two adult kids and four grandchildren."

"What can you tell me about her kids?"

"Trisha Byrd, 43, married with four kids, lives in Seattle. Tony Byrd, 46, single, no kids, lives here in Miami and *ding, ding, ding*, works for Customs Office down at the docks."

"Shit. Run everything you can access on Tony Byrd, details about his job, financials, etcetera. Tech you take the personal route, his Facebook page, homestead, friends, anyone close to him. Nola was sending him her special kind of warning by killing his mother. She's holding something or someone else over his head, though."

"This Nola woman is sick," Genie grumbled as both her and Tech's fingers flew over their keyboards.

I couldn't disagree. It was getting late in the afternoon, though, and I needed to shower and prepare for the long night ahead, so I let them know I would check back for an update.

In my bedroom, I pulled out a burner and called Sheriff Eric.

"Sheriff," he answered.

"Can you get the speed boat into Miami South, slip 2643 yet this afternoon and the cabin cruiser into Miami Center City slip 4727 by tomorrow afternoon?"

"I'll take Tobias and move both this afternoon. I'll have Carly pick us up after she closes."

"Thanks. How's Lenny's foot?" I asked.

"Gone. But he doesn't seem to care that the doctors had to cut off what was left. He's already back at the bar," Eric snorted.

"The doctors released him?"

"Not exactly. But Tobias got his medications and promised the doctor that he would spike his beer with them."

"Sounds about right. Call this number and only this number if you run into any problems. Both the slips are in the name of KNC Enterprises if anyone asks."

"I'll handle it," he assured me.

"Just don't call out too much attention. I can't afford for anyone to be watching either boat."

"I'll leave my badge at home," he said before hanging up.

I took an extra-long shower enjoying the peace and quiet and letting my brain rest for the first time in days. When I stepped out of the shower, I found Bones leaning up against the bathroom wall.

"I would have washed your hair," he grinned.

"I bet. How's the research coming?" I asked, grabbing another towel to dry my hair with.

As angry as I was at Bones earlier, I had to accept that he was only trying to support me when he came to Miami. I couldn't do anything about it now, so it was wasted energy to fight with him.

"Complex. Wild Card wasn't kidding. That place is a maze. It will take me all night to memorize the mansion, and I don't understand enough of the land and water markings to know where the points of entry are."

"Charlie can help you with the waterway accesses and elevations. She'll be around tonight too," I said.

"I thought she was on recon tonight?"

"No, she's assigned to stay here."

"Then why is she dressed like a drug addict?"

"What?" I said, stomping past him to go out to the main room. "Charlie!!"

"Before you start yelling—," Charlie's voice called from the kitchen.

"You can't go!" I had shouted before I turned the corner.

Stepping into the kitchen, I stopped in my tracks. Charlie was indeed dressed up like a strung out street kid. I had to look twice just to make sure it was her.

"Look, the timetable is too tight. You can't send three Yankees in without a handler, and chances are their covers will be burned quickly, so I'm the backup plan. If they fail, I step in. I learned from the best, remember? You know I can pull this off without tipping off Nola. And, you need to be at the warehouse."

"And, what if you get hurt?"

"I was the first one of us that wanted to be a cop. I put my life on the line every day when I put on the uniform. I know you worry, but you have to let me do my part in all this. I love Nicholas too."

"You do this smart. No heroics. You gather intel, you watch, you wait. Something goes wrong, you run, Kid. I mean it!"

"I have her back, Kelsey," Jackson promised.

I nodded and walked away.

Passing through the living room, I noticed Grady and Wild Card looking me up and down. I pulled my damp towel tighter around me and hurried down the hall.

In the bedroom, Bones sat waiting for me on the bed. One single tear had slipped past my guard down my cheek. It was enough for him to pull me into his arms and comfort me, pulling me down on top of him.

"She'll be okay. You said yourself that she can go toe-to-toe with you in fighting, and I'm sure she hasn't been sitting on her ass these last few years eating donuts. My guess is that she has kept up with her training just as diligently as you have, just waiting. You have to trust her."

"I do. In every situation except a show-down with Nola."

"That's your fear talking, not hers. Nola holds power over you because of your son. You need to force that shit down and face one situation at a time like you were trained to do."

I took a deep breath and relaxed into his chest. Even with his shirt and my wet towel between us, I could feel his warm skin radiating through. Unconsciously, my hand started roaming his shoulder and his chest. Before I knew what was happening, he rolled me onto my back and started kissing me. The next thing that registered was him inside me, filling me, freeing me from the endless worry that threatened to shred me.

Chapter Twenty-Seven

By the time I had darkened my hair and dressed, it was almost time to leave for the warehouse. Walking into the living room, I found Reggie, Wild Card and Grady waiting for me.

"I thought you were on recon with Charlie?" I asked Grady.

"I was," he sighed.

Reggie and Wild Card started laughing.

"What happened?"

"He kept getting hit on by women at the hotel pool. By the time Penny left to go back to her room, Charlie said they couldn't use him again tonight and sent him back to join our op," Wild Card grinned.

"It wasn't funny," Grady growled.

"It's the spray tan, I think," Reggie winked at me. "It makes him look smoking hot."

"Sure. It couldn't have been the speedo you forced me to wear," Grady snapped, turning to face Reggie.

Reggie chuckled and jumped out of punching range.

I couldn't help it, my mind wandered to the image of Grady in a speedo. And regardless of the fact that I thought most men looked horrendous wearing one, the image of Grady in one was enticing.

A hard slap to the ass brought me back to reality.

I looked over at Bones and grinned. He rolled his eyes.

Grady looked at me with an ever-so-slightly raised eyebrow.

"Ok, so, Tech, do you have our comms ready?" I asked, blushing a bit.

"I have a dual setup for you, and one channel only for the rest of the team. If I tell you to switch to channel two, you're going to move this switch up a notch, and then you will be able to communicate with Charlie. Otherwise, stay on the line with your own team and trust me to handle it."

"Deal. Don't eavesdrop on them unless you give me the green light. I can do that," I said, inserting the earpiece.

Tech raised an eyebrow at me indicating he had little faith that I would follow the plan but turned to hand out the other earpieces to the team.

Bones snorted and went back to his blueprints. "Be safe, Babe."

"What? No lecture that I shouldn't go?" I asked Bones.

"I trust Grady and Wild Card to keep you out of any real danger," Bones grinned.

"But not me?" Reggie asked.

"Two weeks ago she led you by the nose to go after three dangerous bikers without backup," Bones answered with a raised eyebrow to Reggie.

"Well, there is that," Reggie chuckled.

The guys went to load the SUV, and I cornered Tech in the kitchen.

"I'm wearing one of Carl's brooches," I said pointing to the piece of jewelry. "It's eyes-only for you and me unless I say otherwise, understand?"

The brooch was one that recorded video, and since I was entering private property illegally, I really didn't need it advertised that there would be evidence. In reality, it wasn't smart to record what was about to happen, but since I wasn't completely sure what we would find in the warehouse, I thought it best to have a backup plan that could prove we were the good guys.

"Smart. I'll cut off remote access and run directly to one of the new laptops only. No one else will know unless you tell them," Tech assured me. "Now get going before they leave without you."

I kissed Tech on the cheek before hurrying out the door to jump in the backseat. I was surprised to find Grady in the backseat with me instead of Wild Card or Reggie. He grinned, and I turned away to look out the window as Reggie drove the SUV south.

"We know the building and site layout, but what exactly are we walking into tonight?" Wild Card asked turning around to face me from the front passenger seat.

"Well, I would really like to know that myself," I hedged.

"So, we're walking in blind?" Wild Card grinned.

"Not exactly, but close. Max has a history of running his various import-export businesses through the warehouse district. Word on the street is that dirty cops are covering up some new action he has moving through this particular warehouse. There's also a waterway access that he would find useful. I'm guessing that the building will have some security systems and inside we may find whatever his current outgoing cargo is, but with Max, you never know what he's moving."

"So, did you happen to mention to Bones that you were completely winging this op?" Grady grinned.

"Hell, no. That would freak him out."

Reggie grinned in the rearview mirror, and Wild Card and Grady chuckled.

"So what's the plan if we find something?" Grady asked.

"If it's drugs, we walk away. If it's human and alive, we get them to safety and sit and see what happens."

"Sounds like as good of a plan as any to me," Wild Card grinned, turning back in his seat.

Grady snorted.

"You're free to exit at any time. You don't have stay. We can handle this," I said.

"And miss all the fun?" Grady grinned.

My earpiece beeped and then Tech's voice transmitted over the line.

"Kel, can you switch to channel two?"

"Already?" I asked looking at my watch.

It was only 7:30. I didn't wait for a reply but switched to channel two.

"What's up?"

"Sara relayed that Penny is to meet Nola at the Square Mall on Lancaster in half an hour. We have Jackson heading there now, but it sounded off," Charlie said.

"That's because it is," I warned. "Nola won't go somewhere as public as a mall. Jackson, hang back on the far Southside of the mall. You'll have the best visual from there. My guess is that Nola will pick Penny up at either the South or West entrance and jump across the highway into Center City," I said as I started to bite my thumbnail. "Something has her jumpy. Charlie, you drop Maggie in the mall to watch Penny and then head across the bridge to the backside of the district. There are abandon buildings to the North. My guess is that Nola will be heading that way. Your drug addict disguise will blend in with the neighborhood."

"That's spreading us kind of thin," Charlie said.

"You wanted the op. Just keep your head down and stay in touch with Tech and Jackson. Jackson, if you have the time, you will be picking Maggie back up, but if you don't, she can catch a cab. Do you copy?"

"Copy. We'll let you know how it goes. You at the warehouse yet?"

"We're just pulling into the parking lot about two blocks away. I need to switch back to channel one. Any questions?"

"We're good," Charlie answered.

"Good here," Maggie said.

"Yeah, Yeah, get back to your own shit," Jackson chuckled.

"Everything okay?" Reggie asked.

"At the moment, but something has Nola spooked, so stay alert," I said climbing out of the car and gathering my pack. The guys put their packs on as well, and we all checked our weapons and turned the safeties off.

A half a block away from the warehouse, Reggie and I split off to the North as Grady and Wild Card continued to the East. The plan was to scout the perimeter to check for activity before we moved in closer.

"I have a visual on two armed guards walking the perimeter. They will be in your line of site in approximately three minutes," Wild Card whispered over the earpiece.

"Copy," Reggie responded quietly.

Reggie and I crouched between some bushes and waited. The two guards rounded the corner just as two other guards came from the other direction. All four stopped to talk to each other, while Reggie and I held our positions. A minute later, one of the guards pulled a rolled smoke from his pocket and started to share it with his fellow guards. Reggie and I grinned at each other.

Two more minutes passed, and the guards slowly crumpled to the ground.

"Four guards down, any more movement?" I asked over the comms.

"Negative. Do you need help with the cleanup?" Wild Card asked, sounding a bit concerned.

"Negative. Explain later," Reggie chuckled. "I know it was you. I just don't know how you managed it," he grinned at me.

"Chills sent a runner down with free samples. It may have been a bit laced," I grinned back.

"With what?"

"You don't want to know," I grinned as we moved further to the North to make an approach.

Reggie covered my six, as I snuck up behind the fallen guards and relieved the sleeping soldiers of their guns and walkies. Arms full, I snuck back around to some crates and hid the collection behind a stack of wooden pallets.

"At least if they wake up, they'll be more likely to hightail it out of here rather than call in that they were drugged and robbed," I said to Reggie as he caught back up with me.

"God, I miss hanging out with you, Sis," he said, pulling my head over to kiss my cheek.

"Okay, Okay, let's focus," I laughed moving forward. "Report on East side of building?"

"All clear. Moving North now," Grady reported.

"Team two moving East," I responded.

The North side of the building was inactive, and a few minutes later we met up with Grady and Wild Card at the rendezvous point.

"Hold or go in?" Wild Card asked.

I checked my watch. It was only 8:00, but if anyone else was coming, they would most likely wait until later in the night.

"The guards are already down. We have to move in," I said.

"Kelsey, hold," Tech said over the earpiece. "Switch to channel two."

"I only have a minute," I said over the channel two line.

"A town car picked up Penny and took her over the bridge. I didn't have time to pick up Maggie. Penny's purse was thrown from the window while crossing the bridge and I lost her in traffic," Jackson breathed heavily in the earpiece.

"Charlie, report," I called out.

"I can't get her to respond," Jackson said. "I've tried twice, nothing but silence."

"She might be listening and not responding because she's too close," I answered. "Tech, track her. I put one of Carl's masterpieces in her pocket before she left."

"And, that's why you're in charge," Tech said over the earpiece. "Got it. Hang on. It was an audio tracker, let me see if I can pick anything up."

"Don't patch it through yet," I said, hearing something on the earpiece. "Everyone, silence. Charlie, if that was you, tap twice."

Two barely audible taps came across the earpiece.

"Copy. If your hurt, or in danger, tap twice, again."

Nothing.

"Ok, Tech, patch in the audible."

Penny's voice: "I didn't make a deal with the FBI. I don't know who bugged the purse."

Nola's voice: "Well, I guess it's not really a concern, either way."

Click... Pffing... Pffing.

Nola's voice: "Let's go."

I could barely make out footsteps as they drifted further away.

"Charlie?"

"Shit, Kel. Shit, shit, shit," she whispered.

"Not a word, Charlie. You wait for them to clear out, then wait another 10 minutes and meet up with Jackson. No one speaks out loud of what happened or calls it in," I said.

"I can't just leave her there," Charlie said.

"You don't have a choice, Kid," Jackson relayed. "If you call it in, Nola will know someone witnessed the shooting. Just hang low and I'll pick you up in 10 minutes."

Wild Card put a hand on my shoulder and gave me a questioning look.

I shook my head for him to wait.

"Tech, anyone else listening in on this line?"

"No," he answered. "Bones is outside with Bridget taking a smoke break."

"Everyone needs to keep this quiet. We'll discuss it later. I'm switching back to channel one," I said and broke the connection.

"Everything okay?" Reggie asked.

"No. But it can wait," I answered as I started a forward approach.

Chapter Twenty-Eight

Once we were gathered alongside the building, I climbed on a nearby dumpster and carefully pulled the awning style window up. To my relief, not only was it unlocked, but there were no security bars on the inside. Holstering my gun, I pulled myself up through the window and quietly rolled to the floor. Switching to night vision goggles, I called the all clear and moved to the doorway to scout the hallway.

Reggie was the second one to enter, followed by Wild Card, who had to be pulled up through the window due to his recent gunshot wound. Reggie covered visual surveillance out the window as Grady slid fluidly through the narrow space.

The others switched to their night vision goggles and followed my lead down the hall. Reggie and Wild Card covered our six, as Grady and I danced a rotation of checking one doorway at a time until we arrived at the stairwell.

We moved up silently to the fourth floor. We didn't speak, but we were all on high alert for any noise. It was quiet, too quiet, as we slipped back out of the stairway. Ten feet in front of us loomed a large doorway that was open into the main room. We approached, guns raised.

One step before entering the room, Grady and I both reached out simultaneously grabbing the other and stepped back. Reggie and Wild Card were on our heels and froze as we now all shared the same space.

"What is it?" Reggie whispered barely loud enough for me to hear with his mouth leaning over my shoulder.

"Motion sensor at the doorway," I answered just as quietly.

I motioned for everyone to hold and approached a smaller doorway off to the side. This one was to a small janitorial room that had a mop sink and some supplies. There was no indication of sensors, so I went in and inspected the wall. The interior wall between the two rooms was old plaster board.

Reaching into my boot, I retrieved a switchblade and started cutting through the plaster. Reggie reached down into my other boot, retrieving my other blade, cutting as well. Grady and Wild Card kept watch. After cutting through the first layer, we quietly set it aside and began to work the other side. It didn't take us long before Reggie reached out to brace the plaster as I tipped it out of the way. We had a big enough hole to get through, but a large metal cabinet partially blocked our passage.

"Damn it," Reggie whispered.

"It's fine. I can fit," I said as I squeezed through.

"You can't go alone," Wild Card said.

"Let me do a quick circuit. There might not even be a need to be in here. Meanwhile, you can cut another hole and be ready if I need you," I said, before turning and moving forward.

"Kelsey," Wild Card said, trying to stop me.

I didn't answer his call.

The main room was L-shaped, and up around the corner, I was soon out of their view. I held my position waiting, watching, listening.

I heard movement on the other side of the room, but I was too far away to see, even with night vision goggles. I slowly approached.

By the mid-way point, I could make out metal cages, and could see movement inside of them.

"Stay quiet," I called out. "I'm here to help."

"Please," A woman cried. "I want to go home."

More movement stirred within the two cages, and I could make out at least four moving bodies. I scanned the area again, but it didn't appear that there were any guards around.

"Quiet," I repeated. "When I get the lock open, I need everyone to stay quiet and wait for me to open the second cage. I will take you all out at once, but you have to do what I say. There are alarms on the building, and if we set them off, then we'll be trapped."

"Si, Si," one of the women answered.

I quickly picked the first lock, thanks to Bridget's specialized training, and braced my foot on the bottom of the door to keep it shut until I picked the next lock. When I had both removed, I opened the cages and helped pull the woman out. Two of the women were carrying small children.

"Is there anyone else in the cages?"

"No, it's just the two children and us four women," the woman next to me whispered.

"Okay, stay close and hold hands. Do not go through any doors. I'm going to lead us back to my friends. They'll get us all out of the building."

The women were too terrified to do anything but follow orders, and I was able to quickly get them to the access hole and start feeding them through to Wild Card. Grady and Reggie started to lead them back the way we came, and soon, Reggie and I were helping lower each woman and child one at a time to Grady through the window to the outside while Wild Card kept watch down below.

When the last woman was passed through, I pulled my earpiece and motioned for Reggie to do the same.

"Do you trust me?" I asked Reggie.

"Why do I get the feeling that that trust is going to be put to a test, Kelsey?"

I put my earpiece in his hand. "I won't be alone. Tech has a way to find me if he has to, but I need you to go with Grady and Wild Card and get the women and children out of here. I need to go back upstairs and see if I can find anything else."

"I'll go with you," Reggie said.

"No. There are six victims to escort to safety. If Wild Card and Grady are caught, they will need the extra firepower to get the women and children out. I'll be fine, promise," I said leaning in to kiss his cheek before I disappeared down the hallway.

As I traveled back up the stairs, back through the cut out plasterboard and through the large L-shaped room, my mind kept remembering all the times I went rogue, and it had turned out wrong. I hoped this didn't become one of those times, because if it did, Reggie was going to blame himself.

When I reached the cages, I stopped again to listen. Nothing. My Spidey senses were even calm, so that was a good omen. I ventured past the cages and came upon three doorways. Carefully inspecting for sensors, I moved forward into the first room. The room was empty. I moved to the second and found the same. The third room was what I was looking for – Max's lair.

A king size bed was situated on one wall with an oak desk on the far wall. I moved to the desk. A laptop sat open, and I brushed my gloved hand across the mousepad. The screen lit up, calling for a passcode. Moving the goggles to my backpack clip to keep them in the dark, I typed "Nola" and laughed when it worked. *Dumbass.*

I pulled a flash drive from my bag and entered the commands to copy the files to the removable drive. While the files were copying, I pulled my pen light out and checked the rest of the desk and room. A clipboard hung on the wall with various data that I couldn't make out, so I took a few pictures of it with my burner phone. Looking back at the laptop, I pulled the remove-able drive and placed it back in my pack. It was time to leave.

Back at the doorway, I slid the goggles back on and waited for my eyes to adjust. When my vision was clear, I turned to my right and found a small stairway. I followed it downward, but it ended on the second floor. I looked around, but there didn't seem to be another access to the first floor. I would have to make my way across the building to where we entered.

Moving cautiously down the hallway, an empty room stood on my right. I entered and peered out the window.

Man, I was having a lucky night.

Another dumpster sat directly below the window.

Pushing the window up, I heard a click. Recognizing the noise, I dove out of the room and pulled myself into the fetal position around the hallway wall.

A loud explosion erupted as the building shook and debris flew in every direction.

"Time to go, Kelsey," I said to myself as I ran back toward the window again.

Hoping that the grenade wasn't forceful enough to move the dumpster from below, I swung myself out the now much larger opening and plunged downward.

The dumpster had been pushed away from the building and caught part of my body weight as I flipped backward off from it, bouncing against the brick wall and landing on the paved parking lot between the brick wall and the dumpster. I half-laid, half-sat, on the ground with ears ringing, and trying to catch my breath.

Eventually, I was able to sit up and confirm that I was in one piece. I started to stand when I saw police lights heading toward the building. Two cop cars pulled up, undercover cars with portable lights, followed by a black SUV. My old boss, Trevor Zamlock exited out of the first car followed by Officer Eckert, one of Trevor's cronies in the Vice unit, from the second car. Stepping out of the shiny black SUV was Max Lautner himself, followed closely by one of his armed goons.

I slid my burner phone from my back pocket and was pleased to see that it was still in one piece. I turned on the video recorder and held the phone out as far as I dared from behind the dumpster.

"What the hell is the hole in the side of the building?" Trevor asked Max.

"I had a grenade rigged to the window," Max answered. "There must be someone up there."

"Damn it," Trevor said. "Where are the guards?"

"I don't know. I just got here too, remember?"

"Eckert—Come with me. Let's go check it out," Trevor growled, leading the way into the building.

Max and his goon stayed behind in the lot, but it didn't take Max long to start pacing.

"Go walk the perimeter and see if you can find the guards. Damn it. I pay them good money to protect this building," Max yelled at his man.

The goon took off in a jog to the North, and I turned the video off on my phone and stuffed it back in my pocket. This was the moment I was waiting for.

Sliding out the far side of the space, I moved along some crates until I could pass in the dark shadows across the lot and start working my way to the other side of Max's SUV. Once there, I checked again for the goon, Trevor, and Eckert, before I slipped around the corner and placed a gun to the back of Max's skull.

"Nice and easy," I warned. "I don't have an issue with dropping a bullet in you and calling it a night, but your chances of survival increase if you cooperate."

"Fuck," Max whispered.

"Slowly, walk backward around the back of the SUV to the other side," I ordered.

He followed instructions, and once tucked behind the security of the SUV, I pushed him against the truck and relieved him of his gun, dropping it into the nearby grass. I turned his phone off and slid it into the outside pocket of my pack.

"Let's go. And, don't even think about calling out for help," I said pushing him with the barrel of the gun toward the grass path around the next building. "Keep moving. Head to the marina and lower your hands to six inches away from your sides."

"You know, Officer Harrison, for years I have been telling Nola that her paranoia about you was unfounded. No way – I said. No way is Kelsey Harrison still looking for us. We're in the clear."

"Never doubt a woman's instincts," I said. "Even if the woman is batshit crazy."

Chapter Twenty-Nine

Twenty minutes later, we were at the marina. I moved closer to Max, lowering my gun to the back of his ribs and gripping his arm tight.

"Just remember, anyone stops us, and you're a dead man. Move. Slip 2643."

When we reached the slip, I roughly encouraged Max to get into the boat, and I stepped in behind him. I swung my pack to the floor and while focusing my gun on Max, dug around blindly for flex-cuffs. Finding them, I pushed Max onto the back bench and secured one of his hands to the lower grip-running bar. Confident that he couldn't go anywhere, I went to the driver's seat and opened the hidden compartment and removed the boat keys. I started the engine and untied the dock ropes, dropping them inside the boat.

My phone vibrated in my back pocket, and I pulled it out. It was Reggie.

"I'm okay, but I'm going to be delayed a bit longer. Did you make it out?"

"We're clear. None of the women or children are injured, so we were waiting to see if you made it back before we took off."

"Don't wait around any longer. You have dirty cops up by the warehouse. Move out. Turn the GPS on and follow it to the location marked 'Help.' The women and children will be safe there. Then follow the word 'Safety' back to the safe house. I'll be there in a couple hours."

I hung up before he could argue with me and turned the phone off. I knew the brooch was still on, and Tech could still track me if needed, so I pulled the boat out and drove out of the marina.

Once in the open waterways I opened the throttle and let the boat bounce and skip off the top of the water at high speed. I knew the route well and was far enough out that I didn't have to worry about too many eyes watching. About three miles down the coast, I cut the throttle back, turned inland at a slower pace before bringing the boat to an idle and shutting it off.

"Now that we have some privacy, where's Nola? Where's Nicholas?" I asked swiveling the chair around to face Max.

"You think you can point a gun at me, and I'll just give you all the answers," he laughed. "You won't shoot an unarmed man without cause. Maybe back in the marina when it could mean you getting away, but out here? No, you don't have the stomach for it."

"Ah, but I can do much worse than kill you, Max," I grinned. "I can get word to Nola that you gave her up," I whispered, leaning toward him.

"You wouldn't dare," Max snarled. "You know that would be just as bad as killing me yourself."

"No, see, that's where you're wrong, Max. I've never had any moral issues with bad people killing other bad people. It's the original form of Justice before we corrupted it with all these rules."

"I don't know where your son is, okay? She never told me," he said.

"Not good enough, Max. You need to give me something," I said leaning back in my chair.

"No, I don't," he said before he jumped up and dove off the side of the boat.

"SHIT!" I said, standing up too late to stop him. On the bench seat laid a small pair of nail clippers and pieces of the shredded flex-cuffs. "Max, No! Sharks!"

I ran to the side of the boat, but Max was already swimming at a good clip toward the rocky shore. Moving back to the driver's seat, I started the boat and throttled at slow speed his direction, approaching him from the side.

This area of the ocean was invested with sharks. Several shipwreck sites were just below the surface providing protection and a plentiful food source for the nest. Max wouldn't make it to shore before he became dinner.

Almost to him, I watched in horror as his leg was dragged under, followed by the rest of him. He screamed before the water covered him completely. Cutting the throttle again, I searched the sides of the boat for any signs of him.

Out of nowhere, he surfaced a mere ten feet from the boat, and I tossed a rope to him. He screamed wildly and thrashed around, but managed to wrap the rope around his arm and hand and I dragged him in as fast as my arms could move. Once to the side, I reached down and gripped his arm, bracing my feet against the side of the boat and leaning back to pull his weight up and into the boat as he continued to scream.

I could see his and my own arm, just crossing over the edge of the boat, when suddenly there was a change in the weight to leverage ratio, and I fell backward to the floor of the boat.

I stared in horror, as I realized that I was still gripping tightly to Max's arm, which was no longer attached to his body.

I screamed.

And, screamed. I was full out freaking as I jumped up and threw the arm away from me and it tumbled back over the side of the boat, splashing into the water.

I stood there, violently shaking, covered in blood, listening to the waves and sharks as water splashed.

There was no way Max could still be alive, but I still waited.

I'm not sure how long I stood watching, but by the time I convinced myself to leave, my teeth were chattering loud enough to echo in my ears, and I could no longer feel my feet. I adjusted the throttle, steering carefully out of the shipwreck zone before opening up the speed to return to the marina.

As I entered the gateway, I decreased the speed to the no wake requirements, and slowly meandered the passageways to my slip.

"Tech, if you're still up and watching this, I think I could use a ride. I'm not feeling so good. Can you send someone to get me?"

The sound of the waves, slapping the side of the boat was my only reply. I pulled into my slip and tied the front rope down. I looped the back rope around the post before

I noticed the blood coating it. I dropped to my knees and cried. Not for the loss of Max, he wouldn't be missed. But for the horror of the scene that I had witnessed and the part that I played in it.

I spent a good five minutes crying before I sat up and leaned against the inside of the boat wall. I still gripped the bloody rope, holding the boat in place, but had failed to bother to tie it off. I heard boots pounding against the docks, heading my way, but didn't turn to look.

"She's here," Tech called out, before jumping in the boat next to me. "Shit, Kelsey."

"Tie the boat off. I'll get her back to the truck," Grady said as he pulled me up off the floor and wrapped me in a blanket.

After I was wrapped tight, he picked me up and carried me back down the dock. I heard Tech following us, but I leaned my head into Grady's shoulder and didn't say anything.

Grady held me the entire drive back, and by the time Tech pulled into the driveway, my teeth had stopped chattering.

Tech opened the door and with their help, I managed to stand on my own feet and walk up the path to the back porch and up into the house. The house was quiet, and only Bridget was standing in the kitchen when I walked in, closely followed by Tech and Grady.

"Holy shit," Bridget said, staring at me, hands going to cover her open mouth.

"I'm okay," I said. "Can you get me out a couple garbage bags?"

Bridget jumped for the cabinet to retrieve the bags and handed them to me. I nodded to Tech to stay with her to keep her calm. He looked worried, but nodded back. Grady followed me as I snuck through the living room, past several open bedroom doors, until I was at the end of the hall to the room I claimed as my own.

Once inside, I tucked the blanket in one of the bags and proceeded to fill the next one with everything except my phone, bra, and underwear.

"Are you okay?" Grady asked, stepping up to balance me as started to sway.

"I will be," I answered as I opened up a hidden wall safe behind a bookcase and stuffed both bags inside. "I just need a hot shower."

I locked the safe back up, closing the bookcase door and went to the bathroom. I turned the hot water on full blast and stepped in, relishing the scalding water stripping my skin of Max's blood. I took my bra and underwear off and let them drop to the floor of the shower. I lathered and scrubbed until every part of my body, including my scalp had been properly exfoliated.

I large hand reached into the shower, and I instinctively jumped back. The hand turned off the water and passed me a towel.

"You're clean. I promise," Grady's voice said from the other side of the curtain.

I dried off and stepped out around the curtain to an empty but steamy bathroom. Laying on the counter were a pair of sweat pant shorts and my favorite MSU t-shirt. I eagerly changed into the comfort clothes and wrapped my hair up in the towel.

Walking back into my bedroom, Tech, Bridget, and Grady waited for me.

"I'm okay, now. Promise," I said. "Tech, I need you to bring me the laptop you recorded me on. Eventually, I may need to deal with what happened tonight, but I need to find Nicholas first. I'll lock the laptop up with my clothes for safe keeping."

"Are you sure that's wise?" Grady asked. "I can get rid of everything. I can burn the clothes out back, and Tech can wipe the laptop."

"No," Tech said. "Kelsey's right. We need to keep it all."

"Why don't you two explain what happened out there tonight and let me decide. You both are still in shock."

"Get the laptop Tech," I said.

I walked over to my phone and called Eric.

"Sheriff," he answered.

"I need your help," I said.

"Tonight? I just got home from helping you," Eric chuckled.

"It's serious, Eric."

"What do you need?" he asked.

"The speedboat is back in the slip, but it's covered in blood. I need it moved to a secure location so that the evidence is preserved."

"Are you okay?" Eric asked.

"Yes, but Max is dead," I answered.

"Alright. I'll get it cleared out tonight and store it in my boathouse. Are you sure you don't want me to have someone set it on fire?"

* * *

"No, for right now, it's best if we keep everything locked up until I know the coast is clear."

"You sound pretty shaky. I'm not sure this is the best idea you have ever had."

"You can ask me again in a couple days, but my answer will be the same. Lock the boat up."

"I'll handle it," he said, disconnecting the call.

I opened up the safe again, sliding the laptop that Tech handed to me on top of the garbage bags.

Tech was grinning at me.

"What?"

"Have you ever stayed anywhere that doesn't have hidden rooms and hidden safes?"

"No. Not since I was a kid. I like them," I smirked.

Bridget came back in with a tray of food, and I ate most of it, while Tech caught me up on miscellaneous updates.

"So basically while I was out there rescuing hostages, almost getting blown up by a grenade, filming dirty cops and taking a boat ride from hell, you sat at your computer and got zilch to help the investigation?" I grinned.

Bridget giggled and jumped on the side of the bed.

"What grenade?" Grady asked.

"What filming of dirty cops?" Tech asked.

I grinned at Bridget. "Boys," I said shaking my head.

"What's going on in here?" Reggie asked, wiping the sleep from his eyes. He tossed himself on top of the far side of the bed.

"Kelsey was just about to explain something about almost getting blown up by a grenade," Grady updated Reggie.

"Thanks a lot," I said tossing a pillow at Grady.

"Damn it. I knew I shouldn't have left you!" Reggie yelled.

"If you'd been with me, I wouldn't have been able to jump out of the way in time, and we both would be dead."

"What's all the yelling?" Jackson asked coming in to take up the last available space on the bed.

"That's what I want to know. I thought everyone was sleeping," Maggie said, walking into the room. Charlie followed in behind her.

"I'm telling a few bedtime stories, want to hear?"

"I want to hear," Bones said, sauntering in to join us.

"Me too, but can you tell them in the living room, because there's nowhere for me to lay down in here," Genie grinned from the doorway.

Since everyone was now wide awake, we moved into the living room. Bridget made popcorn and we all settled with blankets and pillows on the floor. I explained my night's events up until I slipped away from the dumpster. Everyone knew I was leaving something out, but between the grenade, the flash drive, the clipboard photos, and the video I played of the dirty cops working with Max, they were satisfied with the parts that I had shared.

Bones wasn't happy about the grenade part of my story, and Reggie was bummed that the closest he got to any real action was watching the guards pass out from their laced joint. Genie and Tech moved laptops into the living room to download all the data I brought back.

"You going to fill us in on how you managed to get laced dope to the guards?" Charlie asked.

"Chills."

"Man, I love that guy," Charlie grinned. "Too bad one of these days one of us is going to need to arrest him."

"Hear you there," I nodded.

"Who's Chills?" Bones asked.

"Her gang-banger drug dealer of a friend," Reggie answered rolling his eyes.

Bones gave me a disapproving look, and Grady laughed.

"Now why doesn't that surprise me?" Grady said.

"Kelsey?" Genie said. "You remember that guy from Customs Office, Tony Byrd? The son of the woman that Nola killed?"

"Sure," I said, taking another handful of popcorn.

"This shipping schedule you found in Max's office lines up with Tony's work schedule perfectly. And, the shipping schedule shows that three 10ft by 10ft crates are being shipped tomorrow night."

"Shit. We can call it in and set up a sting, but I can't promise after everything that went down at the warehouse that the plan won't be changed."

"It's actionable intel," Maggie said. "We can't gamble that they will change the plans and then have women and children shipped out. I'll call Agent Kierson and warn him that we don't know if the information is valid anymore, but to set something up. What time is the shipment going through?"

"Ten o'clock tomorrow night," Genie said.

"My brother works at the Customs Office in North Carolina if you need a contact," Grady offered.

Maggie nodded and went to the kitchen to make a call.

"Hey, why is everyone up without me?" Wild Card asked walking into the living room.

We all looked at each other. No one had even noticed Wild Card had been missing from our story time.

"You needed your rest. You're recovering from a recent gunshot wound, remember?" I grinned, trying to cover.

"Yeah, that's it," Jackson chuckled.

"Especially after tonight, when you couldn't even do a three-foot pull-up to get in a window," Reggie teased.

"Man, that's sad, brother," Bones grinned, while reaching behind me to absently rub my back.

Charlie saw the gesture and gave me a wicked glare before getting up and going back to her room.

"Is Charlie okay?" Bones asked.

"She will be," I answered and got up to follow her.

"What are you doing, Kelsey?" Charlie asked before I had time to close the door.

"Charlie, either Bones will understand when he hears what happened to Penny or he won't. But I won't take a chance on tomorrow night's sting getting messed up, just to have her body moved to the morgue. It won't make any difference if we wait, but can seriously hurt us if we call it in or tell Bones."

Tech, Maggie, and Jackson slipped in the door and closed it behind them.

"She's dead, Charlie," I said. "There is nothing you can do about it. Just like I can't do anything about what happened to Max. What's done is done, and we will face it after we survive tomorrow night."

"I don't know what happened to Max, and I don't want to know," Maggie said. "But I agree with Kelsey about

Penny. She worked in trafficking women and children. Regardless of Bones' mixed up feelings, she's not worth risking this operation for."

"She was a bitch," Tech said, throwing himself on the bed beside Charlie. "She tried to poison Kelsey earlier this week, so consider it karma."

"I should have stopped it," Charlie insisted.

"You couldn't. You're forgetting that we heard the audio feed. There wasn't enough time to stop Nola without killing her. And, if you'd killed Nola, you'd have killed any chance of finding Nicholas," I said.

"Bones is our friend," Jackson said. "He's going to be pissed at Tech, Kelsey, and me, but he won't hold it against you. He'll know that it wasn't your fault, so quit feeling so damn guilty. And, he's going to be pissed at us whether we tell him tonight or after the raid tomorrow night. It's not going to make a big difference, so we might as well hold off."

"She really tried to kill you?" Charlie asked with teary eyes.

"Yes. And worse than that, she was a snob. And, I mean she could put our mothers to shame with her high-snobbery. You would've hated her," I grinned.

Charlie couldn't stop herself from the slight smirk that split her lips.

"It still doesn't feel right to have Bones work the op tomorrow night without knowing about his dead wife," Charlie said.

"We couldn't send him away if we tried," Tech shrugged. "He can't stand to be away from Kelsey."

"Do you love him?" Charlie asked me.

"That's a complicated question. Remember when I had that strange addiction to seafoam candy?" I grinned.

"And, you would eat about 10 pounds of it a day," she nodded. "I had to wean you off them like an addict – Yeah, I'm not likely to forget that."

"Well, it's something like that," I smiled.

"Damn. I remember how you described that seafoam candy. Yum."

Chapter Thirty

Blackness surrounded me when I woke. The house was still. I checked my Spidey senses, but they were still asleep. Something woke me, but whatever it was, we were safe.

Grabbing a sweatshirt from my bag on the floor, I pulled it on over my head and padded down the hallway. At the entrance to the living room, I counted at least four sleeping bodies, wrapped up in blankets. A noise stirred from behind me, and I backtracked down the hall to the first bedroom door.

Opening the door, I turned on the light and rushed over to Charlie.

"Charlie, wake up," I whispered, shaking her gently.

Charlie bolted up into a sitting position, covered in sweat and breathing heavily.

"Shit," she said, throwing her arms around my shoulders.

Her body trembled as I held her, stroking her hair back as she curled into my side. It was a familiar act. I had been holding Charlie after her night terrors since before she was old enough to go to school.

Time felt like it stood still, but eventually, she calmed her breathing and pulled away.

"You okay?"

"Yeah. Did I wake anyone else?" she whispered as she wiped her face with the back of her hands.

"I don't think so," I said. "You didn't tell me you were having the nightmares again."

"We had bigger problems to deal with. I have them handled."

"How long, Charlie?"

She sighed, leaning back into the pillows. "Since Nicholas disappeared."

"Charlie—,"

"I'm fine, Kel. It's not every night. Just when things get a bit ramped up."

I sighed. I couldn't say that I hadn't had my own share of nightmares over the years. "You need more sleep."

"I'm not sure I can."

"Come on, Kid," Jackson said from the doorway. "You can snuggle up with Reggie and I. Reggie makes an awesome nightmare force-field," he grinned.

Charlie returned the grin, crawling out of bed and following Jackson to their room. I looked at the clock. It was only 5:00, but I knew that I wouldn't be able to fall asleep again.

Back in the doorway to the living room, I noted that the War Room light was on. I stepped inside, finding Tech working on his laptop.

"You should be sleeping. You look like hell, and I need you alert tonight," I scolded him.

"I tried, but those bastards in the living room snore like crazy and I couldn't stand it any longer," Tech grinned.

"Charlie moved to Reggie and Jackson's room, so go steal her bed for a couple of hours."

"Sold," he said getting up and passing me his laptop. "I have Max's files up if you want to go through them.

Goodnight." He crept down the hallway, sliding into Charlie's assigned bedroom.

I carried the laptop into the kitchen, setting it down to make a pot of coffee. While it brewed, I slipped out to the porch to smoke a cigarette. The breeze drifting across the backyard was warm against my skin and the smell of jasmine teased my nose as I sat in the Adirondack chair on the deck and propped my bare feet on the railing support in front of me.

The screen door opened, and Grady walked out carrying two cups of coffee, handing me one, as he sat in the chair next to me.

"Thanks."

"Did you sleep okay?"

I knew he was asking if I had nightmares about Max. I was surprised to realize that I hadn't had a nightmare about anything. I had slept soundly until Charlie had woke me.

"I did. Not a single bad dream," I grinned.

"Good. From what I hear, he wasn't worth losing sleep over."

"No, he wasn't."

"You're not what I expected at all," he chuckled.

"What did you expect?"

"Reggie described you as adventurous. Jackson said you were crazy. Bones described you as beautiful. Donovan described you as a soldier."

"What about Wild Card?"

"Haunted," Grady answered quietly.

"And, what do you think?"

"I think they were all correct," he said turning back to look at me. "But I think Pops described you the best when

I visited the ranch last summer and met your horse, StarBright. He said his Baby Girl was a survivor, just like her horse."

My eyes filled with tears, but I blinked them back, unwilling to shed tears today.

"That horse saved me," I whispered a few minutes later.

Grady sipped his coffee and turned toward me, waiting for an explanation.

"After Nicholas was taken, nothing mattered but finding him, no matter how dangerous it was. I was out of control. I didn't have a plan. I didn't know what I was doing from one day to the next. When Jackson and Wild Card took me to Texas, I was like a caged animal, waiting to release my rage on the world.

"Then I met StarBright. I stole her from her owner's barn. She was hurt, scared, angry. I walked her and her baby brother back to Wild Card's ranch. I worked with her all day, every day, for weeks until she finally started to trust me.

"And, while helping her, she helped me. As she healed, a part of me was able to heal. To let go of the mind-numbing fear, to bury the anger, to make peace with the pain, and to patiently wait. That's the piece I needed the most, patience. If I was going to get Nicholas back, I couldn't face Nola head-on. I needed to play the game. I needed to prepare for war."

"Do you think Nicholas will be at the mansion tonight?"

"No," I sighed. "Nola won't trust him being there with so many people around. He's too valuable to her. She'll move Nicholas somewhere remote, but safe. She won't be there either."

"If we survive tonight, I'll help you hunt her down."

"If *I* don't survive tonight, will you help them," nodding to the house, "hunt her down?"

"You have my word," Grady nodded.

"Thank you."

Chapter Thirty-One

"You sure you have the mansion memorized? There are a lot of passageways," Grady asked from his side of the kitchen table.

"I'm sure," I answered, while I continued to take notes on Max's computer files.

I had a list of several properties that I needed Tech and Genie to check on. Any one of them could be where Nola was hiding or keeping Nicholas.

"And, how will you know where to find the door releases to gain access?"

"She'll find them," Tech grinned, entering the kitchen, followed by Bridget and Charlie.

"She's been building hidden rooms and hidey-holes since our first apartment, so she knows how to spot one," Charlie grinned.

"I've counted three so far in this house," Tech said.

"I'm up to five," Bridget grinned.

"You're both off," Charlie laughed. "There are nine hidden releases in this house leading to either storage, a room or an escape passage."

"Ten," I grinned. "You're losing your touch, Charlie."

"Damn it," she laughed. "It has to be in this kitchen then."

Tech, Bridget, and Charlie started searching the kitchen. I laughed and saved my research for Tech to review.

"I need to go get dressed. Find Maggie and let her know we have a breakfast appointment and need to leave in a half an hour."

Twenty minutes later, I reentered the kitchen to find every cabinet and appliance door wide open and emptied of its contents. Maggie, Tech, Bridget, Wild Card, Reggie, Jackson, Genie and Charlie were standing in the middle of the chaos looking completely frustrated. Grady and Bones sat at the table drinking coffee, grinning.

"You still haven't found it?" I laughed.

"No. You have to tell us. It's driving me crazy," Maggie said.

"Do you guys know?" I asked Bones and Grady.

"Yup," Grady grinned.

"No, but I haven't looked. I was having too much fun watching," Bones grinned.

"Well, Grady, show them," I smiled.

Grady reached over and slid a release on the base of the deep window sill. The sill popped up, displaying a row of handguns and two sniper rifles.

"Noticed it yesterday when I threw my hat on top of the sill. The sill is extra wide for this style window, but not wide enough for a window seat or plants."

"Nice," Maggie said, admiring the guns.

"Damn, Cuz. You've gotten even better," Charlie said.

"Thanks, but it's time for our meeting. Let's go."

"Sorry, I can't stay to help clean this mess up," Maggie laughed and hurried out the door after me. "So, Charlie said there are ten hidden locations. Where are the other nine?"

"Two exits, one in my bedroom and one in the laundry room. The War Room is the only hidden room, but there are two hidden cabinets in that room, two in my bedroom and one in the living room."

"Including the window sill, that makes nine."

"There is a drop down ladder in my bedroom that goes to the attic with access to the roof. The roof has pegs for a sniper's nest," Charlie said.

"Nice," Maggie grinned.

I gave Maggie directions to drive, and twenty minutes later I pointed out the house as we drove by. I had her drop us off two blocks away and circle back. She would walk up to the door alone, and warn our Aunt and Uncle that we would be coming in on foot through the back door. Charlie and I knew the neighborhood well and had dressed in running shorts and shoes for the occasion. Jogging up through the back alley, we pivoted quickly to the back porch and walked through the back door five minutes later.

"About time," Uncle Hank said from his favorite chair at the kitchen table. "I'm starving. Both of you get in here so we can eat."

Charlie and I both helped Aunt Suzanne move breakfast dishes to the table before sliding into our familiar chairs. Maggie sat across from me sipping her coffee, looking amused.

After Aunt Suzanne said grace, we all attacked the offerings, filling our plates to the edges with cholesterol and starch filled goodies.

"So, what do you need?" Uncle Hank asked.

"My badge for 24 hours," I answered filling my mouth with butter fried potatoes covered in ketchup.

"It's on the wall in the living room, just waiting for you," he said.

"I need you to go high up the chain with the paperwork, and keep it out of the computers," I said when I had swallowed enough to speak.

Uncle Hank stopped eating, fork midway to his mouth. Aunt Suzanne sucked in air through her teeth and stared at me.

"Dirty cops?" Uncle Hank asked.

"Three," I nodded. "And, one of them is internal affairs. We also have a dirty ME and someone inside the DA's office."

Charlie and Maggie were listening but were content to let me converse about the details as they continued to shovel the breakfast into their mouths. Maggie had loaded up on Texas style cinnamon French toast fried in real butter and drowned in syrup. She kept moaning as she ate. Charlie had a pile of the fried potatoes, smothered in ketchup with an extra layer of table salt, just to further stress out her arteries. On the side, she had biscuits and sausage gravy, which I had somehow missed as part of the offerings.

"Shit," Uncle Hank sighed setting down his fork. "What's the plan?"

"Everyone goes down tonight," I said as I squeezed two biscuits onto the side of my own plate. "We have a multi-level attack plan. If I'm carrying my badge after the dust settles it's reported as a unified task force established to shut down Pasco and corrupt city employees. Without my badge, it goes down as the FBI crippling this city's reputation."

"Well, Good Fucking Morning to you too!" Uncle Hank scowled, throwing his napkin on the table. "Why does this feel like blackmail instead of a favor?"

Maggie cringed, looking at me nervously. Charlie snorted. I grabbed the gravy and drowned my biscuits and potatoes.

"Relax, Uncle Hank. Kelsey's going in one way or another and knows you have her back. The rest is how you're going to feed the story to the Commander so he will sign off on her temporary reinstatement and agree to keep it quiet, and out of the books until tomorrow."

"You want me to go straight to the Commander? I don't have that kind of weight," Uncle Hank complained.

"But Aunt Suzanne does," Charlie grinned.

We turned to Aunt Suzanne, and she rolled her eyes, getting up from the table.

Aunt Suzanne was the only person I knew that still had a landline phone. She dialed a number she knew by heart and waited for the other line to answer. We all openly listened to her one-sided version of the conversation.

"Hi, Ivy. I was wondering if the Commander was working today or if he took the day off since it is Christmas Eve?"

"Perfect. Can you both come over to our house? I can't explain why, over the phone, but it's important. And, come hungry, we have a large table filled with breakfast."

"Splendid. See you in 10 minutes."

Maggie grinned at Charlie and me.

"Aunt Suzanne and the Commander's wife co-host the annual policeman's charity ball together," Charlie grinned.

"Nice," Maggie said. "So how exactly are you guys related?"

"We sort of adopted them. We didn't know anybody when we moved down here, and Uncle Hank was our initial training officer when we joined the force," I said.

"For all of about 3 weeks until you both were pulled into different operations," Uncle Hank rolled his eyes. "But they were in over their heads and needed someone to keep an eye on them. I invited them over for dinner, and Suzanne declared them family. They've both been a pain in my ass ever since then."

Aunt Suzanne playfully smacked Uncle Hank upside the back of the head, as she walked by.

Forty-five minutes later, the Commander had agreed to my reinstatement and would hold off on filing the paperwork until the next morning. Maggie left out the front door, and Uncle Hank walked Charlie and me to the back door.

"I'm not stupid, you know," Uncle Hank said. "What you're about to do is by far the most dangerous shit you two have ever pulled."

"Probably," I agreed.

"If anyone can pull it off, though, it's my Harrison girls. Be safe, and call us to let us know that you made it out. We won't be sleeping until we hear from you."

Uncle Hank hugged and kissed both of us before we ducked out the door.

• • •

"What are your chances?" Charlie asked as we jogged down the back ally.

"Fifty-fifty," I answered honestly.

"I'm scared," she admitted, stopping to take a break.

"There isn't anything to be afraid of, Charlie. I've accepted the odds. I know that if I fail, you have a whole team of people to step in and help you finish the fight. But I've prepared for the worst and have every intention of walking out of this alive."

"Promise? This isn't like two years ago?"

"No. I'm not planning on going rogue. I need you and everyone else to help me get out of this alive. But I also know that there is only so much anyone can do once I step onto that island."

"It should be me, not you."

"But, I'm the one that has all the stripper experience, remember?" I laughed, and she finally caved and chuckled as we continued on with our jog to meet up with Maggie.

I knew we were both remembering my first undercover assignment. I was fresh out of the academy and assigned to a bikini bar on Ocean Drive. I was so nervous, that when I started pole dancing, I fell flat on my ass in front of everyone, including seasoned undercover cops that were scattered throughout the bar. It took me a dozen more stings to overcome the jokes.

Chapter Thirty-Two

Charlie, Bones, Jackson, Reggie, Wild Card, Grady and I all focused on the site plans and blueprints for the rest of the morning before meeting up with a dozen field agents and a dozen more of Donovan's men at a nearby vacant building.

I split the groups up into tactical teams. Maggie worked with Agent Kierson on the strike teams issuing the warrants for arrest on the mainland, corresponding with the Customs office on a dual strike team for the docks, and assembling the second wave of the assault team to hit the island.

Everyone that we didn't personally know had their phones removed and were not allowed to leave for any reason once they arrived. We couldn't take a chance on a mole exposing the operation.

Charlie and Grady were arguing about who would lead the team on the West side of the island. Bones was already assigned the team to the East.

"I need it to be Charlie," I interrupted their argument.

"Why?" Grady asked.

"Because Charlie knows the tunnels better than you on the West side and because I need you in the boat to drop me off, and to later strike from the beachfront. Maggie's agents will be hidden in the cabin cruiser waiting for your signal to come out, along with Jackson."

Grady turned to Charlie, "Prove it. Tell me without looking how the tunnels run."

Charlie closed her eyes and starting from the Cliffside entrance walked through the directions of the tunnels path, first to the office on the first floor, then up to the second and third floors, and ending with listing the access points to get to the East tunnels if needed.

"Okay, then," Grady grinned. "On the boat is where I'll be."

"Where are we?" Wild Card asked, nodding to Reggie.

"Reggie is with Bones, and you're with Charlie. She knows the property better, but doesn't have as much tactical experience. You'll manage communications for the team as she leads you in. Both teams will split up the rest of Donovan's men, but you won't have agents with you."

They all grinned.

Without FBI agents looking over their shoulder, they had a little bit more freedom to act as they needed to get the job done. The agents would be kept busy on the beachfront securing all the guests and sealing off the front escape.

"You're good at this shit," Grady grinned.

"You have no idea," Reggie laughed.

"The guard towers are still a concern," Bones said.

"There are six guard towers, two for each strike team. Two men are to stay behind at the entrances of each tunnel to take out the towers and keep the exits open. I have already loaded four of Donovan's men up with sniper rifles. And, I had the rifles for the boat loaded last night."

"And, when did you have time to do all that?" Reggie asked.

"After our pajama party, when everyone else went to bed," I grinned. "Once I give the signal, it will be relayed to all three teams to take out the tower guards. They all fall at once."

"Nice," Jackson said, cracking his fingers.

"How are you getting to the playroom?" Charlie asked.

"I'll have Pasco take me there."

"No fucking way," Bones yelled.

"It's the only way. It's his playroom."

"He'll hurt you," Grady said matter-of-factly.

"I know," I answered, holding Bones attention. "I can handle it."

"There has to be another option," Bones said, walking over to me.

"There isn't. I need to be in that room when we strike. It's the only way. You have to trust that I can handle whatever happens," I placed my hand on Bones' chest, and he placed his hand over mine.

"You'll stay on the comms?"

"No. I won't be on the main comms. I'll be on one of Carl's jewelry pieces, and Maggie and Tech will have the only eyes and ears on me. I can't risk everyone reacting to whatever is happening with me."

"I don't like this," Bones growled.

"None of us like it, but she's right," Charlie snapped. "We can't be worrying about Kelsey if we all need to strike in unison. We're her best chance of getting out." Charlie dragged a hand through her hair, a habit I knew she picked up from me when I was stressed. "She was only five years old the first time I feared for her life, and she's been scaring the shit out of me ever since. But she's always walked out alive. A little bruised, maybe a few more scars, but alive. We have to have faith that she can do it again."

"What the hell did you do when you were only five years old?" Wild Card asked.

"She smashed a lamp over my father's head then held a knife to his throat," Charlie laughed. "She's been a badass ever since."

Charlie and I shared a secret smile while everyone else wondered about the rest of the story.

Maggie showed up and sent me back to the safe house to work out last minute details with Tech and Genie. I was glad for the escape. Hours before the operation, the adrenaline was climbing, and while it would help the tactical teams to stay focused, it would hinder my role in the operation.

Back at the safe house, Tech updated me on the comm links and security feeds, as well as some of Max's properties. I sat in the War Room absorbing all of the information and downloading them the details on the tactical teams.

"One last thing," I said. "I lied to everyone. I told them that you and Maggie would have access to my audio and video feed."

"And, how is that a lie?" Tech asked.

"Because neither of you will have access. I've already had Sara turn the feed over to Genie. She'll monitor it from here."

"No way. I mean, don't get me wrong, Genie, your good, but there is no way I'm not in on knowing what's going on."

"You'd be too focused on whatever I was doing, and I need you to focus on the bigger picture. Genie doesn't see me as anything more than another team member, and she has more experience with these missions. She won't be as quick to push the panic button."

"At least let Maggie in on it too," Tech said.

"Maggie has a lot on her plate. She'll be managing the beach strike, the second tactical team strike, the Customs sting and the arrest warrants on the mainland. Genie can handle it."

"She can, but she won't have to do it alone," Agent Kierson said stepping into the room. "It's smart that you're separating the communications, but I'll be with Genie listening in on your portion of the plan so we can decide together when to take action. I won't have it resting on her shoulders if you don't make it out."

"Fair enough," I nodded, agreeing with his logic.

I walked to the back bedroom to start getting ready. The sun was setting, and I would need to leave to pick up Ariel in a little over an hour.

I took a long shower, coating my skin with almond-honey shower gel that helped relax my tense muscles. Afterward, I used the temporary hair dye to turn my hair a deep shade of red, before blow-drying it thoroughly. Meticulously applying my make-up, up-sweeping and styling my hair, and sliding into the evening gown that Reggie had left laying out for me, I was almost ready.

I pulled the bag of jewels that Carl had prepared to track and monitor my movements. The diamond drop earrings contained GPS trackers. The white gold necklace with the diamond pendant served as video and audio, hidden between several lines of amber stones that encircled the center diamond. The sparkling silver shoes that Lisa found for me were retrofit with re-moveable switchblades in the long slim heels. The matching purse held two syringes hidden in the lining with sedatives that Haley had acquired. The thin diamond band that hung around my wrist provided a drop down locket that held a picture of Nicholas for good luck.

Looking in the mirror, I checked one last time to make sure I didn't forget anything. I smiled at the reflection that stared back. It had been a few years since I let Destiny out to play. I felt a little like she was another personality that was hidden inside my head. I blew Destiny a kiss and walked out. It was time.

Chapter Thirty-Three

"Quit twitching," I scolded Ariel as we walked down the dock.

"I can't help it," Ariel said.

"Look," I said grabbing her arm gently. "The worst that can happen tonight is that we die. How many times have you been close to death before? A dozen? More? For me, I can't even count. Just remember that there is a good chance we will actually live, and other than that, do your job. Make the men horny."

Ariel looked at me like I was crazy but pulled back her shoulders and followed my lead past the waiting guests on the docks as our cabin cruiser pulled up. I invited several of the men waiting on the dock to join us for the trip over to the island. They happily agreed and by the time Grady pulled our boat up to the island docks, Ariel and I had men dripping off our sides. With two escorts each, we sailed through the security checkpoint and led to the poolside bar.

We were at the party for an hour before we were summoned to Pasco's table. Wearing a black suit with maroon lining and smoking a Cuban, he leaned back in his chair and watched us approach side by side. My silver dress parted to the hip with each long stride, but he barely noticed me until I pulled back my shawl, draping it over my forearms. Pasco's focus locked in on my breasts that were barely sheathed in a fine see-through layer of chiffon fabric.

I had intentionally switched the strapless bra that Reggie had left out for me, with the under-bust corset that Anne had packed. I was playing a hooker after all, and the overexposure of my nipples was working in my favor to distract not only Pasco but his nearby guards as well.

"Ariel, who did you bring for me tonight?" Pasco asked eagerly, still watching my breasts.

"This is Destiny. I thought that you would enjoy her. She's an independent."

"Independent? Tell me Destiny, did you come here tonight in hopes of me putting you on the payroll?"

I openly looked around at the mansion, pool, and guests before returning my gaze to Pasco.

"No," I grinned seductively.

"But you came for a reason," he assumed.

"Of course," I grinned. "Ariel, go play. The guests came to be entertained, and you have a job to do."

Ariel appropriately waited for Pasco to give her the nod of approval, which he did, with his eyes leaving mine for only the briefest second.

"So, Destiny, what's your reason for agreeing to come tonight?" Pasco asked with sparkling eyes. He was playing into Destiny's hands perfectly.

"To fulfill your needs, of course," I grinned.

Stepping over to him and placing my backside up on the edge of the table, I reached into his cocktail glass and removed two ice cubes. I took turns putting one cube at a time in my mouth before removing them.

Raising one of my legs, I propped a heeled foot on the other side of his chair. I moved the ice under the thin layer of fabric of the dress. I was fully covered, but every man nearby knew I was pleasuring myself with the cold cubes.

I leaned back on the table, pushing my breasts out. The position not only helped to further my goals of selling myself, but also forced the pendant around my neck to have a view of the sky. The rest of the men around me, and possibly Grady just offshore n the boat, had a better view of my hand movements under my dress.

Pasco moved his hand to my calf and caressed my smooth skin. I grinned slowly, before I leaned my head forward, and remained still, as I unfocused my eyes, leaving them blank, dead.

"Well, now I'm truly intrigued," Pasco panted.

Refocusing my eyes, I grinned down at him as I reached over and dropped the half melted cubes one at a time back in his glass.

"Well done my dear. I see you have researched me," he nodded, lifting the glass and draining it in one swallow. He chucked a few of the ice cubes in his mouth and continued to grin.

"It's my pleasure, truly."

"And, what other tricks do you have to show me?"

"I'm not sure you can handle all my specialties. I have many," I grinned.

"Guards," Pasco called over his shoulder. "Destiny and I will be needing some privacy. Prepare my room."

Two of the guards split off toward the mansion, while two others flanked our sides. Pasco stood, placing my hand in the crook of his arm and led us away.

"Tell me Destiny, how much do you charge for your services?" Pasco asked.

"I'm very expensive," I seductively grinned, while looking about the house as we entered.

"As you can see, I can afford it."

I smiled, pausing to admire a framed piece of artwork at the base of the stairs. "A Ruben?" I asked.

"You've an eye for art, too. My, my, aren't you full of surprises."

"If you behave, maybe I'll show you more," I said as we ascended the stairs.

"I can't wait," Pasco said eagerly. "Tell me – The vacant look that you did with your eyes, appearing dead, have you played that role often?"

"Only when it suited my partner's desire," I grinned. "You're not the only man that seeks comfort in the cold flesh. You're just more open about your needs than others."

"And, what are your needs? Desires?" Pasco asked as we began walking down the second-floor hallway. "What is it that brought you here tonight?"

"For a position, of course," I grinned.

"And, what position is that?"

"Your mistress," I answered, opening the door at the end of the hall where two guards were placed. I walked backward into the room as Pasco, and two of his armed guards followed me into the room.

"And, what makes you think that you would be able to satisfy my needs?"

"Well, that's for you to decide after my interview," I grinned as I turned to walk further into the room.

The walls were decorated in deep burgundy wallpaper and heavy brass sconces. I immediately recognized two of the hidden access points but turned my attention back to Pasco before I had found the third. I still had time.

"Only two of your guards?" I questioned with a grin.

"Do you require all four?" Pasco smiled.

"We shall see. Do they get to play too?" I asked nodding to the guards.

"Yes."

"Good," I purred, setting my purse on a table along the wall with the chained rings attached. "Tell me, Pasco, are you one of those men that needs to remain in control? Or have you learned that only by removing control can true ecstasy be reached?" I asked as I slid his jacket off and laid it over a nearby chair.

"You're a dominatrix."

"An expert dominatrix."

"I like to be in control."

"You have four guards. Shall we call more?"

"Ok. I'll play along for now," Pasco agreed.

"I was hoping you would say that," I purred stroking my hands on his chest and slowly undoing his buttons as I stared up at him and unfocused my eyes again.

"Damn," he moaned.

"Have them undress," I requested, as I pushed Pasco's shirt off and pushed him back along the wall.

"If they're unarmed, I'll need the other two guards to come in and supervise."

"As you wish." I slowly dragged his belt through the hoops and slid a leg between his.

"Call the other guards in," Pasco ordered the man next to him.

• • •

The other two guards entered and stood together just inside the doorway. Pasco nodded to the two closest to us, and they began peeling their clothes off. By the time I stripped Pasco of his remaining clothes, the naked guards were already stroking themselves. The clothed guards were eager to see what came next.

"Which is your favorite of the two?" I asked nodding to the naked guards.

Pasco nodded to the darker skinned muscular man on my right.

"Very well," I said, reviewing the wall with the anchor hooks before wandering to the oversize trunk sitting in the center of the room.

The clothed guards moved to stand on both sides of me and observe my selection of two sets of handcuffs. I slid a kneeling bench over to the wall and coaxed the preferred naked guard to step up onto the bench. I then handed him the handcuffs, and he grinned as he cuffed himself to the walled rings.

It was common knowledge that Pasco's tastes spanned across the sexes and through disturbing age categories, in addition to his necrophilia-based tendencies. He was a sick son of a bitch, and I planned on using his sickness against him.

With the first guard in place, I stroked Pasco's chest moving him into position in front of the first guard. I motioned for the other naked guard to attach the already present chains to Pasco's wrists as Pasco stepped in front of the kneeling bench.

"My, my, more surprises," Pasco encouraged as he realized that his favorite guard's body was now pressed tightly behind him.

"I have a few more surprises," I grinned as I stepped over to my purse.

I pulled my lipstick out, descretely slipping the needles into the hidden side pocket of my dress. I walked up to the second naked guard and slowly added a rich red layer of lipstick to his lips, before forcing him to his knees in front of Pasco.

The armed guards stepped around me, one on each side to offer them a better view. I pulled the silk sash from the waistband of my dress and stepped up to cover Pasco's eyes. After the sash was secure, I ran my hands down his body, before adding the hands of the guard kneeling naked before him.

The two dressed guards became excited, and each reached a hand inside their pants and started to pleasure themselves. I made a production of sliding my heeled shoes from my feet, while discretely palming the shortened switch blades.

Turning swiftly, I slit the throats of both armed guards. The guard on his knees was half up, when I threw my weight on top of him, gripped his head and twisted his neck to the side. He was dead instantly.

I pulled the needles and jabbed Pasco and the remaining chained guard with the sedatives. I prayed that the drugs would take effect quickly as they both realized the danger that surrounded them. I stepped up on the kneeling bench and covered their mouths until they drifted to sleep.

"Genie, give the order on the towers and send in the troops," I said, knowing she would be glued to the earpiece.

I stepped off the kneeling bench and ran for the first hidden passageway. I hit the hidden release that opened a section of the wall that contained private video equipment and incriminating photos. Jumping over to the second release, a wall opened allowing Charlie and her team to enter the room. Moving to the far wall, I began scanning for the secret panel.

"Shit, I can't find it," I said.

"Slow that crazy brain of yours down. We're doing good on time, just breathe," Charlie encouraged.

Wild Card and one of the other men moved to the door and held a defensive position. I turned my focus back to the wall. No visible hinges or wall seams. No bookcases. No built in or obvious furniture.

And, then I saw it.

A picture of a young Pasco standing with his mother on a beach. I turned the picture clockwise, and the entire wall popped out and slid behind another wall, exposing a narrow staircase down to the first floor.

I took the gun that Charlie passed to me and led part of our team down into the darkness. At the bottom of the stairs, I reached out and turned on the lights. Seven narrow cells lined the wall, occupied with men, women, and children. I passed Charlie the set of keys hanging on the wall, and she quickly started unlocking the cells as I held a gun at the ready to cover her back.

Moving the victims up the stairs, Charlie took point back through the tunnels with her team split between front, center and rear. I waited for them to be in the clear before I closed the hidden door and moved to hold my position with Wild Card and the other man. We had to secure the evidence or the charges against Pasco wouldn't stick.

Wild Card passed me an earpiece from his pocket, and I turned it on and placed it in my ear.

"East team, status?" I asked.

"Interior third-floor secure, moving to the second floor to start a sweep. Good to hear your voice, Babe," Bones answered. I could hear the grin in his voice.

"West team, status?"

"Ten minutes from our boat, Boss," Charlie answered.

"Beachfront, status?"

"Oceanside is secure, and FBI has breached first-floor interior. Should be meeting up with East team soon, so caution on firing," Grady updated.

"Affirmative, East team in sight of Beachfront team. Tech, direct us to Kelsey's location to secure the evidence."

"Forty feet to the West on the Southside of the hallway," Tech instructed. "Kelsey please advise why Agent Kierson and Agent Genie were holding their breath for the last half an hour."

"Let's just say Destiny is a little more creative than the average agent," I laughed.

"Be advised, East team is directly outside of evidence location, halt any shooting," Tech said.

Wild Card walked to the side of the entrance door, unlocked it, and opened the door for Bones and his team.

"Good to see you, brother," Wild Card grinned.

"Kelsey, cover up, damn it," Bones growled.

I looked down at my erect nipples in the thin fabric and laughed. Wild Card passed me his flak jacket to slide into and helped me cinch the velcro straps, grinning the entire time. He looked up at the naked men chained to the wall. Then looked down to the other naked man wearing bright red lipstick and lying next to the two clothed guards with their hands still in their pants.

"You gave the FBI quite a show, didn't you?" he grinned.

"Probably more than what they were expecting," I grinned back.

It took another half an hour for the FBI to agree the property was secure, and the guests were escorted back to the mainland for interrogation. I stayed to witness the video tapes being registered as evidence and followed the technician from the playroom to the boat to the mainland and then into FBI headquarters, to ensure the evidence arrived safely. Wild Card thought I was being paranoid but nonetheless, he traveled with me the entire way.

Genie came out and hugged me, but didn't say anything.

Agent Kierson arrived and looked like he wanted to chew me out, with a raised finger and a scowl, but remained silent, stomping away.

"I think he's going to have nightmares," Genie giggled. "And, that was really uncomfortable with my boss standing over my shoulder," she blushed.

"What exactly did you do?" Wild Card asked.

"It wasn't Kelsey," Genie insisted. "It was all Destiny. That woman is all kinds of wickedness."

"Who's Destiny?" Tech asked entering the room.

"My naughty alter-ego," I laughed.

"She's beyond naughty. She's absolutely twisted," Charlie laughed.

Charlie and I hugged, and then as everyone else returned from the mission, hugs continued to circulate. I was happy to hear that not one of the good guys was injured in the raid.

Maggie walked out and tossed a black duffle bag at my feet.

"If you want ringside seats, you might want to hurry up and change. They're getting ready to move Trevor and Feona," she said.

"Hell, yes," Charlie grinned.

I grabbed the bag, and Charlie and I chased after Maggie. I looked over my shoulder and called out.

"Genie, I need to know if Nicholas is on any of those tapes. Can you push that to the top of the list?"

"I have a team ready to start. I'll keep in touch," she yelled back.

Chapter Thirty-Four

I changed in the backseat of the FBI's SUV, as Maggie drove with lights on to the police station. I was now dressed in hip-hugger jeans, a white blouse (with appropriate bra), and a lot less makeup. She had even packed my favorite bitch boots, knee length, heeled, black leather. I sighed with relief at feeling a bit like my real self again.

One block before the police station, several other SUV's with blazing red and blue lights, lined up behind us and followed us in. When we pulled up in front of the station, Charlie and I exited the vehicle. Several uniformed officers and plainclothes detectives stepped out of the building to see what was going on. We waited for them to gather.

Uncle Hank greeted me in full uniform and leaned over to kiss my cheek. I think he was pretty happy to see I was alive.

The Commander joined us, also in full uniform and gave me a nod of approval. Several of the officers that were now crowding the street stared at Charlie and me openly before saluting the Commander and stepping back to see both Trevor and Feona being led by the FBI to the front doors in cuffs.

Before they could move up the stairway, I moved forward to block their path.

"You should know," I said to them loud enough for everyone to hear. "You should know that I'll do everything in my power to ensure that neither one of you ever experiences life outside of a prison cell again. I hold you both personally accountable for the disappearance of my son and any suffering he has endured over these last few years."

The Commander stepped forward and removed Trevor's badge from his belt clip. He tossed it on the cement and stomped on it. The already assembling media pressed forward to capture the moment on film. The action was a statement for all other police officers to know that Trevor was forever an enemy of the department.

The officers silently parted as the FBI agents lead Feona and Trevor up the stairs, followed by more FBI agents leading a cuffed Officer Eckert, a dirty internal affairs officer, and a crooked administrative assistant from the DA's office, into the precinct as well.

The media was eating up the whole scene and shouting out questions as Agent Kierson, Agent Maggie O'Donnell, and the Commander stepped up to speak to them.

"On behalf of the city of Miami, I would like to publicly thank the FBI agents who helped expose and arrest corrupt individuals in our ranks. By unifying both sides, we were able to not only bring down a very powerful criminal but save numerous lives in the process. Thank you," the Commander said, stepping back to let Agent Kierson speak.

"On behalf of the FBI, I would like to thank Officer Harrison and the *other* Officer Harrison for their bravery, intellect, and investigative abilities to make tonight such a success in apprehending what we believe to be, all the parties in a sex trafficking organization and assisting in rescuing thirty-seven men, women and children in a multi-location sting operation. Thank you, Officers. You served your country proudly tonight."

The media moved as one to surround Charlie and me, and several familiar faces in uniform jumped in to push them back into some resemblance of order. Questions flew in all directions.

"Officer Harrison, we were under the impression that the two of you no longer spoke," a familiar reporter said.

"That was intentional," Charlie said.

"But you had your cousin committed," the reported said.

"Only because she told me to," Charlie grinned.

I laughed and threw an arm over her shoulder.

"Officer Kelsey Harrison, are you officially back on the force," another report asked.

"My future is not yet clear. But I do have a message that I would appreciate the media's assistance in spreading," I said.

I looked at Charlie, and she gave me a swift nod.

"N…O…L… A…. Come out, come out, wherever you are…" I taunted.

Charlie and I looped our arms, and with a police escort we moved inside of the precinct.

Chapter Thirty-Five

Sneaking out the employee-only exit an hour later, I shook my head in dismay at Uncle Hank's ancient caddy taking up two parking spaces in the small employee parking lot. Sliding behind the wheel of the monstrosity, I pumped the gas petal as I turned the ignition key and the beast roared to life. The low bubbling noises of the muffler rumbled the car as I put the car in reverse. Creeping out slowly, turning inch by inch, I guided the oversized jalopy into the drive.

I exhaled when I had successfully pulled the car into the lane without hitting anything. Shifting the gear to forward, my foot slid off the brake to the accelerator – launching the car backward ten feet and slamming to a stop when it hit the parking lot light post. *Damn it!*

I looked up to see Charlie and Uncle Hank on the back porch of the building. Charlie held her hand out, and Uncle Hank pulled his wallet, shaking his head and handed her some cash. Several officers stood behind them laughing, as I moved the gear shift successfully into drive and drove forward out of the lot.

All the lights at the safe house were on, though it was close to two in the morning. I walked up to the back porch and retrieved my cigarettes that were still sitting on the arm of the Adirondack chair. Lighting up, I admitted to myself that I was stalling. It had been a long day, and the last thing I wanted to do, was tell Bones that his wife was murdered and that we intentionally didn't tell him.

When we were at the station, Charlie gave her statement of witnessing the murder and detectives were sent to process the scene and have the body picked up. Hopefully, the body was still there, I cringed.

"We saw you on the news," Grady said stepping out of the house and onto the porch. "Was that smart?"

"It had to be done," I nodded. "Before now, I had to search in secret, but with Pasco and Max out of the picture, I need all the good guys and the bad guys watching Nola so I can track her down before she sets up business with someone else."

"Makes sense," Grady nodded, looking over at me, raising an eyebrow. "You okay?"

"No," I answered truthfully.

"Anything I can do to help?" he asked, taking a seat in the chair next to me.

"Tonight's mission was a lot easier than what I'm about to face in there," I said, nodding to the house.

"Then whatever it is, I suggest you get it over with."

"If I must," I sighed, taking one last hit off the cigarette.

I stubbed my cigarette out in the makeshift ashtray that was sitting on the stand and walked into the house. Grady followed behind me.

Bridget was in the kitchen and started to say something, but I put my hand up to stop her. It was time to face the music.

I found Bones in the living room with Jackson, Tech, Wild Card, and Reggie, relaxing, drinking beer. Bones smiled when he saw me enter. I walked over and sat in front of him on the coffee table.

"I need you to hand me your beer."

"Why?" he asked, with a curious look and a grin.

"Because you're not going to like what I'm about to tell you, and I would rather you didn't have glass objects in your hands when I do."

"Oh shit," Jackson said, pulling Bones' beer and setting it on the end table along with his own. He got up and stood behind me. Wild Card and Reggie set theirs out of the way as well, and Tech chugged his dry.

"I take it you know what this is about?" Bones asked Tech.

"Sorry, brother, but I do. Kelsey's right, you aren't going to like it, but there was no other option," Tech said getting up to stand next to Jackson.

"Tell me what's going on, Kelsey."

"Tuesday night, Nola found the wire in Penny's purse and thought she was working for the Feds. Then she executed her in an abandon building downtown."

"And, you knew and didn't tell me?" Bones yelled, standing up. "Why didn't her parents call and tell me?"

"They don't know yet."

"How can they not know yet?"

"We had to leave the body. If we had called it in, it could've jeopardized the raids," I answered truthfully.

"You just left her there?" He ran both hands over his head trying to process what I was telling him.

He began pacing back and forth in front of the couch, and Jackson grabbed me from around the waist, dragging me over the coffee table and placing me beside him. Bones looked ready to explode, and everyone stood tense, waiting for the eruption.

"How could you just leave her there?"

"Nola would've known we were here. She would've sent out an alert. Pasco would've gotten away. The other women and children would've been moved. It was too risky," I said.

"YOU HAD NO RIGHT!" Bones screamed. "*You left her there like a bag of trash!*"

"Penny made her own bed." I said, shaking my head. "She was meeting up with Nola to get back in the business."

"You don't know that!"

"YES—I DO!" I turned, dragging my hands through my hair. This wasn't going well and would only get worse if I didn't calm down. "Bones, Penny was communicating with Nola through an email account. She reached out. She flew to Florida. Penny asked for a meeting with Nola! She wanted the power she had when she was with Ernesto. She wanted the rush."

"*You're wrong!* You didn't know her," he yelled coming around the corner of the coffee table and standing directly in front of me. "You selfish Bitch. *You're* the one that had the power trip. *You* had to be in charge of this mission. *You* had to prove how good you are so that everyone would rally around *YOU*! And, for what Kelsey? *Your son is DEAD! He isn't coming back!*" he growled leaning toward me. "You knew he wouldn't be there tonight just like you know that it's *your fault* he was taken in the first place!"

I stood trembling, tears streaming down my face, looking up at the hatred in Bones' eyes as he spewed his filth at me. I felt someone grab my arm and pull me back, and I watched in horror as Charlie stepped up and slapped Bones across the face.

Silence.

"Get out of this house and stay the fuck away from my cousin, you bastard," Charlie hissed.

Her own body trembled in rage as mine trembled in despair.

I dropped to my knees, bracing my hands on the floor in front of me to support me from falling over. Tears blinded my vision. My rapid pulse thumped in my ears, preventing me from hearing. But I felt through the vibrations in the floor as Bones stomped past Charlie and out of the house.

Reggie sat down beside me and pulled me up onto his lap as I cried. I sensed Charlie nearby, but she waited for me to calm down before she said anything.

Finally, catching my breath, I wiped my tears with the back of my hands as Charlie sat down in front of us, legs crossed and pulled my chin over to face her.

"No more seafoam candy for you. Do you hear me?" she playfully scolded.

I nodded, inhaling a ragged breath, as Jackson and Tech chuckled.

"He'll get over it, Kelsey. You know Bones likes to throw things around and get hyper mad. He'll regret what he said when he cools off," Tech said.

"No, he won't, Tech," I said. "And, he meant what he said. I could see it in his eyes."

I wiped my face one last time and kissed Reggie on the cheek. I slid off Reggie's lap and forced myself to once again bury my emotions, as I climbed up from the floor.

"Bridget, do we have any liquor in this place?" I asked as I offered a hand to pull Reggie and Charlie up off the floor as well.

"I stocked the cupboards with all your favorites," she nodded as she started pulling the booze bottles and glasses out.

The door opened and in walked Dallas and Haley.

"It's not my fault," Haley said. "I couldn't stop her from coming back after she saw the news."

"Your mission is over, Darling," Dallas said throwing her oversized purse on the counter. "I bought the perfect outfit for the S&M Club!"

I made myself a drink, ignoring Dallas, as did everyone else. When everyone had a drink in hand, I raised mine in the air.

"Merry Christmas, everyone."

Several people clinked glasses and drank. Charlie leaned her head on my shoulder, and I tipped mine to lean against hers. Neither of us had celebrated Christmas since Nicholas was taken. Every year we would secretly meet in some remote location and drink the holiday away.

Bridget poured a round of shots, and Reggie and Jackson started to sing Rudolph off-key. The off-key singing reminded me of the time Nana got snookered at a family holiday, and two of my brothers had to carry her home.

Charlie and I looked at each other.

"Shit, we forgot to call Nana," Charlie said, having had the same memory.

"It's too late to call now," Wild Card said.

"You don't know our Nana," I giggled.

I put the phone on speaker so that Charlie and I could both talk with her.

"I was hoping you would call," Nana answered. "That wretched Aunt of yours is currently in my house, putting her grubby paws all over my things."

"You're at home?" I asked.

"When I saw the news, I figured it was safe to come out of hiding since Charlie was no longer believed to be grieving the loss of the Great Nana. But when I got home, I saw lights on so I parked across the street. Sure enough, Cecil is in there, going through my belongings. I'm just waiting for Gwen and then we are going to invade."

"No, Nana. Uncle Mark is probably with Aunt Cecil. It's not safe. You need to call the police," I said.

"Why? Mark would never dare lay a finger on me," Nana said.

"Nana, you don't know him like we do," Charlie said. "He'll hurt you and Cecil will let him. Kelsey's right, it's not safe. Please don't go in."

"Write down her address," Wild Card whispered, sliding a pad of paper to me. I wrote the address and slid it back. Grady and Wild Card stepped off to the side of the kitchen.

"Girls, what on earth are you two talking about?" Nana said.

"Dad used to beat me," Charlie blurted out, unable to stop herself. "That's why Kelsey and I moved out so young. He started beating me when I was barely three years old."

"No! Please, God, no. Oh, Charlie, I swear, I didn't know," Nana cried.

"I'm okay, Nana. Kelsey protected me from the worst of it."

"They always said you were at camp or sleeping over at a friend's house. I figured that you two were having too much fun to want to see me when I visited."

"They didn't want you to find out. Aunt Audrey always helped cover it up too."

"How could I have raised such horrible daughters?"

"Nana," Grady said, stepping back over to the counter. "My name is Grady, and my brother Mitch is driving over to meet you. He'll get your daughter and her husband out of your house."

"Can I hire him to beat the shit out of my son-in-law at the same time?" Nana asked.

"I gave him a bit of the background. He seems to be in the mood to handle that for free. If anything gets broken, I can reimburse you," Grady grinned.

"*Pfft*. I don't need your money. I need that man *to bleed*," Nana huffed. "Hang on, Gwen just got here. And, there's another car turning down the street. It might be that Mitch guy."

We could hear a car door open and close and Nana talking to Gwen. It was quiet then for several minutes before we heard Nana again.

"You Mitch?" Nana asked.

"Yes, ma'am."

"I need you to cover my six. Come on, Gwen. It's time to haunt my greedy daughter and her douchebag of a husband," Nana said as we listened to her shoes clack against the asphalt.

Nana left her phone turned on but must have slid it into her purse, because the rest of the audio was muffled.

"Holy hell." "No, Mom, don't" Thwack. Crash. Shattering glass. Cecil screeching. More shattering glass. A man crying. *"Please."* Wood snapping and breaking.

"And, don't ever come back!" Nana bellowed.

The phone disconnected after that, and we all looked up at each other nervously.

Grady's phone rang.

"Grady," he answered.

Grady laughed while he listened. "You should meet her granddaughters. Thanks, Mitch."

"Your Nana and Gwen are just fine. Cecil has a broken nose and soon to be a black eye. Mark was last seen on the front lawn after he was hit by a chair that launched him through the front bay window. He's going to need stitches."

"Damn," Bridget said. "Your brother Mitch doesn't mess around."

"Mitch just stood there and watched," Grady grinned. "Nana and Gwen did all the damage."

Charlie and I clanked our shot glasses and downed the liquor.

"If your mothers are sisters, why do you both have the same last name?" Haley asked.

"There were only two well-to-do families in our small town. Nana's and the Harrison's," I explained. "Cecil and Audrey opted to improve their odds by marrying the only two Harrison brothers in hopes that eventually they would inherit both family's wealth. And, it partially worked. Grandma and Grandpa Harrison died in a car accident, and Cecil and Audrey, in charge of the money, were sitting pretty. But, when Pappi died, Nana pulled the rug out from under her daughters and told them that she re-wrote her will, and unless they straightened up they wouldn't see a dime."

"Did you ever think that car accident was suspicious?" Charlie asked.

"You were only seven or eight at the time. I'm surprised you even remember it," I shrugged.

"I remember you asked Grandpa Harrison for help to get me away from my parents a few days before the accident. You told me that he was going to talk to a lawyer and see what could be done."

"I shouldn't have given you false hope," I said shaking my head. "As far as the accident, it's in the past. Let it go, Charlie."

"So, you do know something," Charlie glared.

"Wait a minute," Grady said. "So, you think that your parents might've killed your grandparents?"

"I wouldn't put it past them," Charlie said as she continued to stare at me.

"What about Nana's husband - Pappi?" Wild Card asked.

"Cancer took him," I answered shaking my head. "Only my brothers, Charlie, and I were allowed to visit the last few months. Nana wouldn't let Cecil or Audrey in the house."

"That's seriously fucked up," Dallas said, passing us another round of shots.

Charlie downed her shot before turning her back to me and walking out of the room. It wasn't the first time she had pressed me for information from our childhood. I knew someday, I would have to tell her everything. I just hoped that when I did, she didn't hate me.

I downed my shot, and then after arguing with Dallas for a good fifteen minutes that she would have to wait until the day after Christmas to go to the S&M club, we called it a night and went to bed.

Chapter Thirty-Six

By 7:00, I gave up trying to sleep and crawled out of bed. I spent the last few hours tossing and turning while having the familiar nightmare of the day that Nicholas was kidnapped.

Throwing on some sweats, I maneuvered down the hall, through the living room, and to the kitchen. Grady was already sitting on a barstool drinking coffee. I retrieved a cup from the cupboard and poured myself a cup.

"So what's next?" Grady asked.

"Everyone goes home," I shrugged. "Charlie and I will stay behind to work the evidence with the FBI and see if anything points to Nicholas or Nola's location."

"I promised I would help. I'm here until it's over."

"There's no need, really. Charlie and I have been at this a long time."

"Ah, so independent," Reggie laughed, stopping to kiss my temple before he poured himself a cup of coffee. "And, stubborn."

"So, decipher this conversation for me, Reggie. Does she want my help or not?" Grady chuckled.

"She wants help but doesn't want anyone to feel like they have to help," Reggie grinned.

"Then I'm staying," Grady said.

"Me too," Reggie said. "Jackson's flying back to the ranch to take care of the horses. Wild Card needs to fly out for another assignment but will be ready to come back when needed. Tech said he wanted to stay," Reggie held up a finger to stop me from interrupting him, "but that you would argue with him about being in Michigan to run security there. So he's flying back with Bridget and Haley. He'll check in as soon as he lands and will be available for research when needed."

I grinned as I sipped my coffee.

"They have you all figured out, don't they," Grady grinned.

"Only when she's acting logical," Jackson said, entering the kitchen with Charlie trailing behind him. "When she goes off the rails, there's no telling what she'll do."

"Like last night's op?" Grady asked with a raised eyebrow to me.

"That wasn't Kelsey going off the rails," Charlie defended me as she pushed Jackson out of the way to get to the coffee pot first. "When Kelsey works a case as one of her cover personalities, it's like she's a completely different person. Destiny was the one that made you feel so unsettled, and whatever you witnessed, I don't want to know about it. Been there, done that."

"I'll never look at ice cubes the same way ever again," Grady grinned.

I ducked my head to hide my blush, but it only escalated when Reggie, Jackson, and Charlie turned to look at me with raised eyebrows.

"What? Destiny had limited resources to work with," I laughed.

"That's sick, Sis," Reggie said.

"Are we really related?" Charlie asked.

"Sounds kind of hot," Jackson grinned.
"Oh, it was hot," Grady grinned.

Maggie entered the kitchen through the back door with two boxes of donuts.

"Good, you're all up," she grinned.

"You're pretty chipper this morning," I grinned over my coffee.

"That's because I haven't gone to bed yet. I was up all night doing stupid paperwork. When I realized it was almost dawn, I went for a drive, picked up donuts and came over here."

"I think you should skip the coffee then," I said, sliding the cup that was placed in front of her away. "You can eat a donut, drink some milk and then crash in my room for a few hours. Genie can get us into the FBI office."

"But you might need me for something," she argued.

"I'm sure we will, but when that time comes, we will need you to be on top of your game, which is only going to happen if you get some sleep."

"Fine," Maggie pouted while digging into the donut box.

My phone rang, and I answered it.

"Kelsey," I grinned at Maggie's still pouting face across from me.

"Merry Christmas," shouts called from across the phone line.

I swallowed down the tears that built as I thought of everyone back in Michigan sitting in the living room opening presents.

"Aunt Kelsey, are you there?" Sara asked.

"I'm here, little-bug. Merry Christmas to you too."

"Thank you for my electric scooter and the playhouse."

"Tell her I like my fuzzy socks and new tv!" Carl shouted from the background.

"I'm glad you both liked your presents. What else did you get?" I couldn't contain the tears as they streamed down my cheeks. I turned to face out the window and Charlie came over and wrapped an arm around my shoulder. We both were thinking of Nicholas and our last Christmas with him.

"Mom got me a necklace and a bike. And, Whiskey got me a girly bed with a pink canopy and matching curtains. And, Hattie and my other Aunts and Uncles got me clothes and games. And, Carl got really cool stuff too."

"Sounds like you are having a great Christmas."

"I wish you were here Aunt Kelsey," Sara whispered.

"I'll be home in a couple of days, and then you can show me everything. The time will fly by, I promise."

"Did you find Nicholas yet?"

"Not yet, little-bug, but soon. I have to get ready to leave, do you want to talk to Tech for a minute?"

Tech took the phone and walked off to talk to Sara as I turned to Charlie and wrapped my arms around her to cry. She was crying too.

Jackson and Reggie came over and wrapped us both in their arms, holding us together, giving us both the comfort we needed.

When we separated, Wild Card passed us a box of tissue, and we saw there wasn't a dry eye in the room.

"Sorry," I mumbled wiping my face and blowing my nose. "We Harrison girls have successfully avoided Christmas for a few years now, and …"

"And, it's hard to deal with," Dallas finished for me. "When you miss one of your children, it's the hardest holiday to survive."

I saw the pain in Dallas's eyes before she drifted out to the living room and down the hall. She had lost a child, Dave's younger brother when he was only ten, and it still haunted her at times like this. It was probably the reason that she was able to get through to me and help me get back on my feet when I needed it the most. She understood the pain.

I excused myself to shower and get dressed for the day. When I was done, I was leaving the bedroom as Maggie walked past me and flopped down on the bed. She was asleep before she landed.

In the kitchen, the rest of us parted ways, with only Maggie and Dallas staying behind. Jackson, Haley, Bridget, Tech and Wild Card left for the airport. Charlie, Grady, Reggie and I left to go to the FBI office to see what evidence had been recorded.

Chapter Thirty-Seven

Genie met us at the front lobby with visitor passes and escorted us up to the third floor. It was obvious that she hadn't slept yet, but that didn't explain the smudged makeup, the red nose, and the puffy eyes.

I waited for the elevator doors to close, before turning to her. "What's wrong?"

"I'm rethinking my career choice," Genie sniffled, pulling a tissue from her pocket. "Those videos, Kelsey, they're the worst thing I've ever seen. My analysts and I keep forcing our way through them, but they're really messing with us."

"How far have you gotten?"

"Maybe ten percent of them. Each of us has thrown up at least twice now. It doesn't smell so good on the third floor."

The elevator doors opened, and as we all started to exit, Grady and I stepped back. The third floor smelled foul from human BO and vomit. Charlie looked back at me with a worried glance as I finally stepped into the large open room and looked around. A half a dozen people sat in front of dual screen computers, most of them crying or looking greyish-green. Another dozen agents walked around either empathizing or trying to ignore what was happening.

"Agent Kierson!" I yelled out into the room.

A door to one of the offices opened, and Agent Kierson stepped out.

"What the hell do you think you're doing?" I asked.

"Look, I know it's bad, but they're trained analysts, they'll get through it," he said.

"And then what? Need therapy for the rest of their lives?"

"Do you have a better idea?" he asked, looking hopeful.

"Get some fans going, open some windows, for starters," I said, before turning my back on him and addressing the room at large. "Everyone, if I can have your attention. I want all analysts to stop watching the videos, save your work and step away from the computers. Everyone meet up on this side of the room."

I pointed to the side of the room closest to the elevators.

"Genie, I need you and your team to make copies of the videos onto individual flash drives and have them all coded to match up with the original recordings. Can you do that without having to watch any of the videos?"

"We can do that," one of the men standing next to Genie said, as he nodded to a few of the other techs and they started working with the evidence.

Agent Kierson returned with fans, and some windows were propped open.

"Okay, now listen up. I don't care what your normal day to day job duties are. If you have ever been up close and personal with witnessing a violent death, move to the center of the room.

Seven agents, including Kierson, moved to the center of the room, along with Charlie, Grady, and Reggie.

"Now, here's where you need to be honest with yourselves. Don't over think this, go with your gut reaction. If you think that you can handle watching twenty-some hours of real life horror films, and not require professional therapy afterward, move to the far side of the room."

Everyone except Reggie and two agents moved from the center of the room to the far side.

"I'm willing to try," Reggie said, looking embarrassed.

"I don't need you to try. I needed honesty, and that's what the three of you gave me," I said. "I know when lives are on the line, you're there, Reggie. That's when I need you by my side."

I patted his shoulder before turning to those on the far side of the room.

"Alright people, start moving some of the desks around. We need 8 desks along the back wall for the video watchers. Facing them will be 4 analysts to research the information that the watchers send them. Each video watcher will record notes on what's on the video and send still shots only of any persons shown in the video to an assigned analyst. The analyst will then work to identify the person in the video. We break every two hours, and that break will require that you leave this room for twenty minutes. We also need everyone that has been up all night to set up shifts to take turns and get some sleep. Let's make this happen."

The room erupted in chaos with desks and computers being moved around and stacks of videos being redirected. Twenty minutes later, though, the eight of us assigned to watching the videos took our seats and had four analysts standing by ready to work the photos.

"Remember to disassociate yourself as much as possible from what you're about to see," I warned the watchers. "These will be violent crimes, and they will at times involve young children. Pasco is also a necrophiliac so the torture will not be over when the victim dies. Remember to take a break every two hours, but feel free to walk away before that if you start to become too disturbed by what you're watching. Good luck."

We each placed a single earbud in an ear and started watching videos.

Two hours later, Charlie tapped me on the shoulder, and I saved my place on the computer. It was time for our mandatory break. We all walked away in silence, opting to take the stairs and walk out to the back parking lot for some fresh air.

"How are you guys holding up?" Reggie asked, looking concerned.

"I think it's safe to say that everyone is struggling a bit, Reggie," Grady answered.

Even the Agents that didn't know us nodded their heads in agreement.

"Is there anything I can do to help?" he asked.

"Yes," I said. "Go talk to the analysts and see if they can set us up with dual computer systems so we can have two videos playing at the same time, but each with their own keyboard and mouse so we don't mess up while taking the notes."

"How does that help to watch twice the gore?"

"It would help a lot, actually," Kierson said, stepping up beside me. "If we are tracking two videos at once, we are less engaged. I'll go with you and help set it up."

Reggie and Kierson moved back toward the building, and I felt someone lightly grab my arm. I turned to see Charlie, looking ashen and shaking.

"It's okay, Kid. It's not an easy job," I said, offering her a hug.

"I can keep going, but not with the video I was assigned. The first one wasn't so bad. The second one is an hour in, and it doesn't look like it will end anytime soon. And, worst of all, I recognize the girl. I don't know who she is, but I've seen her before. And, Kelsey," she looked at me directly, "Nola's there watching."

"Nola's in it? Why is she in it?"

"She brought the girl to Pasco. She's standing in the background smiling, watching them torture her. And, she keeps looking up at the camera and smiling too. It's freaking me out," Charlie cried.

"I can take your spot," Maggie said, stepping up beside us. "I've been updated on the new set-up and am ready to sit in as a watcher. I can finish watching your video."

"No," I said shaking my head. "If Nola's there, I need to see it. Charlie and I can switch videos. Besides, I think a few of the Agents are going to need to drop out."

We turned to face the side lot where two of the agents were puking in the bushes. One of them was an agent I noticed making fun of the analysts earlier in the day for not being able to stomach the videos.

"Relieve the one on the right, but make the other asshole keep watching," I said.

Grady grinned, and shoulder nudged me.

"I can only imagine what the one on the left did to piss you off," Maggie grinned. "He was a dickhead last night when I was here. I have no problem pushing him until he's in the fetal position."

She sauntered their direction, and I lit up a smoke. Technically, I was on federal property, and wasn't supposed to smoke, but I didn't think anyone would dare say anything to me.

"You going to share?" Grady asked.

Charlie also held out her hand, and Kierson walked up and pulled one as well as my pack was passed around.

"Okay, so I'll go on a cigarette run," Reggie chuckled, as he threw an arm over my shoulder.

We all inhaled deeply.

"Genie's up from her nap," Kierson said in-between inhaling the smoke. "She says we are 30% through the videos, and the analysts have kept up with most of the id's. There are a few victims that are not in our system, though, and she wants you and Charlie to take a look at their pictures. It's a long shot, but since they were most likely from Miami area, she figured one of the two of you might recognize them from the street."

"If we don't recognize them, then we can circulate the pictures until we get confirmation from someone that does," Charlie said. "Between the cops and our street contacts, we should be able to chase them down in a few days."

I took another hit off my cigarette, before dropping it to the asphalt and stepped on it. Everyone else followed suit, and we all turned to head back inside.

• • •

Agent Kierson stooped over and picked up everyone's cigarette butts. We openly laughed at him.

"What? Littering is against the law, and we're on Federal property," he grinned.

Chapter Thirty-Eight

Charlie, Grady and I chose to ride the elevator back up, while everyone else preferred the exercise of taking the stairs.

"You okay now, Kid?" I asked.

"Yeah," she sighed. "I'm telling you, Kelsey, I know that girl from somewhere."

"We'll figure it out," I assured her, patting her shoulder.

We stepped off the elevator. Grady went back to his set of computers and Charlie and I tracked down Genie in a nearby glass-walled office.

"You have some pictures for us to look at?" I asked.

"Sure do. Three victims, not yet identified," she answered sliding the photos to us across the table.

I picked up the first photo and didn't recognize the girl. I passed it to Charlie and picked up the next.

"This one looks like a woman that I used to see down at the shelter on 12th street. Reach out to St. Paul's Mission and see if the director can get you a name," I said sliding the picture back to Genie.

"Will do," she said, moving over to her laptop and typing in data.

I picked up the third picture and my knees buckled.

If Charlie hadn't reached out to steady me, I would have landed on the floor. Instead, she guided me back into a chair and took the picture from my hand.

"This is the girl from the video I was watching. Who is she, Kelsey?" Charlie asked.

"Molly McNabe," I whispered back.

"McNabe?" she questioned. "*As in Mickey McNabe's daughter?!*"

"Yes," I nodded. "I found her living on the streets doing drugs after I had put away her only living relative. I helped her get cleaned up and into a good teenage group home. I checked in with her regularly until I knew she was on solid ground again. The last time I saw her was at her high school graduation. I took her father a picture of her in her cap and gown. I never expected to see him cry."

"Wait, now I remember. I used to watch Nicholas play at the park while you would walk the nearby path to talk to Molly and make sure she was doing okay. That's how I recognize her. But, you never told me she was McNabe's daughter."

"Because it didn't matter who her father was. She was a teenager that needed help, and that's what I offered her."

"But her father killed a cop," Charlie ranted.

"And, a lot of other innocent people, but that was never Molly's fault."

"I ran the name," Genie interrupted. "It's a match."

"Ok. So, then this video might be personal. You—," I pointed to the other analyst standing there nervously wringing his hands, "—Pull the video and set it aside. I need to watch the whole thing, but I have a feeling I won't be as useful to the team afterward, so I should watch it last."

The analyst hurried out of the room, almost tripping on his way through the doorway.

• • •

"Am I really that scary?" I chuckled, watching the guy hustle across the room.

"Yes," Genie grinned.

"When you're working a case, yes," Charlie agreed.

"Well, back to work," I sighed and stood up. I glanced again at the first photo that Charlie didn't recognize either. "What's this mark on her shoulder?"

"Looks like a tattoo," Charlie said, leaning over to get a better look.

"Do we have a still of just the tattoo?" I asked Genie.

"No. Agent Peitman worked that video. His still-shots are terrible, and we don't get enough notes off the descriptions either. We'll probably have to re-do some of the videos later before we can cross them off the list."

"He one of yours or from the local office?"

"He's local. He's the tall guy sitting next to Maggie looking like he's ready to hurl," Genie pointed.

Yup, same prick from this morning. I picked the photo back up and looked at the video code on the back before making my way in that direction.

"Agent Peitman," I called out before I was halfway across the large room. "At what point in your training did you fail to learn that a clear profile and portrait picture were critical for facial recognition, as well as, any pictures of identifiable markers such as scars and tattoos?"

Maggie grinned, leaning back in her chair, and continued to watch her videos. Several of the other agents noticeably hit pause on their videos.

"This girl has a tattoo on her shoulder. Where's the close-up of that tattoo?" I asked holding the picture up.

"There probably wasn't a good view of it," he said.

"Well, probably isn't good enough. Go back to this video, start from the top and get us pictures that we can actually use. And, tighten up your notes so that someone else doesn't have to re-do everything you're getting paid to do," I snapped before tossing the picture down in front of him and walking back to my station.

"Why don't you mind your own business," he snapped back just as I was about to sit.

"How about I make it *my* business," an older Agent in an expensive suit and tie said, as he stepped over and leaned onto Pietman's workstation. "I've had enough of your excuses. Do as Officer Harrison has asked or go to HR and fill out your exit paperwork."

"Yes, Sir," Peitman said while rushing to grab the photo and switch his video feeds.

The older agent nodded toward me before turning and walking back to the elevators.

"Who was that?" I whispered to Kierson.

"Special Agent in Charge, Jack Tebbs," Kierson grinned.

"I like him," I grinned. "He's got spunk."

It was after 8:00 by the time we finished watching all of the videos. Charlie and I checked in with Genie to see what additional pictures needed to be identified.

"We have only two that need to be identified. The first one appears to be about sixteen, street kid," Genie said passing us the photo.

Neither Charlie nor I recognized her but promised to circulate the picture in hopes of tracking down someone that did.

"The only other one is the girl from this morning. We have a picture of her tattoo and better facial images, but we still came up empty," she said.

The facial pictures were better, but I still didn't recognize her. I took a closer look at the tattoo and sighed. "Damn it."

"Do you know her?" Charlie asked.

"No, but I know this tattoo," I said. "I recently became friends with the Demon Slayers, a motorcycle club. This is their logo."

I pulled my cell and called Renato. He answered on the first ring.

"Who is this?" he answered.

"Paranoid much?" I said. "It's Kelsey Harrison. Do you have a minute?"

"Hey, Kelsey," Renato laughed. "Sorry, this isn't the number I have in my phone for you."

"No, I have three phones running right now depending on what State I'm in."

"What can I do for you? Are you calling in your marker?"

"I was part of a recent human trafficking bust down in Florida, and one of the murder victims had a tattoo on her shoulder that looks a lot like the Slayers logo. She was about sixteen in the video. Does that ring any bells with you?"

"Fuck, yeah, it might. Can I send you a photo and you can compare them and call me back?"

"That will work. The FBI can do a comparison."

"Give me about 15 minutes. I'll need to break into Nightcrawler's room."

"Shit."

"Yeah. I'll get it to you as soon as I can," he said before he hung up.

Maggie, Grady, Reggie and Kierson came in while we waited for the photo from Renato to be sent.

"You planning on watching that last video tonight?" Maggie asked.

"I need to," I nodded. "I have a feeling it's personal."

"I think it would be good if Kierson, Grady and I watch it with you. We all might pick up on different aspects."

"That's up to you guys. According to Charlie, it's the worst video. I plan on having it on one of the conference room televisions so I can make out more of the details," I said as my phone pinged.

I opened up the attached photo and passed it off to Genie.

"It's her. But I'll want your computer program to confirm it before I call Renato back."

"Damn, it's almost worse when you figure out who they are," Genie said plugging the phone into her laptop. "It's a match."

I called Renato and gave him the bad news. He wanted to take care of speaking to Nightcrawler himself. The girl was his niece, and she had disappeared over two years ago. Renato said he would fly down to tell her parents in Biloxi, Mississippi. I let him know I could meet him if they wanted to speak to someone about her death.

• • •

Chapter Thirty-Nine

"Now that I am sufficiently depressed," I said after disconnecting the call, "It's time to watch another horror flick. This one starring the kid that I mentored for over a year."

I walked out of the office, across the main room, and into the private conference room. Maggie and Kierson were already seated lost in anguishing thoughts of what was to come. Grady pulled out a chair for me before sitting next to me. He pulled my hand beneath the table to rest on his leg, with his hand gently resting above it.

"You sure you're ready for this?" Maggie asked.

"You never get ready for something like this. But I need to see it." I clenched my hand to Grady's leg, and he flipped my hand over, clasping it tightly.

"Pause," I ordered about five minutes later. Thoughts whirled in my brain at high speed, but I focused on the window just behind Maggie's chair, trying to center them. "Maggie, can you call Genie in for a second."

Maggie texted Genie, and moments later she stepped in, careful to keep her back to the screen.

"Did we recover the surveillance video from Pasco's mansion?" I asked.

"Negative. A guard destroyed the hard drive before we could secure it. The computer techs are still working on the damaged drive, but they said it didn't look promising."

"Can you reach out to Tech and see if he can send you a possible unofficial version for this date and timeframe?" I asked writing down the date and time I needed.

Genie grinned and walked out. I looked up to see Maggie grinning, and Kierson scowling.

"Is there any chance we can use the footage he has?"

"No. It would taint everything else you have tagged as evidence, so it's best if you forget knowing anything about it," I admitted before dragging my hands through my hair. "It will take Tech a bit to pull the footage I need, so let's keep going," I nodded at the remote.

"Break time," Grady called over an hour later. "Come on Kelsey, let's go have a smoke," he said as he pulled me up out of my chair and propelled me out the door.

My knees were weak, and my body trembled. My ears rang from Molly's repeated screams. And, Nola's sadistic smile bore into my mind blocking the view in front of me.

"Kelsey," Grady whispered in my ear, "Kelsey, shut it out. Close the door."

I blinked several times and looked around. We were standing in the parking lot, night sky surrounding us, and a cool breeze blowing across the lot.

"I'm here," I nodded and tucked my head into Grady's shoulder.

He tightened his arms around me and held me as I cried. I cried for Molly. I cried for Nicholas. I cried for

Charlie. And, I cried for myself. When would this nightmare ever end?

"Stay with me," Grady whispered. "Don't let her win."

"No," I whispered back as I clung to him. "She may hurt me, but I won't let her win."

"That's my girl," he whispered, kissing my hair.

It took me a good twenty minutes to stop crying and then after chain smoking three cigarettes I was still unsure if I could finish the video. We were sitting on the curb, next to the half-empty parking lot.

"Tell me what I can do to help?" Grady asked, pulling my hand into both of his.

"Nothing," I said shaking my head. "Nola took Molly to punish me. She keeps dropping messages throughout the video, forcing me to watch it. Somehow she knew I was coming."

"But the video was over six months ago. How did she know?"

"Max said Nola never believed that I walked away," I whispered, drifting into my own thoughts while still talking aloud. "She's taunting me. Daring me to find her. To find Nicholas."

"So, what's your move, Kelsey?"

"I fight back."

"How?"

"Knowledge. Bury the fear, and plan for the battle," I answered as if talking to myself.

"Then let's finish this," Grady said as he stood and held out his hand to help me up from the curbside.

I grabbed hold of his hand with what little strength I had left and walked with him back inside the building and up to the third floor. When the doors opened, Charlie, Reggie, Genie and a room full of agents I now recognized but lacked the knowledge of their names, stood silently waiting for me. They offered me their strength in that silence, and I absorbed it, raising my head and walking toward the conference room.

Genie stepped into the walkway, blocking my path. "Tech sent the video feed that you requested. I think you should see it before you decide if you want to keep watching what happened to Molly. But it's upsetting," she said as a tear slipped past her fast-blinking eyes.

She was trying to be strong for me.

"Where is it? I want to see it," I assured her with a gentle grasp on her arm.

She turned and started the video on one of the main television screens in the room.

"Why are we here? Is this where Kelsey is?" Molly asked Nola as they entered the mansion. "Why didn't she just meet me in the park like we used to?"

"Oh, dear, you're so naïve. Did you really think I was taking you to Kelsey? No, dear, you're merely a message for Kelsey," Nola said as she nodded to two of the guards to drag Molly screaming up the stairs to the playroom.

Nola turned to the camera and smiled.

I turned and walked directly into the conference room, grabbed the remote and hit play.

Over two hours later, Maggie hit stop on the video as Pasco left the room and a guard dragged Molly's young body out.

"Wait," I said, holding up my hand. "It's not over."

"That was the end, Kelsey," Maggie said.

"No," I shook my head. "Nola always has to have the last word. Hit Play."

Grady grabbed my hand, I felt him tremble in sync with my own trembling. "Maybe we should take another break. I'm not sure any of us can take any more."

"Everyone can leave, but I need to finish this. I can't come back in this room again." My voice shredded in and out, but I knew it was coherent enough for them to hear me. Tears streamed down my face. I gave up an hour ago trying to fight them off. My skin burned in fury for the hatred I felt toward those that hurt such a soulful young woman.

I looked up at Maggie, and her eyes were strained and puffy from crying as well. Agent Kierson was barely maintaining his control. I looked at Grady, who was staring at me unsure, face flushed, eyes red from the stress and strain.

I nodded that I was okay, even if I was barely surviving what I had already witnessed.

"Let's finish it together then," Grady said, nodding to Maggie.

Maggie took a deep, quivering breath and hit play.

After Pasco and the guards had left the playroom, Nola slowly sauntered toward the camera.

"Did you enjoy the show, Kelsey?" she smiled that evil smile. "Oh, I know, somehow, someway, you will see this video. I'm no fool. You picked the wrong person to go to war with."

She paced around the blood-soaked floor where Molly's body had been.

"I want you to know something very important," Nola said walking back to the camera, speaking deliberately. "I had Pasco make copies of these videos just so I can force Nicholas to watch them."

She smiled that malicious smile again as she turned her profile to the camera before turning her head back again.

"Don't think for a minute that if you somehow find a way to get him back that he will ever forget who his real mother is."

"YOU FUCKING BITCH!!!" I screamed as I launched at the television throwing my fists into the screen. *"I'll fucking kill you, you psychotic whore!"* The television screen shattered as I hit it with everything I had left in me.

I felt my body being dragged back, out of the conference room. I felt warm liquid running down my right arm as I continued to scream and swear at the image of Nola that taunted me inside my own head.

"I'll kill you!" I screamed again, as weight pooled on top of me to pin me down.

Unable to move, I continued to fight until my lungs closed up, refusing to allow any more air to pass. As I faded into oblivion, I saw the scared look on Grady, Charlie, and Reggie's faces.

"Get that fucking sedative away from my cousin, or I swear I'll remove your hand from your body!" Charlie yelled as I drifted back to reality.

"Charlie, it might help her," Grady coaxed.

"No!" Charlie yelled.

"Charlie," Reggie's voice penetrated through my foggy brain. "She needs sleep."

"Not this way. Either help me do this my way or leave. But you're not strapping her down, and you're not drugging her."

"What do we do?" Grady asked.

"Ten-foot perimeter," she ordered.

My vision was clearing, and I was finally able to open my eyes enough to see the three of them surrounding me in a wide circle. They weren't turned to keep everyone away from me but turned in defensive stances against me.

"Oh, this can't be good. I must have really lost my shit," I chuckled.

"Are you, you, again?" Charlie asked.

"I'm not the lunatic that you all tackled to the ground if that's what you're asking," I said.

I rubbed a hand across my forehead and felt something warm drip on my face. Looking up I saw my arm was coated in blood.

"Charlie? Did I hurt someone?"

"Just yourself, Cuz," Charlie said, helping me sit up.

Grady sat down on the other side of me and held my arm out, motioning for a pair of medics to step closer.

"She needs stitches," one of the medics said.

I turned my arm to inspect it myself. "No, it should heal just fine if it's taped up right. If it doesn't stop bleeding, I'll stitch it myself."

"You can't stitch up your own arm," Kierson grumbled.

"It wouldn't be the first time," Charlie grinned.

"And, not the last, I'm sure," I grinned back.

"You Harrison women are insane," Kierson said, shaking his head before stomping away.

We all grinned watching his retreat.

"I think we should introduce him to Nana," Charlie said.

"Are you done bleeding on the carpet now?" Maggie asked as the medics left and she helped us all off the floor.

"For the time being," I sighed. "I need to go home and shower. Some sleep would probably be a good idea too."

"I agree. But there are two victims that are asking for you," she admitted. "Do you want me to send them back to the hotel or have them come upstairs?"

"They're asking for me? Who are they?"

"One is a young woman named Bianca Hernandez and the other is a little boy, age eight named Timothy March. Bianca was rescued from the Custom's sting and Timothy was in Pasco's dungeon."

"Send them up, but make it quick. I can't keep going much longer."

"Are you Sam's sister?" I asked the young woman as she approached.

She nodded through her tears as she continued moving my way.

"Have you talked to him yet? Does he know you're okay?"

"Yes. I called him last night. He said that I could trust you. That if it weren't for you, I wouldn't be here today."

"A lot of good people helped. It wasn't just me. And, some of the information your brother shared also helped to rescue everyone."

"Nola," she said, starting to tear up, "She's so fixated on you. She's watching you."

"I know," I admitted, resting a hand on the side of her face. "I'll be fine. But, I need to find my son. Did you see him when she had you?"

She shook her head. "I was kept in a warehouse for months. Other women and children came and went, but they kept me there. Some man named Max was in charge, but Nola would sometimes come and have Max or the guards hurt me, and she would record it. I think she was using the recordings to scare Sam."

"You're probably right."

"But I heard Nola and Max arguing about your son, Nicholas. Max wanted her to get rid of him, said he had a buyer. But Nola refused. Max said that maybe he would find him himself and send him away to take the matter out of Nola's hands. She pulled a knife on him and told him if he ever dared cross her, she would kill him."

"Do you remember anything else?"

"No, she left after that, and I never saw her again. The next day I was moved from the warehouse to a boat, and then into a crate with other women and children."

• • •

"I know Nicholas," the little boy said stepping closer, his hand clenched tightly in his father's hand.

"You're Timothy, right?" I asked.

He nodded.

"And, you met Nicholas?"

He nodded again.

"Can you tell me where?"

"He was at the bad man's house. Where you could hear the screams through the ceiling," Timothy said not looking away from me.

"When was he there? Do you remember?"

"He was there the first day I got there, but then the next day some lady came and took him away."

I looked up at Maggie.

"Timothy went missing eight days ago," Maggie said in a low whisper.

"Timothy, how did you know to ask for me?" I asked.

"Nicholas told me to be brave. That his real mother was a cop, and she was coming to save us all. He said that his bad mother wasn't being careful, and his real mother would find us."

"Did he say anything else?" I asked trying to stay calm, and not to frighten the boy.

"He told me to tell you that he can sometimes hear trumpets where they keep him most of the time. But the sound of the bugs at night is really loud and usually drowns them out. He can also hear an owl nearby. And, he made me repeat this, lots of times, the sun's ahead of him in the morning when they drive to the bad man's house and behind him by the time they get there."

"Timothy," I said, leaning forward to offer a hug, "thank you for telling me what Nicholas said."

"Thank you for finding me," he said hugging me back.

When he let go, I abruptly stepped out of the room.

Chapter Forty

I walked into Genie's make-shift office and sat in a guest chair. I was mentally and physically exhausted.

"Are you okay?" Maggie asked, taking the seat next to me.

"I have to go to the prison and talk to Molly's father. Do you think you can get me access this late at night?"

"I know the warden," Kierson said. "I'll make the call." He walked back out of the room.

"Everyone else can go home. We all need some sleep."

"Can I stay at the safe house?" Genie asked. "I don't think I could sleep in a hotel room by myself tonight."

"Of course. You all can stay there," I assured her, grasping her hand across the table.

"I'll go with you to the prison," Maggie said, getting up from her chair.

"I'll take Charlie, Genie and Grady back to the house and scrounge up something for dinner," Reggie said, kissing me on the temple before walking out.

Genie followed him out.

"Are you sure you don't want to wait until the morning to go to the prison? It's been a long day," Grady asked.

"I'm sure. Mickey deserves to hear about his daughter's death from me."

"He might not like hearing the news from the cop that put him away," Maggie said.

"He forgave me for that years ago. And, I'm going to need his help," I sighed, getting up and retrieving my shoulder bag. "Grady, I'll be fine with Maggie. Go with Reggie and the others and call it a day. We won't be long."

The prison was just as dreary and depressing as I remembered it. We were led in through the side gates and our weapons were locked down. The warden met us from there and escorted us into the inner realm of the prison to a private interrogation room.

"What's about to happen here?" the warden asked.

"Mickey is going to find out that his daughter was murdered. You'll want to isolate him for the rest of the night," I answered, taking a seat at the table.

"Shit," the warden said, before leaving in a hurry.

"What's my role here?" Maggie asked.

"He'll know you're a Fed. Best if you stay back and let me do the talking," I said, just before the door opened and two guards led a chained Mickey McNabe through the door.

Mickey's eyes bored into me while the guards secured his chains to the cemented-in table. I nodded for the guards to leave us before I faced Mickey.

"This isn't a friendly visit, Harrison," Mickey said.

"No, Mickey, it's not. It's about Molly."

Mickey leaned his head into his hands, breathing heavily.

"Just tell me."

"She was murdered about six months ago. They disposed of the body, but we seized a video of her death. I watched it. It's Molly."

Mickey was always the calm, silent type. He didn't allow emotions to interfere with his work but calculated the possibilities and moved forward. When he raised his head to face me, I saw that same cold, calculating look in his eyes that most people feared.

"Who? Who would dare to kill my little girl?"

"Nola took Molly to punish me. She then delivered Molly to Darrien Pasco," I answered truthfully.

Mickey's hands shook as he processed the information. Tears welled in his eyes, unreleased.

"He's in the system now? Darrien Pasco?"

"Yes."

"And, Nola?"

"She's mine. She has my son."

"But you swear you'll get her?" He asked glaring at me.

"I swear it."

"What else? What else do you need to tell me?"

"I need you to reach out. I'm not going to find Nola with a police bolo, but if I work my contacts, I'll find her. If anyone in your circles spots her, I need that intel. And, I need to know they won't step in on your behalf. I have to find my son, Mickey."

Mickey nodded but didn't say anything. He looked up at Maggie.

"Did you see the video too?" he asked her.

Maggie nodded but didn't speak.

"How long did he make her suffer?"

Maggie looked down at the cement floor, a tear trailing down her cheek.

"Three hours and fifteen minutes," I answered for Maggie.

Mickey sat quietly staring at the cinder block white wall. The only sound in the room was the ticking of the clock above the door. I sat in silence across from him, allowing him to have his moment.

"You have six months, Harrison. I'll reach out to my contacts and send any information your way. But if after six months, you still haven't dealt with her, then I will."

"I'm sorry, Mickey," I said as my own tears started to slip.

Mickey nodded absently at the wall before turning back to me, his eyes glistening and hollow.

"For the last couple years, I got such a kick out of seeing my little girl laugh and talk in that animated way she did with her hands flying around," he said, recalling his visits with her.

I had my own fond memories of Molly dancing around excitedly as she would tell me things that were going on in her life.

"She was getting a degree at the University. She had a whole list of friends. She was happy. And, that was because of you. You put aside your differences with me and helped my daughter to turn her life around. I'll never forget that."

"I'll make Nola pay. I'll make her pay for hurting all of them," I said as I got up and knocked on the door to leave.

Maggie was quiet as we walked back out of the prison. Once we were inside the car, she leaned forward and rested her forehead on the steering wheel.

"Sorry, I should have warned you how intense he can be."

"I would seriously hate to be in Pasco's shoes right now."

"Especially being Mickey has a strict rule of tenfold," I sighed.

"What's that?"

"You act against him or his family, you'll get it back, tenfold."

"That's why he wanted to know how long she had suffered?"

I nodded. Pasco's death would not be quick.

"Pasco deserves whatever he gets," Maggie said as she started the car and drove us out of the prison lot.

Chapter Forty-One

Early morning, I rolled over, trying to hide from the sunlight that streamed through my open window, and rolled right into a warm body.

"What the hell?" I asked, partially sitting up to see who was in bed next to me.

"Morning, Sis," Reggie chuckled, wrapping an arm around me and pulling me into him.

"Morning, Reg," I giggled. "What are you doing in my bed? I thought you were bunked up with Grady in one of the rooms?"

"I had to escape. Kid was having a sex-capade in the room next to ours. I snuck in here about two in the morning."

I had gone to bed while everyone else was eating a late dinner and having a few beers. I was too exhausted to eat or drink anything. But the only men in the house were Reggie and Grady, so it must have been Grady that Charlie was with.

"Why did you go all quiet and rigid?" Reggie asked, turning on his side to face me.

"No reason. Charlie's an adult and can do as she pleases," I said as I crawled away from him and pulled on a pair of shorts.

I dressed for a run and laced up my shoes.

"It's Grady, isn't it?" Reggie asked with a grin. "You're jealous."

Was I? No, that was ridiculous. Charlie and I had never competed for the same man. We had completely different tastes. And, I had Bones, right?

I shook off my thoughts and finished lacing up my shoes.

"I've never been jealous in my life, Reg. It's just not my style."

"It's not your style to fall for a guy, either. But I've seen it happen," he grinned.

"I still have that whole mess with Bones, and that's low on the priority of things I need to deal with," I sighed. "Get some sleep." I kissed his cheek before making my way to the kitchen.

Grady sat at the kitchen bar wearing only a pair of jeans. His dog tags hung against his bare chest, flanked by bunched muscles. I noted a deep scar that started just below his left rib cage and dragged diagonally to the center of his sculpted abs, before disappearing into a trail of fine hair that traveled straight down under his jeans. I ducked my head as I felt my face heat, and retrieving a cup of coffee. Good for Charlie, I thought. He was an attractive man, and more importantly, he would treat her well.

"Good Morning," Grady grinned.

"Morning," I answered politely before looking out the kitchen sink window.

"You upset with me about something?" Grady asked.

"No, not at all," I said, while still looking out the window.

"It wasn't me."

"What?" I asked confused.

"In bed with your cousin, it wasn't me," he grinned when I turned around.

"Then who was it?" I asked, curiosity getting the best of me.

We heard rustling in the hall and turned to see Charlie enter, wrapped in a silk robe, her hair askew, followed by a disheveled Agent Kierson. I had to turn my head away to prevent myself from openly laughing at the shocked look on his face when he realized that his walk of shame had been witnessed.

"Shit," Kierson cursed.

"Lighten up," Charlie giggled. "We're all adults."

"Maybe some of us like to keep our private lives a bit more private," Kierson grumbled.

"Might as well suck it up and stay for a cup of coffee," Maggie said entering the kitchen, followed by a blushing Genie. "There is no sound proofing in this house."

I snorted, breaking the awkward silence and everyone laughed openly.

"I'm going for a run," I announced, setting my cup next to the sink.

"Do you want company?" Grady asked.

"No, she doesn't," Charlie said. "She hates running. She only goes when she has to think shit out. I imagine that's her plan. And, everyone will want to be ready to work when she gets back. That's how my Cuz powers up for the big game."

"Love you," I laughed, kissing her on the cheek and heading out the back door

Grady followed me out on the back porch in his bare feet.

"You were jealous," he grinned.

"Don't be ridiculous. I have no interest in Agent Kierson," I said rolling my eyes.

"I wasn't talking about Agent Kierson," Grady said as he gently turned my chin to face him. "Have a good run," he grinned down at me before walking back inside the house.

"Shit," I cursed to myself.

I so did not need to add more complications to my life, but Reggie and Grady were right. I was jealous when I thought that Charlie had slept with Grady.

Mad at myself for always making things worse, I quickly stretched before I started jogging along the side of the road.

I was a good two miles into my run before my muscles started to heat up and my brain started to slow enough to align my thoughts. I picked up the pace and mentally cataloged the past few days.

We had the information on an assortment of properties that Pasco and Max owned under shell companies that still needed to be investigated. I had Mickey reaching out to his contacts, but I still needed to reach out to mine. I needed to check in with Renato and see if he needed my help in Biloxi. And, I had the message from Nicholas to decipher where he might be being held.

My shirt was getting heavier as it absorbed my sweat. Checking for any oncoming cars first, I crossed the road and started the trek back to the house. I was guessing I had already knocked out four miles in one direction.

I set back into a steady pace as I tried to think if I was missing anything else. Ah, yes. As if all the other projects weren't enough to-do items to schedule in, I had promised Dallas that I would take her to the S&M club tonight. At least I knew some of my contacts would be there so I could kill two birds with one stone.

I was nearing the end of my mental list as I approached the block that the safe house was on. I quickly ducked behind some bushes when I noticed a man standing at the edge of the tree line watching the backyard of the house. I scouted the area and chose to sneak through the neighbor's backyard to come up behind him.

I was ten feet away when he heard me and turned. I ran directly into him and flipped him on his stomach, pinning his arm with my knee behind his back.

"Who are you?" I yelled loud enough to draw attention.

"Shit," the man swore.

Grady and Charlie came flying out of the house, weapons drawn.

"Mitch?" Grady chuckled. "Is that you with your face buried in the gravel?"

"You know him?" I asked, still holding him in place.

"He's my brother," Grady laughed. "Let him up before any of the neighbors call this in."

I released the man, and Grady gave me a pull upward off the ground.

"Why was he spying on the house?" I asked.

"I have no idea," Grady grinned.

"I wasn't spying. I was trying to decide if it was too early to knock on the door when out of nowhere you dive bombed me," the man complained, getting up to dust himself off. "And, you could've warned me, Grady!"

"How was I supposed to warn you when I didn't even know you were coming?"

"Well, point taken, I was sent by the Great Nana to ensure her girls were safe. I see now that they're just as crazy as their grandmother and don't need anyone to protect them," he said glaring at me before turning to Charlie, who stood there grinning with her robe loose, exposing a bit too much cleavage. Mitch openly took advantage of the view, and Charlie challenged him with a grin.

"Ok, show's over. Charlie go get dressed. Grady, drag your brother's ass inside before the cops show up."

On the back porch stood Agent Kierson, looking to be once again the poster child for the FBI marketing plan with his perfectly combed hair and shining shoes. He barely glanced at Charlie as she passed, glared at Mitch and sighed when Grady clapped him on the shoulder, offering support.

"I have meetings and reports to file. Genie and Maggie are going to stay here and do what they can to help until we get called out on our next assignment. Let me know if you need anything else," he said as he walked down the back stairs.

"Will do. And, Kierson?"

"Yeah?"

"She's a tough nut to crack but if you're really interested, don't let her push you away," I grinned.

"I'm not sure that I have the time to even attempt such a fate," he said, dragging a hand over his chiseled jaw. "But I like a good challenge," he grinned.

"I promised a friend that I would take her to The Other Layer tonight. You're welcome to join us."

"The S&M club?" he laughed. "I'll see if I can clear my schedule. This should be fun."

His grin was absolutely devilish as he slid into his company black SUV and reversed out of the driveway. Maybe he would be the one to finally push through Charlie's tough exterior.

"I need a shower and then it's time to get to work. You staying or going?" I asked Mitch as I passed through the kitchen.

"I can stay for a couple days if needed," he nodded.

"Good. Genie, we are going to need Tech and Sara on a conference line. Can you give me fifteen minutes?"

"I'll get them on the line, and we shall await your command," Genie grinned.

After showering and dressing in record time, I felt like myself again, clad in tight jeans, bitch boots, and a comfortable v-neck t-shirt. I applied a healthy layer of makeup and pulled my hair up into a clip. It was time to start the day.

Everyone was waiting for me in the War Room when I arrived. Tech and Sara were on the center television screen grinning at me. Carl was bopping around behind them waving at me as well.

"Good Morning," I grinned.

"Good Morning, Aunt Kelsey," Sara giggled.

"Okay everybody, we have a lot to get through. Tech, where are we at with Max's properties?"

"We've cleared some of them off the list, but the ones remaining are on this map."

The screen changed to a pdf of a map of the lower US with red dots indicating multiple locations. Most of them appeared to be in the Miami area, but not all.

"Good. Print the list of the addresses in or near Miami. Charlie, you take Mitch with you and go scout them out."

The printer behind Genie printed the list, and she passed it off to Charlie. Charlie and Mitch walked out to complete their assignment.

"Genie, can you apply the addresses for the properties that Pasco has to the same map?"

"Uno momento," she mumbled, as her fingers danced on the keyboard at high speed.

The map quickly filled with blue dots.

"Maggie and Grady, I need you guys to scout the blue dots in the Miami area. Anything that looks suspicious—get a warrant and enter."

"Ten-four," Maggie grinned.

"I was told I should never leave you alone with Reggie," Grady grinned.

"You're not," I grinned back. "You're leaving me with Genie, Dallas, and Reggie."

Grady rolled his eyes but left with Maggie anyway.

"Dallas -," I said gaining her attention from her perch on one of the side tables where she was giving herself a manicure. "If we are all going out tonight, Reggie, Mitch, and Grady are going to need something to wear. I think you should go shopping."

She grinned wickedly and sauntered out of the room.

"Sara," I said turning back to the television.

She grinned, leaning forward into the screen.

"I got a message from Nicholas. He was able to tell me that he was usually kept somewhere remote, and about a twelve to fourteen-hour drive West of Miami. Can you use that information to narrow down a location and see if any of the properties fit those specifications?"

"I'm on it. Tech is still going through some of the shell companies too so there might be more properties. We will keep in touch," she said before disconnecting the call.

"Genie, keep working Pasco's files. Let me know if anything else comes up. I have a few errands for Reggie and me to work," I grinned.

"You got it. Don't do anything stupid," she grinned.

Chapter Forty-Two

"Why does everyone always tell me not to do something stupid?" I asked from the passenger seat of the SUV.

Reggie grinned, glancing over at me as he drove down the highway.

I laughed and pulled my cell phone out, calling Tech.

"Did you get that number set up for a hotline?" I asked when he answered.

"Yes, it's all set. We will both get a text if a new message is left and can call in remotely to access. I'll text you the number. I also sent it to Kierson to have the warden get it to Mickey McNabe as you requested."

"Thanks, Tech. How's everyone there holding up?"

"Katie's fit to be tied with her bodyguard trailing her all day," Tech laughed. "Everyone else is busy preparing for Lisa and Donovan's wedding. It's in five days, you remember, right?"

"I remember. I'll be there if at all possible, even if it's to swing in for the celebration and duck back out."

"Good. Donovan said that Bones is flying back into town the morning of the wedding but planning on leaving the next day. Sounds like he's still pissed."

"I get that. I mean, I did leave his wife's dead body in an abandoned building to rot. It might take more than a few days to get over that."

"Maybe I could understand if she wasn't such an evil bitch, but I really don't see whatever he saw in her."

"You don't always choose who you fall for Tech. I mean, most men can't see what you see in Katie either," I grinned.

"Then they're idiots."

"I'll check in later. We just pulled up to the police station, and I need to handle a few things."

"Be safe, and don't do anything stupid," Tech said as he disconnected.

I snorted.

"He told you not to do anything stupid, didn't he?" Reggie grinned.

"Shut up," I laughed getting out of the car.

Inside, I found Uncle Hank at his desk, scarfing down a sausage McMuffin and hash browns.

"Hey, Uncle Hank," I grinned, sliding my ass up on top of his desk.

"Don't you dare tell Suzanne," he warned.

"I'll make you a deal, you get me in to see Trevor, and I won't tell Aunt Suzanne that you chose that crap over her cooking," I continued to grin.

"Bloody blackmail," he cursed, but went over and talked to one of the detectives in the far corner. A few minutes later, he returned with a grin.

"They'll move him to a private holding cell. They can give you five minutes, but it won't be on the books, and there can't be a mark on him when you leave. Do you understand?"

"Got it. Not a mark," I grinned.

Reggie followed me down the back stairway. I pointed out a bench and asked him to wait for me as I rounded the corner to the holding cells. Leaning against the first door, the Commander stood, arms crossed and eyes tightened.

"Commander," I nodded.

"There's not much that goes on in this building that I don't know about. I need to know if you're going in there as a cop or a parent."

"Both. I have questions about my son that Trevor might be able to answer, but I won't jeopardize this precinct's reputation while I'm doing it."

The Commander nodded and walked away. I slipped into the holding cell where Trevor was already waiting.

"I figured they were moving me to see you," he said without looking up. "It was only a matter of time."

"I'm not here to kill you, Trevor. But I need answers."

"They'll kill me if I help you."

"You're already dead unless you plead a deal that keeps you safe. Pasco's behind bars. Max is dead. Nola's on the run. The house of cards already tumbled."

"I did fall for you, you know. It was real for me."

I sat on the bench across from him.

"And, Nicholas, he was such a sweet kid. I was at his fifth birthday party, remember?"

"It's not something I am likely to ever forget. I'll carry that guilt with me to my grave."

"I don't know where he is. I swear I don't. I worked mostly with Max and Pasco. Nola would bring Nicholas on occasion when she came to town and keep him at Pasco's while she did her business, but other than that, she lived somewhere else."

"Where was she living?"

"I don't know. Somewhere close to the coast. She would occasionally come in by boat, but you know Nola. She didn't like to share information, and she never trusted me."

"Well, she was smarter than me on that one. I was a fool to trust you. I let you into my bed and worse, into my son's life."

I rose, approached the door and knocked twice, indicating I was ready to leave.

"I'm sorry," Trevor cried from behind me.

"Rot in hell, Trevor," I said as I walked out.

I asked Reggie to wait in the lobby as I went to the Commander's office. The secretary showed me in without asking any questions and closed the door behind me after I entered. Inside, Uncle Hank and the Commander sat waiting.

"It's time," I said, pulling my badge from my pocket.

"Are you sure?" Uncle Hank asked.

"I can't wear a badge and do what I have to do to get my son back. And, walking away from him is not an option."

"We can put you on leave," the Commander said.

"I'm not the same cop I was when I wore this."

I handed the badge to the Commander, and he sighed and handed it to Uncle Hank.

"On behalf of this city, thank you for your service," the Commander saluted.

I returned the salute, kissed Uncle Hank on the cheek, and left.

Chapter Forty-Three

"Where to?" Reggie asked when we were back in the SUV.

"It's time to even the playing field," I grinned.

"Hell, yes," Reggie grinned.

"Let's start with Chills," I said, pointing to take the side road.

"Shit," Reggie sighed.

I laughed as I gave him directions from the precinct to the highway.

"Can't you just call him?" Reggie whined.

"Relax, I won't leave you alone this time," I grinned.

When we pulled up in front of Chills' building, it was still early enough that the streets were scarce of anything other than a few stray cats and a mile of curbside trash.

We got out of the SUV, and I walked to the rear, opening the back hatch. This was the vehicle that I had Haley pick up in Georgia, so I knew it was already stocked.

I hit the hidden release, and the floor popped up, revealing several weapon choices and flak jackets.

"Grab a jacket and then load up."

Reggie didn't seem too confident about whatever I had planned, but he didn't waste time putting on one of the vests. We both strapped on hip holsters, before adding glocks and spare clips.

Reggie's eyes expanded when I unhooked a 12-gauge pump action shotgun from its compartment and loaded it. I grinned and stepped away from the SUV.

"Ah, shit," Reggie grumbled, hurrying up behind me after he closed the back gate on the SUV.

"Time to wake up the neighborhood," I laughed.

The only other vehicle on the street was a new shiny black Range Rover.

I walked up and shot out the back windshield of the Rover.

I then walked to the side and shot out one of the tires.

"I need to speak to Chills," I yelled when I heard the windows opening in the surrounding buildings. "He comes out, or I'll come find him," I yelled, before reloading the shotgun and shooting out the passenger side window. The shot not only shattered the window but blasted the foam filling from the driver's seat all over the inside of the vehicle. I laughed and looked back at Reggie, who nervously looked up at all the residential windows opening.

"*Fuck*!" I heard Chills yell from above.

Seconds later Chills flew out the front doors of the building followed by a small posse. They were each carrying handguns, but Chills was in the lead and held up a hand for no one to shoot.

"You could have just called!" Chills yelled. "You didn't need to shoot up the Rover."

"I could've called. In fact my friend Reggie here, suggested that very thing. But— I chose not to," I grinned.

"I take it the gloves are off?" Chills asked.

"More like the badge is gone. I'm officially rogue, Chills. Do you know what that means?" I asked before taking aim and shooting the passenger door on the Rover.

"It looks to me like you finally off your rocker, Kelsey," Chills yelled, staring at his demolished vehicle. "Quit fucking with my ride."

"Or what Chills? What are you going to do about it?" I threatened.

"What do you want?"

"Information," I threw a piece of paper from my back pocket toward him. "That's the number I can be reached at. Spread the word. Harrison's off the rails and will come after anyone holding anything back. I want Nola's location."

I stepped back and slid into the passenger seat of the SUV as Reggie slid into the driver's side. Reggie started up the truck and drove us smoothly out of the neighborhood.

"That was fucking badass," Reggie grinned.

"I've always wanted to shoot out his ride," I grinned.

"I thought you were friends?"

"More like mutually respectful of the other's turf. But, Chills needed to have a clear motive to help me find Nola. Within the hour, he'll have runners all over this city passing out my number and spreading the word that I have gone rogue. I'm sure the word on the street has already spread that I was in on taking down Pasco and that Max disappeared. Shooting up the Rover was just a way to speed up the advertising process."

"We should get a dash cam and record all the crazy shit you do. We could make millions," Reggie grinned.

"Take a left, go down three blocks and pull up in front of the barber shop. You need a haircut," I grinned.

"I can wait," he said checking out his hair in the rearview mirror.

I sighed and looked at Reggie. "I need to talk to the Barber!"

"Oh, okay. My bad," Reggie grinned.

I entered the shop first and motioned for Reggie to take a seat in the barber's chair. The old man that owned the place stood leaning against the wall, arms crossed, glaring at me. I walked past him, returning the glare and walked through the back rooms to ensure they were empty.

When I returned, the old man was placing a cape around Reggie, and Reggie looked at me unsure. I nodded to him that it was fine, and took a seat in the other chair, turning it to face them.

"Max dead?" the old man asked as he combed out Reggie's hair and started to shear off the lengthy layers.

"Yes."

"Good. Bastard," the old man spat on the floor.

"What talk are you hearing?"

"Nothing solid. Nola only comes in for visits, so my workload has been heavier than usual lately. It will be nice to take some time off until someone else takes up Max's slot."

He was cutting Reggie's hair at a pretty fast rate but seemed to know what he was doing.

"Where does she visit from?"

"Not sure. She's got a couple guys she keeps close. One's a driver and a guard, big guy, but dumb as fuck. Think she calls him Spike or some shit like that. Another guy is around only on occasion and stays close to the vehicle like he's guarding cargo," he said turning his head to look at me for the briefest of moments before he turned back to Reggie's hair. The pile of hair on the floor was getting larger.

"I need more," I said.

"When the other fucktard guard is around, it's when she comes to town in a black SUV with tinted windows." He gave me another pointed look.

"And, you got a plate number," I grinned.

The old man nodded and pulled out a piece of paper from his supply drawer, handing it to me. He was combing out Reggie's hair again, but cutting less, so I leaned back in my chair and relaxed a bit.

"Probably a bogus number but thought it interesting that they chose a Louisiana plate. A quick jump from a boat or a daytime drive."

"That fits with some other information that I've gathered."

"He needs a good shave," the old man nodded to Reggie.

"No way in hell, old man," I grinned.

He shrugged and took the cape off Reggie, shaking the hair to the floor.

Reggie stood and inspected the haircut. "Looks great. How much do I owe you?" Reggie asked.

The old man shook his head and walked into the back room. I pulled ten grand from my bag and dropped it in the chair with my contact phone number laying on top.

After leaving the barber shop, I called Genie with the plate number and asked for them to concentrate their research on anything related to Louisiana, especially anything near New Orleans.

"Why New Orleans," Reggie asked as he drove us to the mission up on 12th street.

"Nola likes big cities, with lots of crowds, " I answered as I wrote the new hotline number on several more slips of paper. "New Orleans also has its fair share of missing women and children. Plus, Nicholas said he could sometimes hear trumpets at night, so maybe they're bedded down just outside of the French Quarter."

"There are a lot of places you can hear trumpets in Louisiana."

"Yes, but most of the towns and cities aren't big enough to hide Nola."

Three hours later, we had stopped at two homeless shelters, one halfway house, three battered women's shelters, and a drug addiction clinic. My number was circulating at a very fast pace.

"I'm getting bored. We haven't shot anything up in a while," Reggie complained.

"Well, then it's good that I saved the best for last," I said as I directed him to pull up in front of the next building.

"This doesn't look much better than Chills' neighborhood," he said as he leaned forward to get a good look up at the building.

"We have Charlie on our six," I warned so as he wasn't surprised when he looked up to see Charlie pulling up with Mitch behind us.

"This place on her list?" Reggie asked getting out of the car with me.

"I don't know, I didn't pay that much attention," I admitted.

"You checking up on me?" Charlie grinned.

"Nope, I'm here to pay a personal visit. Does Max own the building?"

"No, but he rents out the third floor," Charlie answered. "We were watching to see who comes and goes, but it's still pretty early in the day for this block."

This neighborhood was populated by drug addicts and prostitutes and it was rare to see anyone around before the sun set.

"It's all good. I know who lives on the third floor. Best if you head in a different direction while I stop in to say hi," I grinned as I opened up the back of my SUV and reloaded the shotgun.

"Man, I never get to have any fun," Charlie complained.

Mitch and Reggie grinned and loaded up on firearms as Charlie stomped back to her vehicle and did a quick U-turn to leave.

"Did you get a haircut?" Mitch asked Reggie as we walked through the front doors of the building.

"Yeah. For an old man, he did a nice job," Reggie answered. "Kelsey needed to talk to him so he cut my hair while they talked. Some one-man barber shop down on 10th street."

"Benny's?" Mitch asked.

"Eyes open, boys," I ordered as I led us up the stairs.

"You got giant gonads, Reggie. I would never let Benny cut my hair," Mitch laughed.

"Why?" Reggie asked as we turned on the second-floor landing.

"Take cover," I yelled, diving back down the steps and throwing myself into Reggie and Mitch.

We pressed tight against the far wall and covered our heads with our arms as bullets ricocheted around us. When there was a pause in gunfire, I rolled to the open stairwell and shot the shooter in his hand as he attempted to reload his gun. His gun dropped to the floor as he cried out in pain. I ran up the stairs, two at a time.

Reaching the top landing as he was leaning over to pick up his gun, I slammed the butt of my gun on the back of his skull – knocking him out.

I waited a minute, ensuring he was completely out, before checking his pulse. He was younger than I expected. Just a street kid. I was glad I hadn't killed him.

"Stupid punk kid," I said while kicking his gun toward Reggie. "You both okay?"

"I'm good," Reggie said, picking up the gun.

"I'm good too," Mitch said moving low to get to the other side of the only door on the third floor. "We lost the element of surprise. What's the plan?"

I stepped out and shot the doorknob off with the shotgun. The door was cheap, like everything else in the building, so I expected it to blow a big hole in the door. But I was pleasantly surprised when the entire door was blown off its hinges and fell flat into the apartment.

Setting the shotgun in the hallway, I pulled both my glocks. I stepped cautiously over the door and into the apartment.

"It's Kelsey Harrison. You shoot me, and a shit storm will rain down on your ass," I yelled into the apartment.

Several prostitutes huddled in a corner together. Two more were passed out on the couch, unaffected by the gunfire.

"Come on out, Little Joe. The longer you stall, the more pissed I'll be!" I yelled.

A bedroom door opened, and Little Joe came out holding a gun to a prostitute's head, keeping her placed in front of him for cover.

I motioned for Mitch to cover the prostitutes in the living room and ordered Reggie to watch the apartment entrance. I slowly harnessed one of my glocks and placed both hands on the other.

"I came to talk, but if you don't let her go, I'll kill you instead. Not a big deal to me either way. With you dead, your girls will tell me anything that I want to know."

"I got no beef with you, Officer Harrison," he said as he pushed the prostitute away and slowly set his gun down.

"Kick it carefully my way," I ordered.

"I don't know nothing," Little Joe said as he kicked the gun my direction, holding his hands up.

"I'm disappointed to hear that Little Joe. No knowledge means that I don't have an incentive to let you live."

"Wait, wait, maybe I know something," he quickly said. His hands shook, and beads of perspiration were forming on his forehead. "Maybe Max mentioned how he contacted Nola."

"I'm listening."

"He complained all the time how he had to call a message service and leave a message for the surgeon to call him back. It was like what the real doctors use, like on TV. And, he wouldn't hear back from her for at least an hour which really made him mad."

"What else?"

"I don't know anything else. I swear," he insisted.

I walked up to him, standing directly in front of him and watching him closely. Based on his reactions, I believed he told me what little he knew. I turned to step away, but flipped my glock in my hand around and slammed the butt of the gun into his temple. He stumbled once, before dropping in slow motion to the floor, face first.

I stepped back and turned to the prostitutes. I recognized the one closest to me, huddled against the wall.

"Kara, what the hell are you doing back here?"

"I got nottin better ta do," she shrugged looking down at the floor.

"So what, you got bored? Is your big plan to wait until you die of an overdose or at the hands of an abusive John? Brilliant life choice, dumbass," I yelled at her. "I'm sure that your daughter will be happy when she turns eighteen and looks you up to find out that you died in the same shit hole apartment that you abandoned her in four years ago. What a fucking waste of space you turned out to be."

I paced back and forth as Kara started to cry.

"This is all I know!" she wailed.

"Bullshit! This is all you choose to know."

I pulled several pieces of paper from my bag and tossed them on top of each girl. "I'm looking for Nola. Anyone that helps me find her will have my help getting out of this life, for good. I suggest you decide what you want to do with Little Joe first, though, before he comes to and finds me gone." I kicked the coffee table with a pile of heroin out to the center of the room. "Choose wisely."

I walked out of the apartment with Mitch and Reggie on my heels.

"Do you think they will get high or use it on Little Joe?" Mitch asked.

"Depends on when their last fix was," I answered pushing the building doors open and stepping back out into the sun.

Chapter Forty-Four

I stripped the flak jacket off and threw it along with the guns into the back of the SUV. Reggie and Mitch did the same as I claimed the backseat. I laid down in the seat to rest my throbbing head while Reggie drove.

"Do we need to go to the hospital?" Reggie asked.

"No," I sighed.

"You sure?" he asked.

"Yes," I sighed again.

My cell phone rang, and I answered it.

"Kelsey," I said as I closed my eyes.

"You sound like you need a drink," Tech chuckled.

"I'm heading that direction now."

"Message came in from the prison saying to take a closer look at New Orleans. That's all it said."

"That seems to be the direction my sources are pointing me, as well. Anything in the area look good from the property searches?"

"Property records are kind of a mess in Louisiana. There has been a lot of buying and selling going on, and a lot of the records aren't electronic yet, but we're still digging."

"Ok, as always, keep me in the loop," I sighed. "In other news, I found out that Max used to contact Nola using a phone message service. Search his call history and see if you can track the calls backward."

"I'll get started on it," Tech said before disconnecting.

I closed my eyes and rested for the remainder of the drive.

"Come on, little Sis," Reggie said after opening my car door and pulling me out. "Let's get you patched up."

"Shit, Grady's going to be pissed at me," Mitch said, walking with us up the back stairs.

"Why am I going to be pissed?" Grady asked as he stepped out of the house and onto the back porch.

"Put her in the chair," Charlie ordered, pointing to the Adirondack on the back porch. "We don't need her dripping blood through the house."

Charlie already had a pair of scissors and a med kit. She used the scissors to cut the sleeve off my shirt.

"You tore the cut on your arm back open, but where's the rest of the blood coming from?"

"I got grazed," I admitted leaning forward.

Charlie and I had been through more close calls than either one of us would ever admit. She didn't think twice about pushing my hair out of the way and inspecting the wound.

"You got fucking lucky, Cuz," she hissed.

"I know," I sighed. "Just patch me up."

She shaved as little of my hair as she could get away with, cleaned the wound and stitched it. When she was done, I re-cleaned my arm wound and threw a few tack stitches in the center to keep it closed.

I checked the stitches on the side of my ribs and saw that they were ready to come out. It seemed like a month ago when I got them.

Too many close calls lately.

I started snipping the stitches as Charlie pulled them out with tweezers.

"I'm a little freaked by how good they are with this shit," Mitch admitted.

"You get used to it," Reggie said, coming out of the house and passing a round of cold beers.

"What the hell happened?" Grady glared at his brother.

"Don't blame them," Charlie grinned over at Grady. "Kelsey has a habit of kicking in doors in bad neighborhoods." She turned her attention back to me, still grinning. "So who resided in the third-floor apartment?"

"Little Joe and his harem of heroin addicts."

"Little Joe was stupid enough to shoot at you?" Charlie asked.

"No, but the street punk kid he had manning the door, was too young to recognize me. Maybe the permanent scar going through the center of his hand will instill a little *'think first and shoot later'* logic."

Maggie and Genie joined us on the porch.

"And where were you two during all this?" Grady turned on Reggie and Mitch.

"I was still in shock that Reggie had the gonads to get a haircut from Benny the Barber," Mitch fully admitted.

"I still don't get it. How do you know this barber?" Reggie asked.

Genie turned white and looked at me in shock. Charlie and Maggie turned to look at me and broke out laughing.

"Who's Benny the Barber?" Grady asked.

"He's a hitman for hire," I shrugged. "Mostly works straight blade jobs, but will take an occasional bullet job when the money's right or the mood strikes. He doesn't do distance shooting anymore, though. Says it's too competitive, and his eyesight isn't what it used to be."

Reggie dropped his beer. It landed flat on the base of the bottle and shot beer straight up at him before the bottle shattered at his feet.

"You had a hitman give me a fucking hair cut? Are you fucking nuts?" Reggie asked.

"What? I don't know why you're upset. You heard me tell him that there was no way I was going to let him give you a shave! Besides, you have to admit he did a nice job," I smirked.

"Let me guess, he's just another one of your street friends?"

"Hell no. I don't trust Benny at all. But I'm a quicker shot than he is and he knows it. Besides, we've always had an understanding."

"*An understanding*?? Like the one you had with Chills before you blew holes in his new SUV???" Reggie yelled.

"You shot up the Rover?" Charlie laughed. "Oh man, I really missed out on a fun day."

"Woke the whole fucking neighborhood up first thing this morning," I grinned. "The Rover was demolished."

Dallas pulled into the driveway in a brand new silver convertible. She parked and retrieved a half a dozen shopping bags from the trunk before carefully walking through the deep stone drive to the back porch in six-inch heels.

"Nice car," I grinned

"I was tired of the SUV," she grinned back. "Besides, Goat is flying down tomorrow and driving with me back up to Michigan. He even agreed to stop at any of the stores I wanted to visit on the way back."

"I bet," I continued to grin.

"And, I found everything that we need for tonight," she said holding up the bags. "Now I need a drink. I'm simply parched from all this shopping."

"How do you walk in those heels?" Maggie asked as Dallas maneuvered carefully up the steps.

"Walking in them is the easy part. Making sure you don't accidentally stab your partner during a wild round of 'Ride 'em Cowgirl' is the hard part," Dallas said as she entered the house.

Genie spewed her beer all over Reggie.

Charlie laughed as she pulled me up from the chair. Reggie wiped the worst of the beer off his face with his sleeve and entered the house, heading straight down the hallway. The rest of us went as far as the kitchen, and I opened up the liquor cabinet, pulling out all my favorites.

"Bottoms up, ladies and gentlemen. Tonight's going to be an adventure," I grinned as I took a swig of premium vodka.

"What's going to be an adventure?" Mitch asked.

"We're going to an S&M club called The Other Layer," Grady grinned.

"Well, doesn't that sound a bit more interesting," Mitch grinned and winked at Charlie.

"Have you decided if you're going as you or as Destiny, yet?" Charlie winked at me sliding me a glass of ice.

"I was planning on just me, but it really would be a shame if Destiny didn't get to play a bit," I admitted, as I pulled an ice cube from the glass and popped it into my mouth.

"Fuck," Grady swore, grabbing the bottle of vodka and chugging a shot.

I grinned as I pulled the cube back from my mouth.

He took a deep breath and then turned to Mitch. "You're going to want to drink up," he said passing the bottle to Mitch.

"I want to go," Genie giggled.

"You're more than welcome," I said.

"No," Maggie insisted. "Genie is going to stay here with me before you two infect her anymore with your wild ways." Maggie guided Genie back toward the porch.

"But I like their wild ways," Genie giggled.

"Shh, don't encourage them," Maggie laughed.

Chapter Forty-Five

Two hours later, Dallas, Charlie, and I were sufficiently buzzed, completely inappropriately dressed, makeup plastered on, and hair styled in wicked fashion. We walked through the living room and into the kitchen — and froze.

In front of us, stood Grady, Kierson, Reggie, and Mitch, in full-out sexy sinfulness.

Reggie was outfitted in black leather pants, black leather vest, and black cowboy hat. Grady wore blue jeans with chaps, a brown leather vest, and a brown cowboy hat. Kierson wore black leather pants and a leather collar. Mitch wore a white button up shirt that had the buttons undone and the sleeves tore off, black wrist cuffs and was also sporting a black collar.

We stood there staring, absorbing their half-nakedness in all its muscular glory. I heated up when I felt Grady's eyes devouring me with just as much interest. I was wearing a simple halter leather corset with low riding black leather skirt and black heeled boots. I also sported a leather collar around my neck that had fake rubies embedded in it.

"Charlie, you look hot," Grady said to her while his eyes stayed glued to mine.

"Why thank you, Grady," Charlie purred, stepping up to run a single fingertip down his chest as Mitch and Kierson scowled. My eyes flared, but I ducked away. It wasn't quick enough for Grady to miss it, though, which seemed to please him.

"We should get going," I said as I clipped a small 9-millimeter to my leather skirt and grabbed my purse.

"You're not going to be able to take your gun inside," Mitch said.

"I know the owner," I grinned and walked out.

We all piled into Kierson's SUV as it was the only vehicle that would fit everyone. I gave directions to Grady, who appeared to be our designated driver at the moment. When we were a block from the club, you could see a crowd of people already waiting to get in.

"It's going to take hours to get through that line," Dallas complained.

"Not with Kelsey it won't," Charlie grinned.

I directed Grady around the corner and into a private parking garage. I handed him a card to hand to the attendant. After swiping the card, the attendant leaned down to look at me.

"Good evening, Ms. Harrison," the attendant smiled and passed the card back.

I nodded as a reply and tucked the card into my corset as the gate opened and Grady pulled forward.

"Do I even want to know?" he asked, shaking his head.

"I doubt it," I grinned.

At the elevator, I swiped my card again, and the doors opened. After we all had entered, I pressed level three, and we zoomed upward, coming to a smooth stop before the doors opened to what was referred to as The Parlor.

"Welcome, Ms. Harrison," Baker grinned, leaning in to kiss my cheek. "And, I see you brought your beautiful cousin with you tonight. As always, good to see you, Charlie," he said, leaning in to kiss her cheek as well.

"Good evening, Baker," I grinned. "Can you spare two people from security to watch out over a newbie tonight?"

"Certainly. If you would like to wait at the bar, I'll have two of my best sent right up," he said before turning away.

I led everyone to the bar and offered my card to be swiped as everyone placed their orders. We were served promptly, and a waitress was assigned to stand nearby to handle any future requests.

"What's next?" Dallas asked, her eyes lit up like a Christmas trees.

"Go look over that window ledge," Charlie told Dallas, pointing to the far side of the bar.

Dallas took off that way. Curiosity got the best of Reggie and Mitch, and they followed.

Grady stayed, leaning forward on the table, grinning at me.

Kierson leaned back in his chair and openly observed Charlie with a knowing smile.

"You don't want to look?" Charlie asked Kierson.

"At the other floors? No," he grinned shaking his head. "I wouldn't mind taking you upstairs, though."

"You've been here before?" she asked with a raised eyebrow.

"A few times," he shrugged. "I was curious when I found out who the owners were and decided to check it out for myself."

Charlie and I both grinned.

"Well, let's go upstairs then, shall we?" she said, as she pulled a VIP card from her purse.

Kierson stood and pulled her up from her chair, smacking her on the ass as she stepped in front of him to walk to the elevators.

"You two own this place?" Grady laughed.

"Only sixty percent," I grinned. "Baker owns the other forty, and we pretty much let him run the show. Most people don't know we are associated with the club. Our swipe cards come up as Extreme VIP, and that's all the staff needs to know. And, Baker is fine accepting the more public role as the face of the club."

"How in the hell did you end up owning a place like this?"

"I met Baker when he worked at this seedy place downtown. I was doing background research for an undercover job, and he was helping me with my educational needs. He told me about his business plans, and the three of us sat down and worked out the details. I had the cash and needed to diversify some investments. He needed partners and promised that he would keep the club legal. It turned into a tourist mecca. We bought the building and opened one floor at a time, reinvesting the profits for each floor, until the building was completely remodeled."

"Does Bones know?" he laughed.

"No. Nobody in Michigan really knows about most of my companies. I also own a few race horses, part of a casino, a few coffee shops, sizeable shares in several conglomerates and just laid down cash for partial ownership of a shipping company in the area."

"In addition to the resale store you started from scratch that people drive through multiple States to get to? Do you ever sleep?"

"Not much," I grimaced.

"Sorry," Grady said, reaching out for my hand. "That was thoughtless."

"It's fine. This business and a few others, I started before Nicholas disappeared. The resale store was part of my devious plan to continue to build a fortune while biding my time to go after Nola."

"How do race horses fit in?"

"When I was in Texas, I worked with some good racers. I made a deal with another owner to run them through the circuits and split the profits."

"She also helped me get the stock horse business off the ground," Reggie said coming back to the table and sitting.

"So you have the Midas touch," Grady grinned.

"More like she can smell money," Reggie laughed. "Don't get me wrong, Kelsey works hard, but she has a knack turning a nickel into a grand. And, if you ever get a chance to take her to the horse track – just hand her your money and walk away. She paid off my mortgage in one day before the track kicked her out."

"No way," Grady laughed.

"Not shitten ya, brother, just ask Pops," Reggie laughed. "He refused to let her bet for him and went home with twenty dollars. I went home with two hundred grand, and he didn't speak to me for three weeks."

"To be fair, it's not like I have ESP or anything. I'm just good at reading horses," I shrugged.

"So if Reggie made out with two hundred grand, how much did you make?"

"Enough to buy the Miami safe house, a house in Michigan and my start-up cash for the resale store," I admitted.

"Do we have time while we're in Florida to go to the tracks?" Grady laughed.

"Afraid not," I grinned. "My window for returning home is narrowing, and there's still a lot to get done. I'm planning on jumping over to Biloxi tomorrow and then Louisiana. I need to be back in Michigan sometime Tuesday though, if at all possible."

"Donovan's wedding," Grady nodded. "I'm the best man."

"What?" I laughed.

He nodded. "Are you in the wedding party?"

"Last I knew, I was the bouncer," I grinned. "But knowing Lisa, I'll still be in some fancy dress."

"And, why would you be the bouncer?" Grady asked.

"Because everyone except for Kelsey is scared of Lisa's family," Reggie grinned. "Including Donovan."

Dallas and Mitch came back to join us, and Baker returned, accompanied by a man and woman, both dressed in the customary dark security suits.

"Ms. Harrison, I have a group of guest passes to be used at your discretion and the additional security you requested. This is Maddox and Maryanne. They both have been with the club for a few years now."

"Thank you, Baker. Be sure to charge my card accordingly for the additional services tonight and any charges on these guest passes."

Baker nodded and excused himself.

"Maddox and Maryanne, you both are about to begin what I am sure will be a very taxing evening," I grinned. "This is my friend Dallas, and she's a newbie. Unfortunately for both of you, she is also a trouble maker. It will be your job to make sure she doesn't do anything too dangerous and is returned to me at the end of the evening, having enjoyed her visit but without permanent injuries or diseases. She is also not allowed to carry the guest pass. One of you will carry it at all times to ensure she stays with you. If at any point this evening you lose track of her, notify Baker immediately."

Dallas was pouting, but Maddox and Maryanne were trying to hold back their smirks as Maryanne reached out for the guest pass.

"Dallas, behave," I scolded before she jumped up and took off with her bodyguards.

"They have no idea what they're in for," Reggie laughed.

"No, but at least I don't have to suffer through it first hand," I grinned back.

"Where did Charlie go?" Mitch asked.

"She took Kierson on a tour of the club," I said as I passed out the access cards. "Don't lose your cards. You can't get back to the third floor without them," I warned as I got up to leave.

Reggie and Mitch went to the front glass elevators that went to the first-floor dance floor. Grady grabbed his drink and followed me.

"Where do you think you're going?"

"Where ever it is that you're sneaking off to," Grady grinned. "You're up to something, and my guess is that it's trouble."

Chapter Forty-Six

I took the private elevators up to the fifth floor and swiped my card for the door on the right. The door swung open automatically, opening to a long hallway with one-way glass on both sides. The glass walkway overlooked multiple rooms below where audiences could watch various sexual performances.

"Holy shit," Grady said as he stopped to tip his head at a threesome in one of the rooms.

I grinned and kept walking. At the end of the hall, I swiped my card again, and Grady hurried to catch up with me.

"Baker," I nodded in greeting, as I walked into his office and helped myself to his personal bar and expensive brandy.

Baker nodded but looked over at Grady, before looking back at me with a raised eyebrow.

"You can speak freely in front of Grady," I said, taking a seat in one of the guest chairs.

Grady wandered over to the security feeds and inspected the various activities.

"Dallas is in one of those dancing cages," Grady laughed, pointing at the screen.

"I've already had three calls from security asking if they should escort her out," Baker grinned.

"She's harmless, mostly," I grinned.

Looking about the room, nothing appeared to have changed in the years that I had been gone.

"So, spit it out. Where's the money?" I finally asked.

"I would have told you, Kelsey. I was just trying to figure it out on my own."

"Figure what out. Tell me what's going on and why the books are short."

"A woman came in about six months ago with a dozen heavy hitters. She said I needed to pay the toll or else I would be closed down. I told her to go to hell. Her guys trashed the place. Two days later, a pipe bomb was thrown through a window. Luckily, it didn't do much damage before the sprinkler system put it out, but it could have taken down the whole building. I started paying her to leave us alone."

"You broke one of the rules, Baker."

"I know," he sighed, scrubbing a hand across his jaw. "I just didn't want to bother you with it. I thought I could find a way to handle it."

"Do you have a security photo of the woman?"

"Yeah," he said, sliding me a file. "What do you want me to do?"

Inside the folder was a picture of Nola looking up at the security camera. I also recognized several of the other men with her from Pasco's house party.

"I don't want you to do anything. Stop making the payments, and if you hear from them again, call me. If you ever hesitate again, we will be ending our business partnership."

Grady walked over and took the folder scanning through it before calling Genie with some of the details. I was sure that the bank accounts would be a dead end. Nola had planted this trail to get me back in Florida so she could keep playing her games.

"I'm taking the folder with me, but I need you to send a copy of everything, including the access codes to the security system to this email address."

Writing the email address on a slip of paper, I slid it to Baker.

"What if they come back and torch the place?"

"It's doubtful. The woman is on the run, and most of the men in that photo were arrested two nights ago," I shrugged.

Baker grinned. "What would you have done if I would have called you months ago about this?"

"I would have had you make the payments, and I would have followed the money," I snapped back in anger, half standing to lean over the desk. "But now it's too late because I already exposed myself and took down most of her resources. Unfortunately, because of you, she has enough excess cash to stay in hiding longer."

"Wait, that woman is Nola? The one that took Nicky?" Baker asked, getting up from his chair. "Shit."

"Yeah, Shit," I said. "Don't disappoint me again, Baker."

"I'll call you if I see her again. I won't hesitate."

"Good. And, you can make it up to me by setting up a meeting."

I walked over to the security monitors and briefly viewed the feed with Dallas dancing in a cage. It appeared she intentionally caused the cage to oscillate, and poor Maddox and Maryann were desperately trying to stop it from swinging. Dallas fell back on her ass in the cage, laughing. The crowd was loving it, and several other security team members ran over to lend a hand. Grady chuckled over my shoulder.

I shook my head and continued scanning the feeds until I found the one that I was looking for. "This man," I pointed to the screen. "I need to meet with him tonight."

Baker moved over and looked at the screen.

"Are you sure?" he asked, scrunching up his nose in disgust.

I couldn't blame him. The overweight, sweaty bald man was currently in the middle of masturbating as he watched some girl-on-girl action in one of the performance rooms.

I raised an eyebrow at Baker, and he nodded.

"Can I wait for him to finish what he started?" Baker asked.

"Sure. I'll wait here."

Baker shook his head and left.

"Is everything in the building monitored by cameras?" Grady asked from behind me.

He was standing too close. I could feel the heat from his body on my back.

"Everything on the first four floors is monitored. There are no cameras on the fifth and sixth floors, but there are panic buttons. Security teams are authorized to breach any room if an alarm is set off."

"So, the customers don't mind being filmed while they are, let's say, enjoying themselves?"

"We have a reputation for protecting the information, but most of our patrons would rather have someone keeping them safe. Even the politicians prefer safety protocols over the concern of exposure. Besides," I said turning to Grady, "There's a certain appeal to being watched."

"Yes," Grady grinned, stepping away.

He walked over and dragged one of the leather-upholstered guest chairs over in front of two screens. He moved me behind the chair, placing my hands on top of its cool leather back.

A tremor lightly traveled down my body.

"The screen on the right is the man that Baker will retrieve for your meeting," he whispered into my ear as he stepped up close behind me. "The screen on the left though is more interesting, don't you think?"

I looked up at the screen and saw the woman he was referring to. She was standing, legs spread, hands on the back of the chair in front of her, watching the orgy on display below her in the performance room. A man stood behind her, with his hand buried under her skirt. Her eyes drooped, her breathing increased, she seemed torn between watching and feeling.

"What do you think that man is saying to her, Kelsey? Do you think he's telling her he loves her?" Grady asked as he kissed my neck. He slid his rough, calloused hand across my smooth exposed abs.

"No."

"Do you think he's telling her how he loves how her body reacts to his touch?" he whispered. He kissed down my shoulder as his hand stroked down the side of my skirt, and then slowly stroked upward against the skin on the inside of my thigh.

"Yes," I said breathing heavy.

His hand grazed the edged seam of my panties, and my body shuddered.

"Do you think his cock is hard because of her or because of the orgy in the other room?" he asked, as he leaned into me.

I could feel his own desire against my ass, and I pressed myself further into him.

"From watching her. From feeling her," I whispered, as Grady's fingers slipped under the seam and touched my hot skin.

I leaned my head back and to the side as I started to close my eyes. Suddenly, I remembered I was supposed to watch both screens.

"Shit," I said, jerking away, as I realized the room on the other screen was empty. "They're on their way."

I tried to catch my breath as I turned off several of the display screens and Grady dragged the chair back to the desk. I was just sliding into a guest chair to sit, when Baker walked in with the man.

"Thank you, Baker. That will be all for now," I nodded.

Baker glanced from me to Grady, exposing a devilish grin before he stepped out, closing the doors behind him.

Chapter Forty-Seven

"I was told someone needed to speak with me?" the man questioned, looking at me and then at Grady.

"Yes, pardon my interruption to your evening, Mr. Mayfair. My name is Kelsey Harrison. I believe we have some mutual acquaintances."

I walked over and extended a hand as was the respectful thing to do. I hoped that he had taken an opportunity to wash his hands after satisfying himself, but regardless, I would be pouring bleach on mine as soon as he left.

"Kelsey Harrison, yes, I would say we have mutual acquaintances," he grinned and accepted the handshake.

"Please, have a seat. I'll only require a few minutes of your time," I said offering him the high back guest chair that sat beside mine.

Grady moved over to stand by the door, next to Mr. Mayfair's own security man.

"You've been busy lately. I've heard a lot of talk over the last few days. Most of it ends with the whisper of your name at the end of a tall tale."

"I don't wish to discuss anything that may or may not have taken place in the past. I wish to discuss how you can assist me in the future," I smiled.

"And, why would I do that?"

"Because I'm the investor that is buried under three layers of shell companies that just bought out a majority interest in your shipping company."

Mayfair's eyes turned cold as he stood to glare down at me.

"You're lying."

"You were the greedy bastard that believed my lawyer without verifying the facts. Really? Some little old lady needing to invest millions as a silent partner?"

Mr. Mayfair continued to glare at me, as I glared back, unflinching.

"What do you want?"

"Information," I answered. "Certain individuals use your boats to move commodities, and I want to know the who, what, where, and why at all times. You will feed me this information until I say otherwise. If you do not agree to these terms, I'll bankrupt you. If you agree, then when I conclude my business, I'll sell you back my investment at a reasonable price."

"That's blackmail."

"Let's be honest," I grinned, taking a moment to sip my brandy, careful to use my untainted hand. "I've done a lot worse than blackmail someone and so have you."

I handed him a blank business card with an email address written on it.

"Send all the information you have to this address before dawn. If I don't receive anything or if I find out at any time you're holding back information, there will be consequences."

Mr. Mayfair stormed toward the door like an enraged boar, ready to charge. His security man barely had time to jump out of the way before the door was thrown open and Mayfair stormed out. The door slammed shut behind him.

"Was that smart?" Grady asked, sauntering back to the center of the room.

"Yes. He'll call around to see what my threat level is. It won't take him long to find out he needs to get in line. His first call will be to Mickey McNabe, and Mickey will back my play."

"And, if you're wrong?"

"I'm not. But if I were, I could either sink his company or ask for a raid on one of his ships. After the fallout, I take the rest of the control away from him," I shrugged.

"Doesn't that violate some shareholder laws or something?"

"I don't invest in companies that are publicly traded. Some of them have a vast number of investors, but even if I own a small percentage of a business that goes public, I sell off my investment."

"So how did you buy up part of his company without his knowledge?"

"Through a lawyer," I grinned. "Greedy people tend to make rash business decisions."

I returned to the security screens, turning them back on as Baker entered the office.

"Mr. Mayfair didn't seem very happy," Baker tsked.

"Why do you even let him in here?" I asked.

"It's a sex club, Kelsey. They're not all tourists," Baker grinned. "We keep a close eye on men like Mayfair though. And, they're not allowed on the fifth or sixth floors."

I walked behind the bar and pulled out some heavy cleaning solution from under the sink and scrubbed my hands. Grady smirked.

"Yuck," Baker said. "You shook his hand?"

"I thought it would be best to start the conversation amicably before I told him that I was going to blackmail him."

"You're kidding, right? He owns most of the illegal shipping in the South."

"No, he doesn't. He owns forty percent, his son owns five percent, and I own the rest," I smirked.

"Jesus," Baker gasped, sitting back in his chair. "Don't ever tell me how much money you actually have. It would make me feel beyond inadequate."

I grinned as I finished washing my hands and drying them on a nearby towel. I walked back over to the security screens to see where all my friends were at, and what they were up to.

"Shit! We need to go," I yelled after I viewed one of the security screens.

I ran out with Grady hurrying after me.

"Was that really Dallas in one of the performance rooms?" Grady laughed as we ran for the elevator.

"Yes! Room four!" I said, desperately pushing the elevator button.

"Stairs!" Baker yelled, running down the hall and swiping his pass to the stairwell.

We all ran down the stairs and down the hall to room four.

I grabbed a robe off the rack, and Baker swiped his card and swung the door open. I dove into the room, trying to hide my face while I smothered Dallas's half naked body with the robe and Grady helped me drag her out. Baker slammed the door shut behind us as we fell in a pile of arms and legs on the carpeted hall floor.

Chapter Forty-Eight

"If you weren't old enough to be my mother, I swear I would punch you!" I shouted at Dallas as I forced her back into her halter top. Baker and Grady had their backs turned, blocking the view of Dallas as I finished zipping up her skirt and dragging her up from the floor. Maddox and Maryann came running down the hallway.

"You can turn around now," I said to Grady and Baker.

"What do you want me to do with them?" Baker asked, pointing to a dejected looking security team.

"Pay them hazard pay for tonight and let them leave early. They deserve it. It's not easy keeping Dallas in line, believe me. That's why I chose to hire her babysitters."

Dallas pouted all the way back to The Parlor, where I made her sit and wait for the others to join us. I texted Reggie, Charlie, and Mitch that it was time to leave as I paced back and forth, fuming at Dallas.

Grady and Baker continued to chuckle but kept a close eye on Dallas so she couldn't escape again.

"Do you even understand what could have happened tonight? You could have had this whole place shut down!" I ranted.

"Oh, no, she didn't?" Charlie laughed walking up to our table, closely followed by Kierson.

"Oh, yes, she did!" I fumed.

"Do I even want to know?" Reggie sighed walking over from the glass elevators.

"It couldn't have been worse than the dancing cage, whatever she did," Mitch had the nerve to say.

I turned a glare so intense toward Mitch that he stepped back.

"Ok, maybe it was worse," he said, with his hands raised in surrender.

"Much, worse," I said, dragging Dallas by the arm to the private elevator that led to the private garage. "It's a good thing Goat is coming for you, Dallas, because Miami can't handle you."

She continued pouting all the way to the car, and all the way back home. When we entered the house, she went down the hallway to her assigned room and closed the door.

"Kel, you can't be so hard on her," Charlie said.

"Oh, yes I can!"

"She seems really upset," Reggie said.

"Good," I said, slamming around in the cupboards before Grady pushed me away and started emptying them himself. "Look, it doesn't change how I feel about her. I'm just mad right now. And I have a right to be angry."

"It's not fair to take it out on her when she doesn't know that she was putting you and Charlie in jeopardy," Kierson said.

"How was I hurting Kelsey?" Dallas asked, having stepped around the corner of the hallway.

I sighed and sat on one of the barstools.

Grady poured me a brandy and slid it my way.

"We're part owners of the club," Charlie said. "We gave you an access pass, so if the police would have been called, we all could've been arrested for prostitution, or worse. And, the club could've been shut down."

"You own a sex club! Oh, that is so cool. Can I invest?" Dallas asked excitedly.

"You're not helping your case, Dallas. Come on," Reggie laughed. "Let's go watch a movie."

He steered her out of the room as Grady, Mitch and Charlie chuckled.

"It's not funny!" I said.

"Oh, yes, it is. You have the strangest friends," Charlie laughed.

Mitch pulled a beer from the fridge and joined Reggie and Dallas in the living room.

Charlie leaned over to make sure Dallas was no longer paying attention, before taking the stool next to me. "So, who did you meet with tonight?"

"How do you know I met with anyone?"

"You wouldn't have left Dallas in the hands of strangers if there wasn't some other agenda you needed to focus on," Charlie said stealing my brandy.

Grady rolled his eyes but poured me a new glass.

"I met with Baker on the financials. Nola's been extorting money from him. I gave him a good scolding but let him off the hook. He'll call if he has a problem again in the future. Then I met with Mayfair."

"Oooh. That must have been fun. Did you stick it to him?"

"He was fuming," Grady grinned.

"Are we talking about the shipping industry Mayfair, as in Ronald Mayfair?" Kierson asked.

"Yes. I kind of own his ass right now. When I'm done with him I'll throw you whatever's left," I smirked.

"He runs most of the illegal contraband in the southern States," Kierson said.

"Allegedly," Charlie and I said in unison.

"Sure, allegedly, like we don't all know what that means," Kierson said rolling his eyes.

"I need him under my thumb for a few months. Then I'll figure out the best way to exit the arrangement and turn over evidence for you to convict his sorry ass. But right now, he's a valuable lead."

"You can't trust him," Kierson bellowed.

I shook my head and looked up at Grady. "Does he remind you of someone?" I asked.

"You mean Donovan?" Grady grinned. "Yeah, they seem to have the same worry-wart gene."

Kierson stomped over to the fridge, pulled a beer, and stomped out of the kitchen and into the living room.

"What's next on the agenda?" Charlie grinned toward the living room before turning her attention back to me.

"I need to go to Mississippi, then Louisiana. I'll head North for the wedding after that if I don't turn up anything right away. You can go back to work. Reggie and Grady can fly North and keep an eye on things until I get back up there."

"And what makes you think we are letting you fly solo?" Charlie asked.

"She's not," Maggie said, entering from the hallway already wearing her pajamas. "I'll be with her and stay in contact with Kierson and Genie. We've already worked it out."

"I promised I'd help," Grady said looking at me.

"The wedding is leaving my family too exposed. Donovan's good, but he's distracted. I need them protected. Nola may be looking to punish me for Max and Pasco, and my Michigan family would be the easiest target."

"I'll go with them to Michigan," Charlie nodded, agreeing with my logic. "You're right to want to take extra precautions. I took leave from the department today, so I'll fly up with them and help with security."

I pushed my glass of brandy away and stood to hug her. "Thanks, Kid. I'll feel better knowing you're there."

I went to the back bedroom that I had claimed as my own and changed into comfortable shorts and a Detroit Lions t-shirt. I had some work to do before I could sleep, so I slid my feet into a worn-out pair of tennis shoes and went out to the SUV.

Opening the back hatch, I pulled the release on the hidden compartment, and the back opened to all the weapons. I pulled the guns that had been used and moved to the porch with a cleaning kit to clean them.

Grady stepped out onto the back porch, sat a cup of coffee next to me, and he reached for the shotgun. We both worked in silence as we cleaned each gun and set them aside.

● ● ●

"Whatever it is, just ask," I said, while I reached for the last glock.

"Bones. What's he to you?"

"I don't honestly know," I sighed. "I know he's important to me, but it was never a priority for me to figure out what exactly our relationship was. And, it's still not. But neither is deciphering whatever happened between you and me at the club tonight."

"Because of Nicholas," Grady nodded, understanding.

"Yes."

"Is Bones in love with you?"

"He said he was, but I really don't know if that was real. It's hard to separate emotions with so much drama going on around you constantly."

"About the Penny thing, he'll forgive you."

"I hope he does forgive me. But I won't feel guilty about it either way."

"And, when you get Nicholas back? Then what?"

"I'm going to hug my son for a month solid, and then the next month, I'm going to sleep," I smiled.

I loaded up an armful of guns and carried them back to the SUV, stowing them in the hidden compartment as Grady carried the rest of them to me.

"Are you expecting trouble in Biloxi?" Grady asked as he secured the rest of the guns and I put the flak jackets back in their place.

"No, but I might find some in New Orleans. Maggie and I will raise the red flag if we run into a problem."

"Stay focused and alert. Don't worry about your family in Michigan. Charlie and I will make sure security is tight."

"I appreciate that," I sighed, running my hands through my hair.

As Grady closed up the back of the SUV, I looked around the quiet neighborhood. In the distance, I could hear a family out entertaining in their backyard and a dog barking. The familiar scent of Jasmine filled the air around me, and the skies above me were clear to a mass of stars that shined brightly. It was peaceful.

"You're going to find him," Grady said pulling me into him with an arm wrapped around me.

"I just hope I find him before it's too late," I said, pulling away and walking to the house.

I knew that Grady was only trying to comfort me, but I couldn't handle it. I felt restless and emotionally exposed. Time was running out. I could feel it like a hot rash covering my body. Finding Nicholas was the only thing that mattered.

Thank you for reading Kelsey's Burden: Friends and Foes. I hope you are still enjoying the series, even after I left you with a bit of a cliffhanger. Sorry – it couldn't be helped! Rest assured, Book Four will sooth your frazzled nerves!

Kelsey's Burden: Blood and Tears

After years of searching, Kelsey is finally making progress in the search for her son and her nemesis, Nola. But can she find them before time runs out? Or will Nola outsmart her again and go into hiding?

As her world becomes less and less stable, and her desperation consumes her, can she hold it together long enough to reach him and the end the war once and for all? And, which of the alpha males in her life will be standing by her side when the dust settles?

To save Nicholas and stop Nola will be a bloody fight to the end — Book Four: Blood and Tears.

Updates for new releases will be provided via an emailed newsletter for those registered on my email list. To register, simply email me at AuthorKaylieHunter@gmail.com.

Information regarding release information will also be posted on my Facebook page: Author Kaylie Hunter and on my Amazon Author Page.

About the Author –

I must have been around the age of nine, running about with my best childhood friend Julie. We roamed the neighborhood and nearby woods with a good amount of freedom. And while we were far from troublesome as kids, we didn't have what some would call good sense.

One day, we lucked upon some old cans of paint and used brushes near the community dumpsters. This was a prize to be found for sure. What in the world should we do with them? Having crossed off the list several ideas that we knew would lead to an adult noising around in our business, we finally decided the best idea was to paint our favorite climbing tree that grew just inside the woods.

So off we went, carrying our new-found supplies to our favorite tree. Each armed with a brush, we proceeded to paint the enormous maple tree's bark as we ventured higher up, paint cans in hand. A good distance up, the endeavor was taking too long, and we were starting to get bored. The tree was never going to be done before dinner at this rate. So, we did the only sensible thing that we could do—we climbed higher up the tree and poured our remaining paint down the sides, coating all the nearby limbs and trunk in a thick coat of white.

We cheered at seeing our results. Oh, we are so smart! And, then we realized our mistake. We still needed to get out of the tree!

I can't say how high we were from the ground other than a good 15 hardy climbing-limbs up, but we reached the consensus that our only way out of the tree was to jump. We counted it out and went for it. I remember my body ricocheting off two branches before landing hard on the packed ground. Ooof. I laid there beside my best friend, neither of us moving, as we stared up at the white painted tree, gasping to catch our breaths from our deflated lungs.

And, then without a word, we dragged ourselves out of the woods and went limping home. Next time, we'd remember to plan an exit strategy.

Thank you for your support!
Kaylie Hunter

<u>Kelsey's Burden Series:</u>
Layered Lies
Past Haunts
Friends and Foes
Blood and Tears
Love and Rage

Printed in Great Britain
by Amazon